Praise for *Murder Between the Lines*

"Intrepid journalist turned amateur sleuth Capability 'Kitty' Weeks is in tip-top form in her second outing. As World War I rages in Europe, New Yorker Kitty stumbles on the unexpected death of a schoolgirl— and the more she investigates, the more it looks like murder. Radha Vatsal succeeds once again in fleshing out a strong-willed, ambitious, and thoroughly delightful young heroine, who struggles against the society's restrictions on so-called career women, while solving crime—and writing news stories—with aplomb."

—Susan Elia MacNeal, *New York Times* bestselling author of the Maggie Hope series

Praise for *A Front Page Affair*

"A delightfully spunky heroine defies convention as an investigative reporter in this engaging historical mystery. The small factual details of New York life are gems."

—Rhys Bowen, *New York Times* bestselling author of the Molly Murphy and Royal Spyness mysteries

"This first in a planned series is a nice combination of mystery and thriller seasoned by historical facts and a look at women's lives before woman's liberation."

—*Kirkus Reviews*

"This lively and well-researched debut introduces a charming historical series and an appealing fish-out-of-water sleuth who seeks independence and a career in an age when most women are bent on getting married, particularly to titled Englishmen. Devotees of Rhys Bowen's mysteries will enjoy making the acquaintance of Miss Weeks."

—*Library Journal*, Starred Review

"A spirited debut… Vatsal deftly intertwines the tumult of the era, from emerging women's rights to spreading international conflict, into this rich historical."

—*Publishers Weekly*

"The fascinating historical details add flair to this thoroughly engaging mystery starring an intelligent amateur sleuth reminiscent of Rhys Bowen's Molly Murphy. Vatsal's debut will leave readers eager for Kitty's next adventure."

—*Booklist*

"An impressively well-written and consistently compelling read from beginning to end, Radha Vatsal's *A Front Page Affair* is the first book in what is justifiably expected to be an outstanding series featuring rising journalism star Kitty Weeks."

—*Midwest Book Review*

"Vatsal has clearly done her research on the geography and fashions of the period, but the novel's strength lies in its exploration of complicated wartime politics, and the difference between neutrality and innocence. Rich with period detail and cameos from a few historical figures, *A Front Page Affair* is an appealing beginning to Kitty Weeks and her world."

—*Shelf Awareness*

"Reading a well-crafted historical mystery is always a pleasure and with *A Front Page Affair*, Radha Vatsal delivers precisely that."

—*The Big Thrill*

"Vatsal ramps up the action in Kitty's simple, rule-driven world to show how American women are beginning to shape their country in previously unheard-of ways. Delightful, intriguing, and relevant historical fiction!"

—*Historical Novels Review*

"This is a well-thought-out mystery novel, combining historical fiction and feminism with a determined and brave protagonist ready to chart new mysteries and new paths for herself."

—*Mystery Scene*

"Vatsal's debut...doesn't read like a first novel. First novels aren't supposed to be this self-assured, or detailed, or full of three-dimensional characters (both real and fictional) who vividly bring the 1910s to life... Framed against the backdrop of World War I, and tackling cultural issues that still resonate today, it's impossible not to let yourself slip into the novel."

—E. A. Aymar, *ITW Presents: The Thrill Begins* Debut Author Spotlight

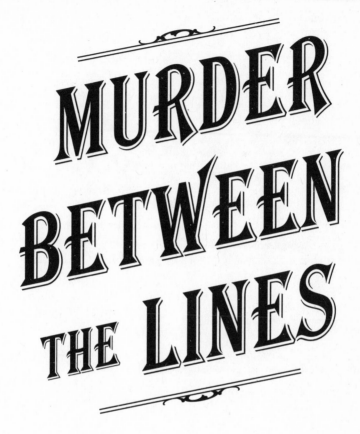

MURDER BETWEEN THE LINES

RADHA VATSAL

sourcebooks
landmark

Published by Sourcebooks Landmark, an imprint of Sourcebooks, Inc.
P.O. Box 4410, Naperville, Illinois 60567-4410
(630) 961-3900
Fax: (630) 961-2168
www.sourcebooks.com

Library of Congress Cataloging-in-Publication Data

Names: Vatsal, Radha.
Title: Murder between the lines / Radha Vatsal.
Description: Naperville, IL : Sourcebooks Landmark, [2017] | Includes
  bibliographical references and index.
Identifiers: LCCN 2016052526 | (pbk. : alk. paper)
Subjects: | GSAFD: Mystery fiction.
Classification: LCC PS3622.A885 M87 2017 | DDC 813/.6--dc23 LC record
available at https://lccn.loc.gov/2016052526

Printed and bound in the United States of America.
VP 10 9 8 7 6 5 4 3 2 1

Chapter One

D id you or did you not remove the book from Ruth's desk?" Miss Howe-Jones, headmistress of Westfield Hall, stared down at the pupil in her chilly, slate-floored office, a panorama of portraits of graduating classes hanging from the walls. "Stand up straight, Virginia, and look me in the eye. No blubbering."

Hair braided in two loops on either side of her head and tied with white ribbon, Virginia attempted to do as she was ordered, but her lower lip trembled, and her eyes filled with tears. She couldn't have been more than eleven or twelve years old.

Ladies' Page reporter Capability "Kitty" Weeks shifted uncomfortably in her carved, high-backed visitor's chair. She really ought not be here; minutes ago, she had offered to leave, but Miss Howe-Jones had insisted she remain and observe. "We run a tight ship at Westfield," the headmistress had said, lips breaking into a thin smile before beginning her interrogation.

Kitty glanced out of the leaded glass window. Snow fell in gentle drifts, covering the school's Gothic campus. A group of girls, bundled in coats and hand muffs, chatted and giggled as they shuffled along in two lines under the supervision of a schoolmistress.

"I'm waiting, Virginia." Miss Howe-Jones spoke firmly.

She wore her salt-and-pepper hair swept off her forehead in a bun and sported an old-fashioned, high-collared blouse with a heavy jeweled brooch clasped at her throat. Beside a potted poinsettia on her desk lay a copy of *The Automobile Girls Along the Hudson.*

"I just wanted to read it." Tears rolled down Virginia's cheeks.

"See, that wasn't so bad. All you had to do was admit the truth."

"Yes, Miss Howe-Jones."

"So much grief over nothing." The headmistress handed the book over. "Please return this at once. And which penalty would you prefer? Delivering mail or tidying up after lunch?"

Virginia didn't hesitate. "Delivering mail, please."

"Very well. You will begin tomorrow and then continue after the holidays."

"Yes, Miss Howe-Jones." She wiped away her tears with the back of her hand.

"That's all. You can go now."

Virginia dropped a quick curtsy and left the room. Miss Howe-Jones turned to Kitty. "I know you won't report this incident, but I did want you to be aware that we don't rely on corporal punishment at Westfield, and our students—all boarders—benefit from the manner in which I handle discipline. I'm responsible for sixty girls, Miss Weeks, ranging in age from eleven to eighteen. By the time they leave, all my pupils—even little Miss Virginia—will be fully equipped with strong moral characters. They never forget the lessons they learn from me, and they take those lessons with them as they fulfill their duties as daughters, wives, and mothers, or as exceptional students at Bryn Mawr, Barnard, and Radcliffe."

"I've heard wonderful things about Westfield Hall." The school, in the northern reaches of the Bronx, was reputed to be one of the finest girls' academies in the country. That was why Kitty's editor at the *New York Sentinel* had chosen to feature it in Saturday's issue of the Page and had arranged for her to visit a few days before the students left for Christmas recess.

"Let's take a look around, shall we?" Miss Howe-Jones stood.

Kitty followed the principal out of the office and through the reception room. At nineteen—she'd turn twenty in March—the pretty, dark-haired reporter wasn't much older than many of the school's students.

"I believe you started the school yourself," Kitty said.

Miss Howe-Jones nodded, striding down the hallway. "Thirty years ago with just ten students. Even then, I had a way with the girls. I never used harsh punishments, and in addition to a well-rounded education, I provided wholesome meals, plenty of exercise and fresh air."

"And what subjects do your pupils study, Miss Howe-Jones?" Kitty asked.

"Well, we make sure all our girls have already mastered the basics of reading, writing, and penmanship when they enter," the headmistress replied, "and we offer English, German, and French, as well as Greek or Latin—each girl must choose one, but some do both—history and geography, natural history, music, art, domestic science, health, hygiene, and mathematics."

"Lessons are restricted to no more than five hours a day. The girls play tennis and badminton and go on hikes in the spring and fall. They cross-country ski and skate on the pond in winter. And twice a year, they undergo full physical examinations by the nurse to ensure that they're all in good health... But here we are. Take a look."

Behind a closed door fitted with a glass panel so one could keep an eye on things without disturbing the class in progress, three rows of girls, all in white blouses and cream- or peach-colored cardigans, repeated a drill led by an energetic schoolmistress.

"Madame Pouille, our French teacher," Miss Howe-Jones whispered.

"*Êtes-vous l'homme?*" Madame Pouille enunciated each word clearly and loudly, her piercing voice audible from behind the closed door.

"*Je le suis.*" A chorus of girls responded.

"*Êtes-vous sa mere?*"

"*Je la suis.*"

Kitty smiled. She had loved her French lessons and had an excellent ear for languages.

"We have German across the hall," Miss Howe-Jones said. "Some parents have threatened to remove their daughters from the class, but I've explained to them that education is education. A language is a language. We must keep it separate from politics."

She was referring to the European war, which had recently crossed the one-year mark, and although the United States was officially neutral, people still took sides—increasingly against Germany and Austria-Hungary, and in favor of England and its allies, France and Russia.

Kitty, who had studied French and German for ten years at her boarding school in Switzerland and had friends on both sides, felt the effects of the struggle keenly. "I think German is a wonderful language."

"Do you?"

The headmistress's suspicious look suggested that she thought Kitty was taking fairness too far. After all, mellifluous French was said to be the language of culture, while guttural German sounded stiff and formal.

"Ah, there's Miss Howell."

A young woman in a long tartan skirt with leather buckles at the side made her way down the hall. She had a trim, athletic figure, a confident gait, and a fresh complexion. Kitty took a liking to her at once.

"Georgina, come meet Miss Weeks," Miss Howe-Jones called. "She's a reporter at the *New York Sentinel*."

"A reporter for the *Sentinel*?" Georgina Howell gasped, hurrying over. "At the Ladies' Page?" Her eyes widened as Kitty smiled. "You write those wonderful interviews? Did you do the one with Anne Morgan as well? I loved it!"

Kitty's editor, Helena Busby, wouldn't have cared for the schoolgirl's gushing response. She believed that crediting writers by name was déclassé, too much in the vein of the "yellow press" that showed off its female writers, often derisively known as "stunt reporters" or "sob sisters." Miss Busby credited Kitty only as "Our Correspondent" or "Special Ladies' Page Journalist," and so, despite the popularity of some of her stories, Kitty wasn't well known—and she preferred it that way. There was no reason to court publicity. She'd make a better reporter if she could blend into the background.

"Don't jump on Miss Weeks, Georgina!" Miss Howe-Jones corrected her.

But Georgina couldn't stop staring. "I'd love to do what you do."

"You have plenty of time before you decide," Miss Howe-Jones said. "At least six months."

Kitty laughed. "That's right. Choose with care." In the public's mind, newspaperwomen were just a step removed from actresses and a stumble away from streetwalkers or any other female whose profession entailed conversing with strange men and roaming unsupervised about the city. It explained why Miss Busby preferred not to use names and clung to the conventions of propriety.

"When they do work," Miss Howe-Jones went on, "Westfield Hall graduates take up teaching or nursing, librarianship or charitable endeavors."

"The more ladylike pursuits." Kitty understood the headmistress's caution, although she didn't agree with it.

The principal nodded. "Exactly. Georgina, I'd like you to show Miss Weeks the yearbook and then take her over to the science lab when we're finished, but for the moment, please return to your studies."

"Yes, Miss Howe-Jones." Georgina curtsied.

"Georgina is one of our best pupils and our head girl," Miss Howe-Jones said with pride as her student disappeared down the hall. She opened the door to a classroom, and Kitty found herself transported to a world she had forgotten about, although barely a few years ago, it was the only world she knew.

Chalk dust flying as she wrote, a teacher jotted a mathematics question on the blackboard. "A parlor is 15 feet 9 inches square. The height of the ceilings is 11 feet 6 inches. What would be the cost of plastering the walls and ceilings at $0.33 per square yard? How much would be saved by having the ceiling calcimined at a cost of $0.18 a square yard? And what would be the cost of wainscoting the outside hall, which is 30 feet long, 8 feet wide, 12 feet 8 inches high, at a cost of $0.40 a square yard?" The teacher turned to face the class and noticed Kitty and the headmistress standing in the doorway.

"Reporter from the *Sentinel*. Don't mind us." Miss Howe-Jones waved her hand. "In mathematics," she whispered to Kitty, "we focus on problems of a practical nature. Ones that our girls might face in life. It keeps them engaged."

The teacher held out her chalk. "Perhaps our visitor would like to try for herself and see how she fares?"

Kitty blushed as a room full of faces turned to stare at her. "You will have to excuse me, ma'am. I'm a bit rusty at the moment."

They moved on to a geography lesson in the room next door. "It's so important to be fully acquainted with the world, don't you think?" Miss Howe-Jones held the door open, allowing Kitty to enter first.

"Who will read from Morton's, page thirty-three?" A bespectacled school mistress who was nearly as round as she was tall held a textbook in one hand and pointed to a globe on her desk with a stick.

Hands shot up.

"Go ahead, Miss Appley."

Miss Appley stood. "East of Tibet is the plain of China, which we may call the 'Yellow Land,' as it is the home of the yellow people and much of its soil is yellow. The Huang He—*He* means *river*—carries so much of this soil that it is called the Yellow River. It is also sometimes called 'China's Sorrow,' because of the great losses of life and property caused by its floods."

"Can anyone name another important river in China?"

Again, several hands shot up.

Kitty realized she missed being in school. She had enjoyed the easy camaraderie of school friends and the excitement of learning something new each day, but more than that, she missed the security that came from believing that every problem could be solved and every question had a right answer.

Most of the world now spinning beneath the teacher's fingers had gone up in flames and the noxious effects of Europe's war could be felt as far away as Asia, Africa, and the Middle East. Even all the way to New York City, as Kitty had learned this past summer when she inadvertently stumbled upon evidence of wrongdoing by those who should have known better.

"I'll send for Georgina." Miss Howe-Jones beckoned Kitty outside. "You should take advantage of your time with her to see the school from a student's perspective."

Minutes later, Kitty was heading back down the hall, following the head girl's brisk footsteps.

"So you'd like to be a reporter?" Kitty asked now that they were alone.

Georgina grimaced. "Miss Howe-Jones hates the idea. She wants me to go on to Bryn Mawr and study the classics. I think it's her dream to have one student at the pinnacle of each realm—that female professor? That society matron? That botanist? All Westfield women. But why not something different? It's so old-fashioned."

"And what happens if you don't agree with her?"

"No one disagrees with Miss Howe-Jones." Georgina opened the door to a closet-sized office. She picked up the mock-up of a large volume lying on the desk. "This is a Westfield Hall tradition. Our annual yearbook. I'm the editor."

"May I take a look?"

Georgina Howell handed it over, and Kitty flipped through the pages.

"We include essays and photographs from events during the year but"—Georgina pointed as Kitty neared the end—"this part is everyone's favorite."

Beneath photographs of the girls, arranged alphabetically by surname, a few lines of description summed up each student of "The Graduating Class of 1915–1916."

Of stature, Joan is passing tall,
And sparsely formed and lean withal.
Mistress Mary, who does not want to vote,
To home and its beauties her time shall devote.

"Do you write this?" she asked.

"The entire yearbook committee contributes."

Kitty read on. A photograph of a beautiful, composed young woman was followed by the words, *I strove with none, for none was worth my strife.*

And then, beneath a round-faced student: *"Baby" we call her not unkindly, Merely because she seems in manner set, And hates the little epithet.*

"Isn't this a bit mean?" The faces and nicknames in the yearbook reminded her of so many bugs pinned to a board, their peculiarities neatly labeled for all to examine.

Georgina shrugged. "It's just a little teasing. That's part and parcel of being here. What doesn't kill you only makes you stronger."

Kitty didn't agree. The headmistresses at her boarding school had been members of the Theosophical Society. They followed no set religious practices and urged their charges to seek the truth themselves. Moreover, they discouraged close friendships. No "best" friends, no groups, no name-calling. Of course, such behavior occurred, but it was never condoned, and it never would have been enshrined in print.

"Should we move on?" She checked the time on her wristwatch.

The fresh snow squeaked under Kitty's and Georgina's boots as they passed a frozen pond and made their way to a low-slung structure adjacent to the main building.

Georgina had come out only in her cardigan.

Why was it, Kitty wondered, that schoolgirls never seemed to need jackets? "Aren't you freezing?" she asked.

Georgina shook her head, and her breath came out in white puffs as she answered. "It's only a few minutes." She knocked on the door to the lab.

A voice from inside called, "Come in!"

"I'll leave you here." The head girl rubbed her bare hands together to warm them. "Come back to Miss Howe-Jones's office when you're done." She turned and ran back to the main building.

Kitty stomped the snow off her boots and entered the lab, which was bright and crowded with equipment. Fish of different sizes and colors swam in a tank. Plants grew under an electric light. Tortoises crawled around another tank, and a glass display case held a stuffed owl perched on a branch, a robin about to take flight, and a dusty rabbit, frozen and stuffed in death, as well as a chipmunk against a painted backdrop of foliage. She marveled for a moment at the taxidermist's art. Then she turned to face a chart on the wall, which illustrated layers of the earth and different types of rocks, while another listed the periodic table of the elements. Tables in the center of the room had been set with lilies on white sheets of paper, petri dishes, and sharp knives, one for each student.

"You must be Miss Weeks." A dark-haired woman with a plain but kind and intelligent face rose from a chair and held out her hand. "I'm Mrs. Swartz. Miss Howe-Jones told me to expect you."

"This is wonderful." Kitty gestured around her with amazement.

Mrs. Swartz smiled. "It's out of season to be dissecting flowers in winter. We're late this year. When the girls return from vacation, we will begin with insects as part of animal classification."

Kitty itched to pick up one of the knives and cut into a blossom. Her own botany lessons had been restricted to sketching from nature. "Are all your lessons so"—she searched for the word—"physical?"

"I find that girls learn best when they can use their hands, but science education isn't what it used to be." Mrs. Swartz sighed. "Even as recently as when I was a student, we were taught physics and chemistry. Now, it's all nature study: leaf gathering and bird-watching. Some of the parents object to my dissections and even the most basic chemical experiments."

"You were taught chemistry and physics?" Kitty had been taught neither.

"Oh yes." Mrs. Swartz took down a couple of books from

her shelf. One was titled *Juvenile Philosophy.* "That's physics." The other—*Conversations on Chemistry.* "Take a look at the publication dates."

Juvenile Philosophy was structured as a series of conversations between a mother and daughter and had been published in 1850. *Conversations* went as far back as 1809. Kitty had learned a bit about light and heat and rain, but of the topics in *Conversations,* written to offer the public, "and more particularly...the female sex," an introduction to the subject, Kitty knew nothing. In it, a woman by the name of Mrs. B. and her female protégé spent entire chapters discussing the difference between latent heat and chemical heat, oxygen, nitrogen, hydrogen, and sulfur, metals and alkalis.

"Why don't they teach this anymore?"

"I suppose," Mrs. Swartz said, "that it's not considered feminine. These days, the ablest girls study the classics or go into the general field of education."

A clatter sounded from an adjacent room. "Elspeth!" Mrs. Swartz called. "What is going on in there?"

"I'm sorry, Mrs. Swartz. I dropped something."

"We have a visitor here," the teacher said. "Why don't you come out and say hello."

Silence. Then a figure in an apron and goggles emerged, removing thick white gloves from her hands.

"Meet Miss Elspeth Bright, one of my brightest students," said Mrs. Swartz.

The girl pulled off her goggles and smiled, revealing perfect pearlescent teeth. Her eyes were an incandescent silvery gray, her hair silvery blond to match.

Kitty sucked in her breath.

The young woman held out her hand, and dumbly, Kitty shook it. Elspeth Bright must have been a bit younger than her; still, it was Kitty who felt intimidated. Miss Bright was radiant; she ought to have been in an advertisement for dental paste.

"So, do you have any questions for me?"

"Don't be forward, Elspeth." Her teacher corrected her, but mildly.

"You know what they say, Mrs. Swartz. Those who wait, wait in vain."

Mrs. Swartz raised her eyebrows as though she was accustomed to Elspeth's quick rejoinders but not entirely pleased by them.

"Are you a student of science, Miss Bright?" Kitty asked.

"You could say that."

"What are you studying now?"

"I'm *working* on something." Elspeth Bright emphasized the word *working*, clearly insulted by the insinuation that she was a mere schoolgirl. Teacher and pupil exchanged glances. "Let me put it to you this way, Miss Weeks. In the words of the great Sir Isaac Newton," she continued, "'I don't know what I may seem to the world, but as to myself, I seem to have been only like a boy'—I'd say like a girl—'playing on the sea-shore and diverting myself in now and then finding a smoother pebble or a prettier shell than ordinary, whilst the great ocean of truth lay all undiscovered before me.'"

"That's an inspiring sentiment. Do you study the natural world then, Miss Bright?"

"I study chemistry and physics. Molecules, atoms, energy—"

"All right, Elspeth." Mrs. Swartz stepped forward. "Time to return to your classes. Miss Weeks, if you wish to speak further with Miss Bright, you must first obtain permission from our headmistress."

"Or if you'd like, I can tell you more over vacation." Elspeth Bright reached into her pocket and handed Kitty a card embossed with a Manhattan address.

"Elspeth!" Mrs. Swartz sounded dismayed.

The Westfield Hall article would run on Saturday, but that didn't worry Kitty. She sensed that Elspeth Bright might deserve a story of her own.

CHAPTER TWO

The rest of the week passed quickly. Kitty caught up on her Christmas shopping and soaked up every last detail the papers reported about President Woodrow Wilson's weekend wedding to Edith Bolling Galt in a quiet ceremony at the bride's home in Virginia. The year 1915 was inching to a close, but the president's remarriage, while in office and to a widow, made it feel like the end of an era. Kitty could almost see the ticker tape falling outside her window.

She arrived at work on Monday, December 20, to find formidable Helena Busby, who ruled the Ladies' Page with an iron hand, in a furious mood. The beanpole figure kept her head down and shoulders hunched as she made her way through the clatter of the typists' hall—otherwise known as the hen coop—like a pedestrian forcing herself through gale-force winds.

"My office, five minutes," she said to Kitty and Jeannie Williams, her other assistant, both of whom sat at the front of the room.

"What's gotten into her?" Jeannie said as she gathered her papers. She had once been a typist herself but had been brought on to the Page to take over some of the more mundane tasks when the workload became too onerous for the editor to handle alone.

"No idea," Kitty replied. Miss Busby in a foul mood never boded well. She watched the clock at the front of the hall. The hand hit the five-minute mark.

"Shall we?" Kitty rose from her seat.

The two young women made their way down a narrow corridor, past the Weekend Supplement editor's office to the alcove at the back that served as Miss Busby's doorless, windowless office.

"He's done it," Miss Busby said as they entered. "He's betrayed us. All of us. Each and every one of us."

"Who has, Miss Busby?" What could be so dire? Kitty feared the worst. Could Mr. Eichendorff, their publisher, have decided to put the Ladies' Page out of business?

"The president...Mr. Wilson." Miss Busby looked on the verge of tears.

She had disapproved of the president's engagement since it had been announced in October. Mr. Wilson, whose wife of nearly thirty years had died a few days after the European war broke out in August 1914, had been a widower for just over a year when he told the public that he would be marrying Mrs. Galt, the widow of jeweler Norman Galt. And now this "blue-eyed descendent of Pocahontas," as the press had dubbed her for claiming native ancestry, who drove around Washington, DC, in her electric motor car, had become First Lady to the nation.

"He could have turned back," Helena Busby said. "He could have changed his mind. Instead, he's chosen to betray Mrs. Wilson's memory and so betray all of us. One year. One year—that's all it took for him to forget. *Men*," she spat out, "can be so fickle."

Kitty wondered whether Miss Busby spoke from experience, whether her heart had once been broken. "The country seems to be happy for them," she observed mildly. "And the president's daughters"—all three were grown, and two were married—"seem to approve."

"That's because the world has lost all sense of propriety." Helena Busby shook her head, and her chandelier earrings swung back and forth. "To think that I cheered him on, that I put my faith in this deserter."

Although Kitty secretly concurred that the marriage did seem too soon and too sudden, she also thought they must put personal feelings aside and think of their readers when it came to the stories they chose. Saturday's Ladies' Page should have included some commentary about the momentous event, but Miss Busby had refused to allow a single word to be printed on the topic. At least, to both Mrs. Galt and the president's credit, the ceremony had been simply and tastefully conducted. According to news reports, the forty-three-year-old widow exchanged vows with the fifty-eight-year-old widower in front of just forty guests. The bride wore a gown of black chiffon velvet; the service had been Episcopalian; and the decoration consisted of scores of orchids in shades of mauve and purple, as well as American Beauty roses. Invitations had gone out with the president named as a private citizen—Mr. Wilson—in keeping with the private nature of the proceedings.

"Now, upcoming assignments." Miss Busby squared the corners of a stack of papers on her desk with a determined thump.

Kitty had an idea of what she might like to write about—girls in science—but she wouldn't propose it until she fleshed the piece out fully, and that would require speaking to Elspeth Bright first.

"I have this weekend's story set," the editor continued, her jaw clenched. "I always write the Christmas feature myself. We will work on something special for the New Year's issue and fill the remaining columns with so much fluff—holiday trivia, whatever—that nobody will notice we haven't said a word about that *interloper.*"

Kitty arranged to meet Miss Bright on Wednesday afternoon at Tipton's, a tearoom on Madison Avenue. A thick blanket of fresh, white snow covered the streets. Soon, the white powder would be dark gray from automobile soot and the footsteps of hundreds of pedestrians, but for the moment, it was pristine, and the city looked like it did in holiday postcards: lights, wreathes, candy canes, and trees in every store window, vendors selling roasted chestnuts, shoppers hauling hefty bags, carolers singing on street corners. Just three shopping days left until Christmas.

Rao, the Weekses' chauffeur, pulled the Packard up in front of the restaurant, and Kitty climbed out, adjusting the stole around her neck. She stood on the sidewalk for a moment, absorbing the atmosphere around her. Manhattan at holiday time was like nowhere else. One could buy anything one's heart desired: player pianos; fox, lynx, and Russian sable sets; bonbons; port in Delft jugs; hosiery fine enough to be pulled through a ring; evening slippers; enameled watches; even Tecla's cultured pearl necklaces for seventy-five dollars or real pearl ones for a fortune.

This was only Kitty's second winter in the city. She had arrived last spring after a decade at school in Switzerland and, before that, had traipsed around behind her father as he conducted business across the Near and Far East. She had been born in Malaya, where her mother had died shortly afterward. Her father, Julian Weeks, never remarried and left his only child in the care of maids and a succession of governesses. Now that they lived together again, he gave Kitty a fair amount of freedom. He was busy with his investments, his club, his books, and his papers and allowed her to do pretty much what she wanted so long as she didn't get into trouble.

"Hello." Miss Bright waved when Kitty came in. "I ordered tea and sandwiches for both of us." With her pale complexion and fair hair, she looked as striking in her white wool jacket as she had in the gray school cardigan.

Tea arrived in a porcelain pot covered with a knitted cozy, followed by cucumber, chicken, and egg-salad sandwiches on a tiered tray borne by a deft waiter. Kitty poured.

"I saw your piece in the Ladies' Page on Saturday," Miss Bright said.

"What did you think?"

"It was complimentary."

"Too complimentary?"

"I don't know…" She took a bite of one of the sandwiches. "The pranks the girls play go too far sometimes. But I suppose all of us need to blow off steam now and then."

"Don't you like it at Westfield?"

"Miss Howe-Jones runs the place like a fiefdom," Elspeth said. "She told me her method builds character."

"Oh, yes. She's very proud that she doesn't use corporal punishment."

"I saw her question one of the girls."

"Virginia?"

"How did you know?" Kitty brought the china teacup to her mouth.

"Virginia's delivering all our mail. You see, that's Miss Howe-Jones's trick. She creates certain visible tasks, which we all know are punishments. When one of the girls does them, we can tell that she's done something wrong, but we don't know what."

"That must be awful."

"It's embarrassing. Personally, I'd prefer a nice hard rap on the knuckles, and then it's all over. No lingering guilt or curious stares."

"Before I forget to ask," Kitty said, "do your parents know you're speaking to me?"

Elspeth laughed. "They'd have conniptions if they thought I was meeting a reporter. I just told them I'd be out walking. Fortunately, my parents are very busy and don't ask many questions. My father is a scientist, and like me, his mind is always on his work.

"And now, may I ask you something, Miss Weeks? Why do you write for the papers? If you don't mind my saying so, you don't look like you need the money."

"Ah." The girl was nothing if not direct. "You're correct, Miss Bright. I don't."

"Well then?"

"I like to learn about the world, about people. And I want to make something of myself."

"We're kindred spirits then. My studies are more than just a hobby. I hope to go on to Cornell University when I finish at Westfield. I know it's coeducational, and our headmistress doesn't approve, but competing with the men will force me to become better at what I do."

"That brings me to my point." Kitty leaned in toward her. "I'd like to understand what exactly it is that you're working on, then write about it for the Ladies' Page."

"Why, Elspeth, fancy seeing you here!" A fashionable woman in a black hat with black feathers towered over them.

"Oh, hello, Mrs. Marquand." Elspeth Bright looked up.

"Out doing some shopping?" The woman glanced pointedly at Kitty.

"Catching up with a friend. This is Miss Weeks." Elspeth Bright made the introductions. "Mrs. Marquand's daughter also goes to Westfield Hall, and the Marquands live down the street from us."

"That's right." Mrs. Marquand's smile stretched to reveal her teeth. "Just a few blocks north of here. Between Park Avenue and Fifth."

If that was an invitation for Kitty to reveal her address, Kitty didn't take her up on it.

"Mama still busy with her women's caucuses, Elspeth?" the older woman asked.

"She is still busy with the Congressional Union, yes."

Mrs. Marquand remained standing beside them for a few moments. Then, when no further chitchat appeared to be forthcoming from either of the girls, she said, "Well, enjoy yourselves." She settled herself at a nearby table.

Elspeth ran her hand across the back of her neck. "So, Cornell. That's where I'd like to go."

"That's commendable." Kitty was fascinated.

"I know I have talent. And I have a practical turn of mind as well. Madame Curie won a Nobel Prize. If I work hard"—she kept her voice low—"why not another woman someday?" She shot a sidelong glance at Mrs. Marquand. "My tea's getting cold. Should we eat?"

They finished a couple of the sandwiches. Her neighbor's presence clearly constrained Elspeth, who kept darting looks in the older woman's direction.

"Why don't we speak again before you return to school?" Kitty realized they wouldn't make much headway under the present circumstances. "I'm not in a rush to write my piece, and I'd like to hear more before I submit a proposal to my editor."

"I'd enjoy that very much." Elspeth offered to pay the check, but Kitty wouldn't allow her. They said good-bye to Mrs. Marquand and headed out to the sidewalk.

"I'm terribly sorry," Elspeth Bright apologized once the door closed behind them. "It's hard for me to talk when I know someone else is listening. And Mrs. Marquand is the nosy type."

"Not to worry. May I give you a ride home?" Kitty offered.

"No, thanks." Elspeth Bright shook her head. "I'm just a short walk away—and besides, I love this weather." A light flurry of snow had begun to fall, and it scattered around her pale figure like a Christmas scene in a Viennese globe.

"I'll telephone you next week."

"Perfect. I don't go back until the new year. Can you believe it—1916? I'll be eighteen and off to college in the fall."

"I'll look forward to our next meeting." Kitty held out her hand.

"Likewise, Miss Weeks. And who knows? By then, I may have some news that will surprise you."

"Now you really have my attention."

Elspeth Bright smiled. "Merry Christmas, Miss Weeks."

"Merry Christmas, Miss Bright."

Kitty crossed the street and climbed into the waiting Packard. A cloud seemed to have lifted. She felt light and optimistic and full of hope for the future.

Chapter Three

Julian Weeks had invited "old friends" to Christmas dinner, and Kitty, who couldn't recall when she last met any of his acquaintances from his travels in the East, waited with anticipation for the arrival of the Lanes, a brother and sister pair, whom he had known in China. The Weekses' spacious apartment in the New Century building on West End Avenue was looking its best—the fire had been lit, and Kitty had decorated the Christmas tree in the corner with ornaments and candles. She went around putting a match to every candle so the tree blazed bright.

"I don't see why you set such store by this German bonfire," Mr. Weeks remarked.

"A Christmas tree isn't German," Kitty replied. She wore a gauzy yellow gown and a pearl bracelet that her father had presented to her that morning. She had given him a Waltham automobile clock, advertised as a perfect gift "for the man who has everything."

"Queen Victoria and Prince Albert popularized it, and what were they?"

"All right, all right." Kitty laughed. "It's a German tradition. You've made your point."

Ever the contrarian, Mr. Weeks enjoyed confounding received

wisdom. He referred to Santa Claus as "the Dutchman" and had gleefully informed Kitty that poinsettias had nothing to do with Christmas—they were a Mexican shrub brought to the United States by an American ambassador of the same name.

"If it were up to you," Kitty said, stepping back to admire her handiwork, "we wouldn't have any traditions at all."

"It's not the traditions I mind," he replied. "It's not knowing their past that's dangerous."

"I beg your pardon. How is not knowing that Christmas trees are German or poinsettias Mexican a danger to anyone?" Sometimes, she felt, her father pushed matters too far.

"They are our enemies—"

"They're not supposed to be our enemies." Kitty felt combative. The United States was not at war with anyone, neither Germany nor Mexico.

"What they're *supposed* to be is neither here nor there. You read the papers, my dear. You see what's happening—"

"Pancho Villa and his bandits have been making mischief, and German spies are up to no good. What does that have to do with tradition?"

Mr. Weeks sighed. "One day, you will understand me."

"I don't think I will." Kitty kissed the top of his head. Her father's heart was in the right place, but she thought he often argued just to needle her.

They had a drink together and watched the snow start to fall again before the Lanes arrived at seven on the dot.

"What a lovely place you have here." Sylvia Lane looked around. A smattering of freckles dusted her pert nose, and she wore her shining red hair in an elegant chignon, a shahtoosh shawl draped carelessly over her smooth shoulders. "Much nicer than being stuck in a hotel. Don't you agree, Hugo?"

"Absolutely." Hugo Lane projected the casual ease of a world traveler. He looked in his midforties, about ten years older than his sister. "We haven't made any permanent arrangements, but Sylvia is keen to set up our own place soon. Thank you for inviting us."

"Have you moved permanently to the city?" Kitty asked.

"That's our plan, as of the moment."

Kitty served mulled wine from a cut-glass bowl, and together, they discussed the Lanes' time in Russia.

"I don't think we ever told you"—Miss Lane brushed away a strand of her hair and turned to Kitty's father—"but for a month, I filled in for the grand duchesses' regular tutor."

"For the Russian princesses?" Kitty said, amazed.

"For the Romanov girls, yes. The Grand Duchesses Olga, Tatiana, Anastasia, and Maria." Miss Lane gestured in the air. She had a delicate build, like a porcelain doll.

"What was it like?" For Kitty, the words *grand duchesses* conjured up visions of balls and palaces and splendor on a scale that would dwarf mere mortals. Anna Karenina, Vronsky, troika rides on wintry nights.

"Let's just say that my sister is a teacher," Mr. Lane said. "And I don't think those girls do much learning."

Mr. Weeks asked about the mad monk Rasputin, and Mr. Lane replied that he had become the tsarina's favorite by keeping Grand Duke Alexei's hemophilia in check and that the tsar was playing with fire by resisting changes that would give his people more say in the government.

"They'll bring him down if he's not careful."

"Really, Hugo?" Julian Weeks sounded skeptical. "The Romanovs have ruled that country for three hundred years."

Hugo Lane grinned. "So they keep reminding us." The dynasty had celebrated its third century in power with great fanfare just two years ago.

Sylvia Lane mentioned the sinking of the Japanese liner *Yasaka Maru* and wondered whether it might lead Japan to join in the war on the side of the Allies. Mr. Weeks told them about Secretary Daniels's report in which the naval secretary maintained that in order to catch up with other fleets, the United States would require the construction of new vessels to the tune of one and a half billion dollars.

Kitty kept quiet and listened. There was so much going on these days that it was hard to keep up with it all. She made sure everyone's glasses were filled and that Mrs. Codd, their cook, was on track with dinner.

They dined at nine on fish soup, roast beef, rack of lamb, Brussels sprouts, and green beans with almonds. Grace, the Weekses' maid, served sorbet, candied pecans, and plum pudding doused in rum for dessert.

Kitty woke up early the next morning, groggy from the full meal and late night. The Lanes had left after eleven. Kitty pulled back the curtains herself, since Grace and Mrs. Codd had taken the twenty-sixth off. Looking out the window, she noticed that some of yesterday's snow had melted away. Kitty slipped into her dressing gown and padded off to the kitchen to prepare tea for herself and coffee for her father.

"Thank you, Capability." Mr. Weeks was reading the

newspaper at his usual spot at the table when Kitty brought in the tray. "Did you enjoy yourself last night?"

"You seem to know the Lanes very well." She had noticed their use of one another's first names.

"I told you we're old friends."

Kitty's gaze wandered across the front page of the *Sentinel*.

"I think we'll be seeing more of them."

She didn't hear a word her father said. Sandwiched between the headlines 7,200 MEN NEEDED FOR MARINE CORPS and TO FREE THE SEAS AND CURB ARMAMENTS MUST BE CHIEF AIM OF PEACE was another that made her pay attention. At first, she thought it was just a curiosity, but only when she finished reading GIRL SOMNAMBULIST IS FROZEN TO DEATH did Kitty grasp its significance.

"Are you sure it's her?" Mr. Weeks said.

"How many scientists' daughters do you think live on the east side of the park and attend Westfield?" Out of respect for the family's privacy, the article didn't mention names.

"Tell me what happened, Capability." Her father set his paper aside.

"It's the strangest thing. It says she was last seen by her family at Christmas Eve dinner. That was on Friday. Yesterday morning, she didn't come down to breakfast, and she wasn't to be found in her room. The family started to look for her outside, since she was known to be a sleepwalker. The chauffeur discovered her body about half a block away from home, just inside Central Park. She was wearing only her nightclothes, coat, and boots in the middle of winter. There were no signs of any struggle. Her body was half-covered by snow drifts, and the medical examiner ruled that death was due to exposure."

"How bizarre."

"Apparently, too much schoolwork affected her mental health... I can't believe it. I met with her on Wednesday. She was young and so full of hope." Kitty thought back to the afternoon at Tipton's. "She had news, she said, news that would surprise me. She seemed to be in perfectly fine spirits." Other than the awkward encounter with her neighbor, Elspeth Bright had shown no signs of distress. If anything else had been troubling her, Kitty had completely missed it.

CHAPTER FOUR

K itty trudged along behind Mr. Weeks. Fresh air and exercise. That was his solution to her distress. As though he couldn't understand how the unexpected death of someone almost her age might lead Kitty to question the certainty of her own existence. Fresh air and exercise in Central Park, no less—although they wouldn't be near the area where the girl somnambulist had perished.

"Lace up your skates," Mr. Weeks said, sitting on the edge of a bench and tying his. He waited for Kitty and then stepped onto the frozen pond. Why this sudden enthusiasm for ice skating when they could just as easily have taken a walk instead? Although it was still early, there were half a dozen or so other skaters out, and church bells rang in the distance. Kitty and her father glided around the pond a couple of times. In her dazed state, she felt rather like a somnambulist herself.

"Oh, hello!" Miss Lane floated up to them, her brother beside her. "Fancy seeing you here! Thank you again for a lovely evening." Her complexion glowed from the exertion, and she wore a neat fur hat that set off her lustrous red hair to perfection.

Talk about coincidences, Kitty thought. She and her father never went out this early on a Sunday morning. She looked at him and then at Miss Lane, then back at her father again. His face was impassive, as usual.

No. If there was any interest, it came from the woman.

"Will you join me, Miss Weeks?" Miss Lane held out her arm. She chattered on while her brother and Julian Weeks skated side by side, but Kitty was in no mood to be cajoled into light conversation. She gave short, quick answers, then, so as not to seem rude, said she was feeling tired and that she would sit down and watch.

"Are you sure?" Miss Lane asked.

"Positive." Kitty made her way to a bench and untied the laces to her skating boots.

Mr. Weeks and Mr. Lane made space for Miss Lane, and the trio skated around and around, while Kitty sat alone, thinking.

"*Guten Tag, Herr Musser.*" Kitty arrived at work early and went straight to the paper's archives, known to staff as the morgue.

"*Guten Tag, fräulein.* To what do I owe the pleasure of such an early visit?" The grizzled archivist and his team of young men filed and indexed every story the *Sentinel* printed so that reporters could use them for reference. "Did you miss Herr Musser over the weekend? 'Where is my old friend,' you asked yourself? Or perhaps you have a question that you believe only I can answer." He grinned as he spoke, his English heavily accented, although he had lived in New York most of his life.

"You read my mind, Mr. Musser. I was wondering if you

happen to know who reported the piece on the girl somnambulist." Kitty often came down to the basement to chat in his
native German, and he would regale her with tidbits from
obscure articles.

"Let me see." He stared at the pile of papers in front of him.
"When was that?"

"Yesterday."

"Oh, yes." He called to his assistants in the back. "Lewis, you
know who wrote the somnambulist story?"

"Page one?" a voice replied.

Kitty nodded.

"Yes," Musser shouted.

"Phineas Mills."

"Phineas Mills," Musser told Kitty. "He's a new fellow. Why
are you interested?"

"I'd like the name of the girl who died."

"She was a sleepwalker?"

"So they say."

Musser stroked his walrus mustache. "It's a terrible affliction.
My sister had it. We used to wake up in the morning and find
cheese and bread crumbs scattered all over the kitchen, and she
had no memory of getting up at night, let alone eating the next
day's breakfast."

Kitty thanked the old man and headed upstairs, hoping that
Mills would be on the early shift. A glass partition on the sixth
floor separated the newsroom and its "real" reporters, all men,
from the rest of the *Sentinel*'s employees. As in a gentlemen's
club, women weren't allowed to even set a foot inside.

Kitty knew the procedure: she knocked on the pane of glass

and waited until one of the reporters noticed her. He called out something to the other men.

A few minutes later, Mr. Flanagan, a reporter with whom she had worked previously, stepped out, trailing the odor of cigarette fumes. "What brings you upstairs today, Miss Weeks?"

"I'm here to see Mr. Mills."

"Uh-huh. For anything in particular?"

"He covered a story that I'm interested in."

Flanagan raised an eyebrow. He wasn't a bad sort, but he had no patience for female reporters and believed they didn't possess the rationality to write an objective account of events. "Back to your old ways, Miss Weeks?"

"Not at all, Mr. Flanagan. I just thought I might know the victim."

"I see… You know what comes of that. First, it's sympathy, then it's curiosity, and then, the next thing you know, you're knocking at doors, asking one too many questions—"

Kitty interrupted him. "All I want is a name, sir."

"That's how it begins." The reporter turned on his heel and sauntered back inside, the odor of one too many cigarettes wafting out again.

A few minutes later, a curly-haired fellow appeared. "I'm Mills. You're looking for me?"

Kitty introduced herself. "I heard you wrote the piece about the scientist's daughter—the girl somnambulist who died?"

"Yes. That was terribly sad. She was so young."

"Would you mind telling me her name?"

Mills jangled the contents of his pocket. "The parents wanted to keep it quiet."

"I think I might have known her."

No response. The jangling continued.

"Was it Bright?" Kitty couldn't contain herself any longer. "Elspeth Bright?"

A pause. And then, "That's right."

"Oh." Kitty crumpled. Up until that point, she had been hoping—not very optimistically, but hoping nonetheless—that she had made a mistake.

"I'm sorry," the reporter said. "Was she a friend?"

"An acquaintance, but I liked her. She had so much promise."

Kitty could hardly believe that the girl who had been ready to show the men at Cornell what she was capable of was dead. She felt the loss more deeply than she would have imagined.

"She was about to turn eighteen." Mills exhaled. "What a shame. Frankly, I had no idea that sleepwalking could be so dangerous. But the medical examiner confirmed that she died of exposure, and how else would a young woman with her home just paces away freeze to death?"

Kitty slowly made her way downstairs, where Jeannie Williams waited for her.

"Miss Busby wants to see us."

The two girls headed to the alcove.

"So, ladies, what do we have for this coming Saturday?" Miss Busby held out her planner. "I hardly need remind you that it will be the first of January."

Kitty remained silent.

"Jeannie's covering New Year's resolutions," Miss Busby went on. "Everyone loves those. How about you, Miss Weeks?"

"I do too," Kitty replied.

Miss Busby glared. "I'm not asking what you like to read, Miss Weeks. I am asking what you plan to write for this weekend."

"Of course." Kitty smiled apologetically.

"Pull your head out of the clouds, young lady. I expect some ideas from you *tout de suite.*"

Back at her desk, Kitty flipped through old interviews, hoping for inspiration. She turned to *Journalism for Women*, Arnold Bennett's excellent guide on the subject. When at a loss, she found it spurred her creativity. Mr. Bennett observed that in the early years, the "sole subjects deemed worthy of a newspaper's attention were politics, money, and the law… Formerly, newspapers had a morbid dread of being readable." But things had changed, and now the "aim is to be inclusive, satisfying the public curiosity and at the same time whetting it; for the more the public knows, the more it wants to know. And it refuses any longer to make a task of newspaper-reading. It demands that it shall be amused while it is instructed, like a child at a kindergarten."

So, he advised, reporters should wake up in the morning and come up with ideas like "Queer Ways of Sleeping" or "How to Economize Space in a Small Bedroom."

Or, Kitty thought, why not disorders of sleep? Why not somnambulism, its causes, effects, and remedies?

"For New Year's Day?" Miss Busby didn't sound pleased when Kitty suggested the idea. She tapped her pencil on her desk in annoyance. "How is it relevant? No, give me something festive, Miss Weeks. We are looking forward to, not dreading, what lies ahead of us."

When she finished working at lunchtime, Kitty asked

Rao to take her to the East Side, where her friend Amanda Vanderwell lived. While Amanda was away in Europe working as a nurse's aide, her snooty mother had warmed toward Kitty, and from time to time, Kitty liked to pay her a visit. But today, she had an ulterior motive. Mrs. Vanderwell knew everyone in society, and Kitty suspected she might know the Brights and be able to provide more color—or gossip—on what had happened.

Gilbert, the Vanderwells' wizened old maid, opened the front door to the narrow brownstone building. She was such a fixture in the household that she was only known by the nickname that Amanda had given her as child, its origins lost in the hazy mists of time. Strains of triumphant music came from the parlor as Kitty entered. Amanda's portly mother sat on a bench, eyes closed, chubby fingers flying up and down the baby grand. Amanda had told Kitty that Mrs. Vanderwell aspired to become a concert pianist in her youth, but her grandparents had discouraged their daughter's ambition. Now, Mrs. V. played for her own pleasure, to calm her nerves, and—Kitty recalled Amanda whispering mischievously—to make everyone else feel hopelessly untalented in comparison.

The final notes of the piece died down, and Delphy Vanderwell opened her eyes. "Ah, it's you, Capability. I thought I heard someone… Turn on the light, Gilbert."

Gilbert doddered over to a table lamp. The Vanderwells were old money, but there wasn't much of that left, so they took pains to keep costs low wherever possible, especially when it came to newfangled luxuries like electrical expenditures.

Mrs. Vanderwell picked up her rings from the top of the

piano and coaxed them back on. "So nice of you to visit, my dear. I have wonderful news; Amanda says she might be back in January. About time too. I think all this tending to the wounded has made her pretty melancholy."

"I can't imagine her like that." In fact, it was Amanda who loved to tease Kitty for being too serious.

"Well, that's what she sounds like in all of her letters." Mrs. Vanderwell moved over to the couch. "And as it is, she won't make any promises. She says she will come home only if replacements arrive to take her place. And how are you?"

Kitty sat back. "To be honest, Mrs. Vanderwell, I need your help."

Gilbert shuffled in with tea and toast on a tray, and Mrs. Vanderwell gestured for Kitty to pour for them both.

"A girl I met passed away," Kitty said. "I thought you might know the family. Her name was Bright."

"Elspeth Bright."

Kitty put down her cup. "So you do know her."

"I know her mother. At least, we were great friends until Ephigenia took up the suffrage cause. Ever since then, she's neglected anyone who doesn't attend all those tiresome meetings. She certainly neglected Elspeth. Why else send her away to school? We have plenty of perfectly fine schools in the city."

"Did you know Miss Bright was a somnambulist?"

"I recall Ephigenia mentioning something of the sort when Elspeth was a child. I thought she'd grown out of it."

"I'm sorry," Kitty burst out. "I just don't believe she would die—and to freeze to death all of a sudden. It's too grotesque. Like a story pulled from a dime novel."

"Well, it certainly happened," Mrs. Vanderwell replied without losing her composure. "The funeral service is this evening." "Will you go?"

"I haven't been invited. They want to keep it private. Understandably so. A child's death…" Mrs. Vanderwell sighed. "I don't know what I would do if anything ever happened to my Amanda. Did you know Elspeth well? Are you quite cut up about it?"

"It bothers me." Kitty picked up her tea again. "Miss Bright was just an acquaintance, but I find what happened to her troubling. She gave no sign of being someone who might die at any minute. And if something like that could happen to her, well then, why not to any one of us? Why not to me?"

"Do you suffer from somnambulism as well?" Mrs. Vanderwell's motherly features creased with worry.

"Fortunately not. What I mean to say is that Miss Bright seemed perfectly healthy, and she was young and in good spirits."

"Appearances can be misleading, Capability. But I can tell it's been a shock for you. Why don't you see my nerve man? He may be able to help."

Kitty shrank back. "I don't want to take any medicines."

Amanda's mother smiled. "You young girls are all the same. You think you can manage everything by yourselves. In my day, we never hesitated to say yes to a little pick-me-up. There's no harm in taking some tonic or pills just to tide one over."

"I'd rather not, Mrs. Vanderwell." That was how too many ladies became addicted to one kind of medication or another.

"He may be able to explain to you how it happened. The causes behind somnambulism and that sort of disease."

"He would do that?"

Amanda's mother brightened. "He will if I ask." She patted Kitty on the knee. "He's terribly busy, but he owes me a favor. You'll see, my dear. You won't regret it."

CHAPTER FIVE

A bust of bearded, bald Hippocrates sat near a malachite pen holder and vellum-paged notepad. Volumes with titles beginning *Disorders of...*, *Disturbances to...*, and *Abnormalities in...* covered the shelves to the right of the physician's desk.

"Please have a seat," Dr. Flagg said in a surprisingly thin, high-pitched voice. "I'm glad to be able to squeeze you in."

His office reeked of rubbing alcohol and—or so Kitty fancied—the fears and hopes of his patients. She shot a glance at the glass-fronted cabinet arrayed with shining metal instruments, the padded leather examination chair with its leather straps and metal buckles.

"I hope Mrs. Vanderwell informed you that I begin all consultations with a physical exam. Of course, we will have a nurse present."

"No," Kitty squeaked. She patted her forehead with a handkerchief. "I'm here on behalf of someone else."

"I beg your pardon. I wasn't aware of that."

"My friend is a somnambulist, or, rather, was a somnambulist. And as a nerve specialist, Mrs. Vanderwell said you would be able to help me understand her condition."

Dr. Flagg scowled, evidently displeased.

"Mrs. Vanderwell told me you were an expert," Kitty went

on. "I wouldn't have troubled you, but I work for the *New York Sentinel*, and my editor thought I should write a story about the disease. We would quote you as a source." In many cases, Kitty found, the newspaper angle made a difference. It stoked people's vanities to think they might be mentioned in an article.

Dr. Flagg removed his gold pen from its holder and held it loosely between his fingers. He blinked once or twice. "I don't care for publicity myself...but my patients do like to feel that they're being treated by the best. Seeing my name in print might boost their confidence."

"Absolutely, Dr. Flagg."

"And you will be charged for the consultation."

"I'm prepared to pay, Doctor." Thank goodness, Kitty thought, that she could afford it and that she had brought along some extra money.

"All right then." He put down the pen. "Let's begin. So where were we? Ah, yes. Somnambulism." He leaned back in his chair. "It's one of the phases of grand hypnotism, along with catalepsy and lethargy—"

"I've been told that my friend walked out into the cold while she was asleep," Kitty broke in to avoid a long, technical lecture. "And she then died of exposure. Does that seem plausible to you?"

Dr. Flagg didn't miss a beat. "Absolutely."

"Oh." Kitty had hoped he would contradict her and tell her that it was impossible, that something less extraordinary had caused Elspeth's death. It wasn't dying from exposure that Kitty objected to; it was the sleepwalking, the idea that she could have been cold enough to die and yet not wake up and run home to safety.

"Tell me more about this young person," the doctor said. "I assume she was young?"

"She was a student at Westfield Hall."

"I see." Dr. Flagg rose. "Of course, that explains it." He pulled a book from his shelf and showed it to Kitty. "Are you familiar with this?" It was called *Sex in Education; or, A Fair Chance for the Girls.* "It's written by Dr. Edward Clarke, who was a Harvard man. Some of his ideas have been contested, but the main ones hold. Would you care for me to explain them to you? They will help you make sense of what happened to your friend."

"Please." The smell of the rubbing alcohol and sight of the instruments in the glass case no longer disturbed Kitty. She sat up straight, ready to hear everything.

The doctor returned to his chair and brought his fingertips together. "First, you must understand that three systems control every living body. These are?" He waited for Kitty to answer.

"Why don't you tell me, Doctor?"

"The nutritive, which controls digestion; the nervous, which controls sensation; and the reproductive, which controls the sexual health of the organism."

A splash of color appeared on Kitty's cheeks. She reminded herself that Dr. Flagg was a medical man. There was no need to feel ashamed.

"The first two systems," the doctor went on, "are identical in women and men. As for the third, the female has a set of organs particular to herself. If properly cared for, they bring vitality and power to her being. If neglected, however"—he paused, allowing the import of his words to sink in—"she is beset by disease and illness."

Kitty had never heard human physiology described with such candor and in such stark detail, and she tried to conceal her embarrassment by staring intently at the marble statue of the Greek physician on his desk.

"You must understand," Dr. Flagg continued, oblivious to her discomfort, "that there are three stages of life. The first extends from birth to maturity—from zero to about twelve or fifteen years. The second, mature phase extends from about fifteen years to forty-five years. And the final stage lasts from about forty-five years to death. It is the *transition* between these stages that is critical.

"Women's organs exhibit a complexity, delicacy, and force, which are among the marvels of creation—but they can also be easily derailed. A habit of regular, healthy menstruation must be achieved during the first transitional phase, by the age of eighteen or twenty. If not"—he emphasized each word—"it will *never be achieved in the future*."

It took a moment for the shocking conclusion to register. "Never?"

"I'm afraid so. The point that Dr. Clarke makes so elo-quently is that girls between the ages of fourteen and twenty must have adequate time to rest and enough time to develop properly. But unfortunately, this is the exact juncture at which girls who attend academies or institutions of higher learning subject themselves to rigorous mental exertion, which diverts energy away from the reproductive system, and this, in turn, leads to hideous mental and physical consequences." He looked at Kitty pointedly.

"Allow me to give you an example. A capable girl, let's call her Miss A., entered a seminary at the age of fifteen. Always anxious, she practiced her recitations standing up for hours on end, which caused terrible effects. She began to hemorrhage monthly. Her skin turned pale, and she started to twitch involuntarily. Eventually, her parents removed her from school, but while the hemorrhages ceased, dysmenorrhea afflicted her for the remainder of her days."

"But that's terrible!"

"Nature is a stern master, Miss Weeks. Of course, Dr. Clarke doesn't claim that education for girls is wrong. In fact, quite the opposite. He wants to make sure that young women have an equal chance for success in *all* aspects of life, which is why he maintains that most education takes place at the wrong *time* in a girl's development. I believe that is what afflicted your friend and led to her somnambulism."

"I see." Could what he had said explain Elspeth's malady?

"Do you have any questions?"

She thought for a moment. The Misses Dancey, who ran the boarding school that she had attended, enforced strict rules. They consulted *What a Young Woman Ought to Know* and instructed their charges to avoid tight clothing and corsets. The girls took adequate rest, light exercise during monthly periods, and bathed regularly. But Kitty herself wasn't yet twenty, and she had been working at the *Sentinel* for almost a full year. "Dr. Flagg, would one know if one suffered from such ills?" She feared his response but couldn't help herself from asking.

"You would feel it, Miss Weeks. You might not care to admit it to yourself, but you would know."

"How?" Kitty persisted. "Are there any telltale signs?"

"Are we still talking about your friend?"

She shook her head.

"Well then. Do you suffer from monthly fatigue?"

"No, Doctor."

"Regular dizziness or lethargy?"

"I'm safe in that regard."

"Do you take care of yourself? Eat well, rest adequately?"

"I do, but I also work."

"Oh yes. I forgot about that… For how long?"

"Since the beginning of the year, but I work half days." Kitty and Miss Busby had agreed upon that arrangement, because Mr. Weeks didn't want her working from nine to five. "Who knows?" he had said with a crooked smile. "It might look like we need the money, or even worse, that you're serious about a career."

Dr. Flagg considered what Kitty had told him. "How old are you?"

"I turn twenty in May."

"You look perfectly healthy to me. But to be honest, any damage that could have occurred has already happened. Now it's just a question of managing the consequences." He checked his pocket watch. "Will that be all, Miss Weeks?"

"Thank you, Doctor." Kitty stood and shook his hand.

"My pleasure. And if you have any other concerns, do feel free to come see me again."

Kitty returned to work in a daze. She had always pooh-poohed girls who coddled themselves and spent a few days each month resting. If only the medical reason had been explained to her properly...

She paused at the entrance to the hen coop. The sore arms and wrists of the typists banging away at their machines for nine and ten hours a day were the least of their worries. She now understood that they might be setting themselves up for terrible futures—futures permanently marred by debilitating illness.

"Are you all right?" Jeannie stood and picked up her things. "You don't look yourself." Not wanting their editor to panic, Kitty had telephoned to say she would be late because of a doctor's visit.

Kitty managed a smile. "Do you feel you work too hard, Jeannie?"

"I'd work less if I could," Jeannie replied as they made their way down the corridor, "and spend more time gadding about and going to the movies. But then again, who wouldn't?"

"Hello, girls." Miss Busby set aside her papers. "Let's discuss resolutions. Jeannie, what do you have for me?"

Kitty's mind wandered. This summer, the editor had had a breakdown as the result of her many responsibilities. Whose turn would it be next? One of the other girls at the hen coop? Jeannie's? Hers?

"Miss Weeks." Miss Busby snapped her fingers. "Miss Weeks, may I have a moment of your attention? Miss Williams and I were talking about resolutions. Do you have anything you'd like to add to the list?"

Shaken from her reverie, Kitty replied without thinking. "I'd like to stay healthy."

"Excellent. All the riches in the world are nothing compared to good health. Write that down, Jeannie." Miss Busby beamed. "And do you know what my resolution is, girls?" The opalescent earrings dangling from her earlobes swayed as Helena Busby nodded. "I have resolved to be more open to change. And so, Mademoiselles Weeks and Williams, I have decided that for our January 1 issue, the two of you will go to Times Square and cover our city's New Year's Eve celebrations."

"The public celebrations?" Jeannie couldn't keep the excitement from her voice.

"Yes."

"At midnight, Miss Busby?" Kitty added.

"Yes." The editor couldn't stop smiling. "You must tell your father, of course, and, Miss Williams, you should ask your landlady's permission."

"You want us out among the crowds?" That didn't sound at all like the Helena Busby Kitty knew, always concerned about appearances.

"Haven't you always told me you want to be a real reporter, Miss Weeks?" Miss Busby replied. "Here's your chance."

Thousands of inebriated revelers thronged in Times Square to bring in the new year. It would be loud, crowded, and rowdy. Kitty did want to be a real reporter, out on assignment, but this wasn't reporting. It was a recipe for being knocked about and manhandled. And the story wouldn't do much for the Page or its readers. In the end, it would be so much more fluff, just another account of a festive evening, though on a far grander scale than she had ever witnessed.

"I'm finished." Kitty rushed into the apartment and threw herself onto the couch in her father's study.

He remained seated in his armchair. "Finished with what?"

"I don't want to work anymore. I've made a New Year's resolution to leave the *Sentinel*."

"Don't be silly."

"I went to see a doctor." Kitty hugged a pillow to her chest.

"What for?" Her father's tone changed.

"I wanted to speak to him about the girl who died. I told you about her. Do you remember?"

"Of course, I remember."

"Dr. Flagg, a nerve doctor, said that her death was a result of studying too much. He said that overwork causes all sorts of disorders in girls." She found herself blinking away tears.

"Why are you crying?" Julian Weeks said gruffly.

"I don't know." Kitty patted her eyes with a handkerchief. "I'm not really crying. I'm very upset. I don't know what to think."

"You're overwrought."

"Perhaps."

"Have you eaten?"

"Not yet."

"Let's have some lunch then."

"I know the difference between being upset and being hungry," Kitty said, annoyed.

"Fine. Then I don't think you should stop working. Who is this quack you consulted?"

"He's Mrs. Vanderwell's physician. One of the best in Manhattan."

"You're all worked up because one girl has died."

"Yes," Kitty replied with force. "I am."

Julian looked at her silently. Then he brushed an invisible speck of dust from his trousers. "I think you should put this behind you."

"I can't."

"We all must leave this world sometime, Capability. None of us are exempt."

"I know that, but not so young. Not for no reason."

"You know the reason. You may not like it, but you know it." A hint of annoyance crept into his voice.

"I don't want to believe it's true."

Julian Weeks sighed loudly. "You're impossible... The best way to let go is to say our good-byes as best we can. Why don't you pay a condolence visit?"

It took a minute, but Kitty brightened. "Could I?"

"I don't see why not."

"Well, the funeral was just yesterday... But I'll go," she said, "if you'll come with me."

Chapter Six

L eafless trees creaked in the wind as the black Packard snaked through snow-covered Central Park with the Weekses in the passenger seat.

"I'm only coming along," Julian Weeks grumbled, "because I'm concerned about your health, and you are too young to pay a condolence call on your own."

"Thank you." Normally, Mr. Weeks didn't mind what other people thought, but in this case, Kitty was glad to have him with her. She wouldn't have felt right going by herself to a stranger's house at a time like this.

The Packard emerged from the park, which separated the west side of town from the east, and pulled up, a mere half a block farther, in front of a town house between Fifth Avenue and Madison. A Christmas wreath festooned with ribbons and gold bells still hung from the bright-red front door. Ornate stone carvings framed the windows.

A uniformed maid came to the door and took Mr. Weeks's card. She returned in a minute. "This way please, sir."

Kitty first saw Mrs. Bright playing solitaire in a puffy armchair in the parlor. A rakishly handsome young man stood beside the crackling fireplace; he turned as the Weekses entered and ran a hand through his wavy blond hair. "I'll be on my way then." He nodded at the newcomers.

Mrs. Bright snapped a ten of hearts below the jack and didn't acknowledge his departure. The young man vacated the room with a casual backward glance at Kitty and Mr. Weeks.

"I'm sorry. We don't mean to disturb you," Julian Weeks said, still standing.

Mrs. Bright held on to her cards. "My maid tells me your daughter knew Elspeth?" She gestured vaguely toward the sofa. "Please, make yourselves comfortable."

"My daughter recently met Miss Bright," Mr. Weeks replied. "And when she heard what happened, well, she was distressed and wanted to pay her respects. We won't keep you long."

Mrs. Bright smiled wanly. "I'm tired. Otherwise, you could stay as long as you like. I have nothing left to do, and I'm in no hurry…" As if to illustrate her exhaustion, her words petered off. She placed her hands in her lap. There was something still about her, as though she was accustomed to waiting.

A family portrait above the mantelpiece showed a younger Elspeth with her parents, sedate Mrs. Bright and an impassive gentleman with muttonchop whiskers. Two boys, twins about four or five years old, stood in front of them, both in little white suits with their hair neatly combed and parted to the side.

Below the painting, two bouquets of irises flanked a more recent photograph of Elspeth in a silver frame. She stared dreamily off into the distance.

Mrs. Bright caught Kitty looking. "She's lovely, isn't she?"

"A beauty," Kitty agreed. "I was impressed by her from the moment we met. She told me she wanted to go college."

Her mother smiled. "How did you meet my daughter, Miss—"

"Weeks," Julian Weeks replied.

"I'm a reporter at the Ladies' Page of the *New York Sentinel*. I met Miss Bright while I was writing a story about Westfield Hall, and then I met her again last week at Tipton's."

Two spots of color appeared on the mother's cheeks. "You did?"

"I thought I might write a story about her. She would have cleared it with you first."

Mrs. Bright tilted her head. "I doubt it. If she wanted something, Elspeth would act first and ask questions later... May I ask what you spoke about?"

"Not much, I'm afraid. We were interrupted by a mother of a school friend, a Mrs. Marquand. I had hoped to learn more about Miss Bright's scientific studies and ambitions."

Mrs. Bright nodded. "The Marquands live down the street from us. She's very nosy."

"That's what Miss Bright said."

Mrs. Bright closed her eyes. She kept them closed for so long—at least five or ten seconds—that Kitty wondered if it was some kind of signal for them to leave, but then she opened them again. "You liked my daughter?"

"I didn't know her well, but what I saw, I liked very much."

"Can you be discreet, Miss Weeks?"

Kitty glanced at her father. "I believe so. I hope I am."

Mr. Weeks shifted slightly in his seat but didn't interrupt.

"I could use your help," Mrs. Bright said.

Mr. Weeks turned to look at the woman squarely. "What kind of help, Mrs. Bright?"

Elspeth's mother picked up the deck and separated the cards into two piles. "Elspeth must have had something on her mind, something that was gnawing at her. She wouldn't have walked in her sleep otherwise." The cards whirred as she shuffled them in her lap. "She did it often when she was a child," Mrs. Bright went on. "But we were assured she would grow out of it, and she did. But from time to time, whenever something troubled her, she would wander off into the night. This time, whatever was bothering her led to her death. And I need to know what it was."

"I'm sorry, I wish I could help you, but she didn't tell me anything," Kitty replied. "As a matter of fact, she seemed to me to be in very good spirits."

"She must have had something on her mind." Mrs. Bright held on to the thought as though it were a life preserver. "I'm sure her friends would know."

"Then perhaps you should speak to them," Kitty suggested gently.

Mrs. Bright looked up at Kitty. "Perhaps you could ask them for me."

"I beg your pardon?" Kitty didn't know how to respond. "I don't think—"

Julian Weeks intervened. "My daughter isn't acquainted with Miss Bright's friends, and she wouldn't want to pry into her personal affairs."

"Miss Weeks wouldn't be prying; she would be helping—and at my request. I've been torturing myself, wondering what was on Elspeth's mind. And you know how young women are— they don't tell us old folks anything."

"I'm afraid it's not my daughter's place." Mr. Weeks sounded firm, and Kitty could tell he'd had enough.

"It's just one or two girls." Mrs. Bright spoke with a hint of desperation. "Prudence Marquand and the head girl from Westfield, Georgina Howell. They were both here for dinner the night Elspeth died."

"Thank you for your time, Mrs. Bright. I'm very sorry for your loss. Now Miss Weeks and I must be on our way." Julian Weeks stood.

Mrs. Bright cast an imploring look at Kitty. "Thank you for visiting, my dear. It gives me some small measure of comfort to know that Elspeth had such a powerful effect on strangers."

"That she most certainly did," Kitty said.

Mr. Weeks waited until the door to the Brights' home closed behind them. "I feel sorry for her, Capability, but she has no right to parlay any sympathy you might feel into the idea that you would do a favor of that sort for her. How can she imagine that you would be willing to poke around in her dead daughter's business?"

Kitty climbed into the Packard. "It's ridiculous."

"I'm glad to hear you say that."

The car pulled away from the red door with the Christmas wreath. Kitty hoped that her father would take her silence to mean that she and he were in agreement.

CHAPTER SEVEN

Have you discussed New Year's Eve with Mr. Weeks yet?" Helena Busby inquired the following morning. "Will he allow you to go out?" She had scribbled notes on a copy of the day's paper with headlines announcing MODIFIED CONSCRIPTION FOR BRITAIN and OUR RELATIONS WITH AUSTRIA ACUTE.

"Oh." Kitty's hand flew to her forehead. "I'm sorry, Miss Busby. It slipped my mind."

"Slipped your mind, Miss Weeks? It's the twenty-ninth already, and you are usually so chop-chop with things. Do you not wish to undertake this assignment?"

"I'm afraid I'm not myself at the moment," Kitty confessed.

"Well, you better become yourself again, or I might have to rethink our arrangement."

Kitty took that to mean the arrangement that she and Miss Busby had come to in August, whereby she wrote the feature stories and interviews, and Jeannie handled the regular pieces like contests, advice columns, and so on.

Miss Busby raised her eyebrows. "Do you have any ideas for next month?"

"I thought perhaps I might interview Madame Alice Guy Blaché," Kitty suggested. "She's married, and I believe she owns her own film studio out in Fort Lee, New Jersey. She's been making films since they were first invented."

"What is this fascination with cinema?" Helena Busby burst out. "Pictures, heroines, drama—do you girls ever think about anything else? For next month, we need something different. A piece that straddles tradition and originality, the old and the new—"

"Could you give me an example?"

"Well." Miss Busby paused. "For instance, Mrs. Alva Belmont will be producing a suffragist operetta featuring all the best debutantes in the city."

"Now, that's interesting." Society ladies often put up tableaux or plays to raise funds for charitable causes. And the slate for the first months of 1916 included a Ball of the Gods, a pageant at the Astor, based on the premise that a sibyl had summoned the gods of Egypt, Hindustan, and Greece to the island of Cyprus; a black-and-white ball at Sherry's; and for the first time ever, a photoplay—the old-fashioned term for what many now simply called the "movies"—enticingly titled *The Flame of Kapur.*

Even society was modernizing its offerings, so why not Miss Busby? "Let's interview Mrs. Belmont," Kitty said.

Miss Busby laughed. "You want to interview Alva Belmont?"

"Is there something wrong with that?"

"She's a tyrant. Grown men have been reduced to tears in her presence. And she's been divorced."

"Miss Busby, we can't bridge the gap between old and new if we refuse to speak to divorcées." Mrs. Belmont had parted ways with her first husband, William K. Vanderbilt, and married Mr. Oliver Hazard Perry Belmont, who had died, leaving her a wealthy widow. She had orchestrated the wedding of her daughter, Consuelo Vanderbilt to the Duke of Marlborough, a marriage that had been considered a great accomplishment but ended in separation.

"I hate to say it, but you may be right." Miss Busby sighed. "Times are changing, and we must make allowances. Some allowances," Miss Busby added, in order to clarify that she wasn't giving Kitty free rein. "There's only one problem. I wouldn't know how to reach her."

"Isn't she involved with the Women's Congressional Union?" The group was a suffragist organization, and—if Kitty recalled correctly—Elspeth Bright had mentioned at the tearoom that her mother was a member.

"Mrs. Belmont is the Congressional Union's most important benefactor."

"Leave it to me then." Kitty was beginning to see a way she could use the confluence of interests to her advantage.

Miss Busby stared at the mess of papers on her desk. "Divorced women remarrying, widows in the White House. It's a struggle to keep up. Do you think me terribly old-fashioned, Miss Weeks?"

"I think you run a very successful section of the paper, Miss Busby. You know what appeals to our readers. We attract the best advertisers. I'm proud to work here."

"Really?" The wrinkled face looked up at her.

"Don't doubt yourself now, Miss Busby. It will be a new dawn for the Ladies' Page." And as she said the words, Kitty realized she believed them.

CHAPTER EIGHT

Y ou're back, Miss Kitty." Grace opened the door to the apartment on West End Avenue.

"Do we have visitors?" Kitty held out her arms, and the maid helped her off with her coat.

"Mr. and Miss Lane. They've been here for the past hour."

"Is that you, Capability?" Mr. Weeks called from his study. "Come on in."

Hugo Lane and Mr. Weeks sat side by side in armchairs, smoking cigars, while Sylvia Lane graced the sofa opposite.

"I hope you don't mind the smoke," she said to Kitty. "It's Hugo's bad influence on your father."

Kitty took a seat beside her. "I rather like the smell. So much nicer than cigarettes."

"How was work?" Mr. Weeks blew out a puff, evidently enjoying himself.

"Fine, thanks."

"I think it's wonderful that you work," Miss Lane put in. "Every young woman should if she can."

Her brother laughed. "Don't listen to Sylvia. She'll have you up in arms, petitioning for the rights of women, if you give her the opening."

Miss Lane turned to Kitty. "Do you have any interesting assignments coming up?"

"As a matter of fact, I do." Kitty looked at her father. "I forgot to ask you—in a rare departure from form, Miss Busby wants me to do something risqué. She'd like Jeannie Williams and me to cover the New Year's Eve revels in Times Square."

"I've heard about that!" Miss Lane clapped her hands. "Don't they drop a ball?"

"I don't know, Capability." Kitty's father examined the tip of his cigar. "Those things can get boisterous quickly. Everyone will have had too much to drink. The young fellows will be out to have a good time."

Kitty had anticipated his objection. And to be honest, she didn't care to be pinched or groped in the crowd. "I'll ask Rao to come with us. And afterward, we'll go straight back to the paper and write the story in time for the morning deadline."

"When would you come home?"

"Two o'clock?" Kitty hazarded a guess.

"Two in the morning! That's beyond the pale."

"Oh, let her go," Miss Lane intervened. "She's only going to be young once."

Mr. Weeks stubbed out his cigar in the ashtray. "Suppose something goes wrong?"

"I can take care of myself," Kitty said. "And I won't be alone. I can bring Grace too—I'm sure she'd like to come along."

"Try to remember how you felt when you were her age, Julian," Miss Lane added.

Kitty noted Miss Lane's use of her father's Christian name

and the ease with which she participated in what was a family discussion. "I have to tell Miss Busby by tomorrow."

"And I take it you don't want to disappoint her?" Julian Weeks asked. "I fear I will live to regret this." He looked away for an instant. "But you can go if you must."

"Wonderful." Miss Lane smiled at Kitty. "I will want to hear all about it."

Kitty smiled back at her smartly dressed and unexpected ally. Miss Lane really did look attractive in the peacock-blue jacket that skimmed her narrow shoulders and unexpectedly complemented the coppery-red of her hair.

She telephoned Mrs. Bright after the Lanes left and Mr. Weeks headed out to his club. Although she didn't relish having to ask a recently bereaved woman for a favor, she thought it would provide a good cover if at some point she had to explain to her father why she reinitiated contact.

"It's Capability Weeks," Kitty said when Mrs. Bright came on the line. "We met yesterday."

"I remember you."

"I wanted to say that I would be happy to speak to Miss Bright's friends if that is still something you would like me to do."

"I would—but you must promise me something. I don't want you to tell anyone else what you find out. Rumors spread. I don't want to see stories about my daughter printed in the press."

"Oh no, Mrs. Bright. This is strictly personal, a favor to you." And, thought Kitty, for Elspeth.

"Thank you for understanding." She gave Kitty Prudence Marquand's address. "And as for Miss Howell, she lives at school, so speaking to her might be more difficult. She's a scholarship girl, no parents. It's why we invited her for Christmas."

"I'll do my best," Kitty said and then changed tack. "May I ask you something, Mrs. Bright? If this isn't the right time, please let me know. It won't in any way affect my decision to speak to Miss Marquand and Miss Howell."

"Go ahead. I'm listening."

"This has nothing to do with your daughter." Kitty plunged in. "My editor would like me to interview Mrs. Belmont."

"And you want me to put in a word?"

"Only if you know her, and if it's not too much trouble. I wish I didn't have to ask, but—"

"It's quite all right, my dear. I understand. Even without Elspeth in it, somehow or the other, life goes ahead."

Kitty announced her good news about New Year's to Miss Busby the next morning.

"Glad to hear it, Miss Weeks." Miss Busby beamed. "Just in time. Otherwise, I don't know what we'd have done."

"I've made arrangements to come back late to the boardinghouse," Jeannie added. "Normally, all us girls have to be in before nine."

"Every night?" Kitty said.

"My landlady doesn't make exceptions," Jeannie replied. "I had to tell her that I would lose my job and wouldn't be able to pay the rent!"

"Enough chitchat, ladies." Miss Busby glanced at them from

behind her desk. "Let's finish up here. Tomorrow will be a big night for you both."

"What do you think has come over her?" Jeannie asked as she and Kitty returned to their desks.

"She's feeling old-fashioned. Trying to make up for lost time."

"What will she do next?" Jeannie wondered. "Start wearing short skirts?" Both girls dissolved into giggles at the thought of Miss Busby's spindly ankles peeking out from beneath a raised hem.

Rao drove Kitty to the Marquands' home after work, and on the way over, she mentioned that she would be covering the New Year's Eve festivities and asked if he would accompany her.

"With pleasure, Miss Weeks." The chauffeur tipped his cap. "I'd like to see them myself."

CHAPTER NINE

M rs. Marquand opened the front door and frowned. "Have we met before?"

"At Tipton's," Kitty said. "I'm a friend of Elspeth Bright's."
The door opened a shade wider. "Oh, yes."

"I'm also a reporter for the Ladies' Page of the *New York Sentinel*," Kitty said as she came in. "I wrote the story on Westfield Hall that appeared in the paper two weeks ago, but I'm not here on business. It's strictly private. I was wondering if I might speak to Miss Marquand."

Mrs. Marquand eyed her suspiciously again. "What for?"

"Mrs. Bright wanted to know whether something had been troubling her daughter—whether she had something on her mind that made her walk in her sleep again. I believe Miss Marquand had dinner at the Brights' on Christmas?"

"Yes." Mrs. Marquand led Kitty down the hall. "They invited our family. We were all there."

"Ah, so you're all friends."

"In a manner of speaking. Between you and me, Miss Weeks, I don't have much patience for Ephigenia Bright's suffrage activities." She adjusted her diamond bracelet. "I believe that a woman's place is in the home, and that's where women's rights begin. If Effie hadn't been so busy with whatever it is she does and had paid more attention to her daughter, then—well, one doesn't like to say it—but perhaps Elspeth might not have been wandering out and about like that. As it was, I didn't like to see her out alone with you at Tipton's."

"I see." Kitty felt Mrs. Marquand's criticism to be in bad taste. People had different views on how far a girl could roam unchaperoned and unsupervised. Julian Weeks gave Kitty a pretty long leash, but for the Brights' neighbor, it would seem that even a few blocks was too much. "Mrs. Bright thought Miss Marquand might know something...that Miss Bright might have said something to her, one girl to another."

"And she deputized you to come instead of asking herself?" Prudence Marquand's mother looked at Kitty askance.

"She thought it might be more effective coming from someone her daughter's age. You know how girls are."

Mrs. Marquand put her hand on the bannister. "That I do. Prudence," she called up the stairs. "Prudence. Come on down. There's someone here to see you." She turned to Kitty. "Let's wait in the parlor. Prudence will meet us there."

A sullen, baby-faced girl shuffled in a few minutes after Kitty had settled into a comfortable living room with a fireplace and mantel not dissimilar to the Brights', except there were no photographs here. Only a white porcelain cat and three silver boxes.

"Look sharp, Prudence," her mother said. "Miss Weeks is from the papers. What will she think if you slouch so?"

Prudence Marquand didn't say anything but came and sat opposite Kitty without showing much interest. It looked as though someone else had chosen her red skirt and frilly blouse patterned with tiny flowers.

"Miss Weeks would like to ask you some questions about

Elspeth." Mrs. Marquand maintained her forcefully cheerful manner, but clearly, her daughter's behavior in front of a newswoman was a disappointment.

"I don't know anything." Prudence picked at her cheek.

Mrs. Marquand sighed. "Don't touch, darling."

"I wonder," Kitty said, "would you mind leaving us alone for a moment?"

"Perhaps that's for the best." Mrs. Marquand rose. "Do try to be cooperative, Prudence."

"I don't know why you want to speak with me, Miss Weeks," the girl said once her mother left the room. "We were invited to dinner because we're neighbors and I've known Elspeth for ages, but I didn't like her, and she didn't like me. I am sorry though that she died."

"Oh." Kitty hadn't expected to hear such a blunt account of the situation and that the two girls weren't friends. And Mrs. Marquand didn't care for Mrs. Bright's activities either. She hoped at least the fathers enjoyed each other's company, or it would have made for a very dreary dinner. "May I ask why you didn't get along?"

"Elspeth was a strange girl," Prudence said.

"In what way?"

Prudence wrinkled her nose as she hunted for an answer. "She spent all her time with that odd Mrs. Swartz. And she kept a photograph of ugly, old Thomas Edison pinned beside her desk. We had nothing in common."

"Miss Bright admired Mr. Edison?"

"I suppose so. She must have. It can't have been for his looks"—the Wizard of Menlo Park was in his seventies and hadn't ever been handsome—"but then again, you never knew with Elspeth." Prudence couldn't resist a smirk.

"So, you wouldn't have known if she had anything on her mind the night she died. Any girlish worries, for instance?" Kitty had begun to wonder whether Prudence held a grudge against Elspeth, or whether Elspeth had some secret beau hidden in the background.

"Elspeth didn't have girlish worries. She wasn't very girlish, if you know what I mean."

"I'm afraid I don't, Miss Marquand."

"She dabbled in her science constantly." Prudence pronounced the word with disdain. "Always in the laboratory with her experiments and her beakers. So proud to be different from the rest of us. I mean, who did she think she was—a young fellow?"

"I think it's admirable that Miss Bright was interested in scientific pursuits." Kitty felt sorry for Elspeth. Perhaps the other girls found her strange as well.

"The birds and the bees, fish, flowers—nature drawing—I can understand all of that." For the first time during their conversation, Prudence looked Kitty in the eye. "But batteries?"

"I beg your pardon?" Kitty didn't think she had heard correctly.

"That's right. Miss Bright was working on something to do with batteries."

"She told you so?"

Miss Marquand took a hankie from her pocket and started winding it around her little finger. "I heard her arguing with Dr. Bright that evening when we came in. She said something about batteries to him and how she'd stake her life on what she believed, and then..." The handkerchief stopped moving. "That very night, she passed on."

CHAPTER TEN

K itty returned to the *Sentinel* and hurried straight to the basement. "I need your help, Mr. Musser."

Herman Musser wiped his mustache on his sleeve. He ate lunch at his counter on busy days. "Well, *Guten Tag*, Miss Weeks. Fancy seeing you at this hour." He brought out a jar and offered it to Kitty.

She shook her head. "No, thanks. Are these the pickles that Mrs. Codd made?" She often brought him samples of her cook's spicier experiments.

"Mmm-hmm. My compliments to the chef. This batch is particularly potent. But you were saying—?"

"Elspeth Bright, the girl somnambulist, was studying something to do with batteries before she died, and I was hoping you could help me learn more about them." Kitty made a face. "I know it's probably a vast topic."

"Have you considered speaking to her teachers?"

"School isn't in session. And besides, I think I should understand the subject before I start asking questions."

Musser stepped out from behind his counter. "You don't make this easy, Miss Weeks."

"I thought you would appreciate the challenge."

The fuzzy eyebrows wrinkled. "All right then. Batteries,

batteries, batteries." He shuffled to the wall of drawers that held his painstakingly detailed index cards.

"Batteries," he said again and opened a drawer. He flipped through the entries, then shook his head.

"Is there something wrong, Mr. Musser?"

"There's just too much information. You will be overwhelmed—I am overwhelmed. Do you even know what a battery is?"

"Not really," Kitty admitted. "I know it stores electricity, and it makes things go?"

The old man laughed. "You're as bad as I am. Tell me more about this girl. Did she have any interest in cars, for instance?"

"I have no idea. Her work on batteries may have had something to do with Thomas Edison." Kitty recalled Prudence Marquand's remark about the photograph pinned beside Elspeth's desk.

"That's like a literary scholar who studies Shakespeare. It hardly narrows things down."

"I wish I could, Mr. Musser, but I don't know anything more than what I've just told you."

"Well then, we will have to try again tomorrow. The newsroom needs stories on the Welland Canal business"—German spies had been caught trying to blow up the canal in Canada and thereby disrupt North American shipping routes—"as well as the automobile show and the English bond market. And those must come first."

"You don't have an extra minute?"

"It's not just an extra minute's work. That's the problem." He retreated to his counter. "We'll find you something, *fräulein*. Don't look so disappointed."

"Thank you, Mr. Musser." Kitty had no choice but to wait until his more pressing tasks were finished.

Julian Weeks heard the front door open from his study.

"You're late, Capability," he called.

Kitty peeled off her gloves and handed them to Grace. "I'm sorry. I sent Rao back for you." She joined him inside. Kitty had told the chauffeur to go home after he dropped her off at the Marquands. Now she feared that Rao might have mentioned her little detour.

"I was about to leave." Then Mr. Weeks slipped in casually, "You had a visitor. A young man."

"Who?"

"That Secret Service agent you met over the summer, Mr. Soames. He said he had been in touch."

Kitty felt her ears go hot. "He sent me one letter." She had met Soames briefly before he was transferred to Washington, DC. And after that one letter, he had gone quiet.

"He waited for half an hour, I'd say. Seems a very nice fellow. Intelligent, well-mannered. I liked his conversation."

Kitty collected her thoughts and said, "What did you talk about?"

"Oh, this and that. He asked if he could call on you this weekend."

"And what did you tell him?"

"I said you would be out tomorrow morning and night, so he will try to come by on Saturday afternoon. He leaves for

Washington on Sunday. He must be busy—he's on the president's security detail now."

"Oh." Kitty tried to sound casual when she was both intrigued and impressed. "I didn't know that."

⍟

"Here you go." Mr. Musser slid a pile of papers onto Kitty's table. "On the eve of the year's most festive celebration, the modern girl studies electric storage batteries."

"You know me too well, Mr. Musser."

"All work and no play?"

"Now you're teasing." Kitty picked up the first story.

"Aren't you excited about the news?"

"Which news exactly?"

"That the Austrian government has punished the U-boat captain responsible for sinking the *Ancona* and is offering reparations for all the lives lost."

"Why should I be excited?" Kitty itched to begin her own work. The *Ancona* was an Italian passenger liner that had sunk in November, resulting in two hundred deaths. It was tragic but nothing compared to the numbers this past May when a German U-boat torpedoed the *Lusitania*.

"If Germany follows suit with the *Lusitania* case," Musser said, "it will show that they're acting in good faith, and the warmongers will find it harder to press their cause."

"That's a big 'if,' Mr. Musser. It's been seven months, and President Wilson and his counterparts in Berlin still can't seem to come to an agreement."

"I live in hope, Miss Weeks. The new year will bring good news."

"I'll believe it when I see it, Mr. Musser."

"Ah, the bitterness of young people."

"I don't mean any disrespect, sir"—Kitty suddenly felt angry—"but old men in Germany, England, and Russia decided to go to war, and young men are dying in it."

"I was only joking, Miss Weeks," the archivist said.

Kitty controlled her frustration and returned to her papers. What a strange mood he was in. He and Miss Busby—it was as though Kitty had become cautious and hardened, and they'd become young and optimistic, almost carefree.

Kitty flipped through the stories Mr. Musser had selected for her. In 1908, a Dr. O. F. Reinholt of Newark, New Jersey, had invented something called an aluminum wet storage battery; in 1909, Norwegian inventor Gross claimed he had invented a storage battery. Kitty didn't know what the difference was.

An article from 1907, NEW BATTERIES POWERFUL, said that Frank C. Curtis of Milwaukee, "inventor of the new battery," expected it to supplant "present sources for light, heat, and power, and gave today some remarkable instances of its abilities." These included powering an electric runabout for 150 miles on a single charge (eighteen cells required), powering a motorboat for nineteen hours (eight cells), and powering an electric piano for months (six cells). Each cell weighed about twelve pounds and was made from new alloys.

Kitty's eyes glazed over as she read the chemical description: *ore…precipitates…metal…sulfides…zinc, aluminum, cadmium, ionites…*

If this was what was on her mind, no wonder Elspeth Bright had disturbed sleep.

An article from 1906 had to do with Thomas Edison and was simply titled ENERGY AND MR. EDISON. Kitty skimmed through it once and then read it again, more carefully, finally beginning to understand what all the fuss about batteries was.

The essay explained that mankind was still a child in relation to the problem of energy. For centuries, humans had depended on wind and water for power. The magnificent steam engine, which propelled boats across the Atlantic, relied on vast amounts of burning coal for a week's journey.

But, the article said, "it is not through pure mechanism that energy will be most economically appropriated."

Something clicked for Kitty. All mankind's sources of energy so far relied on physical mechanics—steam mills, windmills, water wheels, the steam engine all depended on actual move-ment or burning—to produce energy. However, a battery relied on the actions of chemicals upon one another to produce power. It was ingenious!

The 1906 story said that although the storage battery held much promise, as yet, it had accomplished little. But that had been written a decade ago, and a different piece from 1911 said Mr. Edison had announced to the public that he had perfected a storage battery for the running of cars and trucks. The problem with previous batteries was that cars needed to be recharged overnight. The new battery could run a car or truck for up to sixty miles and then be recharged in three minutes.

Were those batteries currently in use? Kitty wondered. Then she realized, since she didn't see too many battery-operated cars on the street, probably not. Perhaps they didn't work as well as Mr. Edison claimed. She visualized Elspeth Bright in a lab, wearing goggles and pouring fizzy chemical solutions from one beaker into another. Her thoughts raced. Could Elspeth have concocted her own chemical mix? One that solved the problems of its predecessors and produced incredible amounts of energy while requiring very little time to charge? If so, no wonder she didn't seem like other girls. No wonder she radiated confidence.

Kitty realized this was all sheer speculation, based solely on the opinion of grumpy Prudence Marquand. Her next step would have to be to return to Westfield Hall and speak to Mrs. Swartz, the science mistress.

"Are you ready?" Miss Busby said to Kitty and Jeannie. "Are you all set?" Her eyes sparkled. "I heard that tonight, New York City will celebrate in record-breaking numbers. All the hotels and restaurants are booked, crowds of up to five hundred thousand are expected, and police reserves have been called to be on hand to keep revelers in check. Mayor Mitchel has given 219 establishments special licenses to stay open late, but they all must close at three o'clock.

"My contact at the Waldorf tells me that they're expecting their biggest New Year's Eve in history with five thousand guests," the editor went on breathlessly. "They've been stockpiling favors and noise-making devices since July. The St. Regis has had to turn people away. There will be ice-skating at the

Biltmore. An artificial lake has been created on the second floor of the hotel, and professionals from the Hippodrome will put on an ice show as well."

"Miss Busby," Kitty interrupted the barrage, "you seem quite excited about all this. Perhaps you would like to join us?"

"Me?" Miss Busby giggled giddily like a schoolgirl. "I'm far too old. Besides, the noise alone would make me faint. You are taking your chauffeur along with you just in case you require assistance, Miss Weeks?"

"Yes."

"The most important thing is not to be daunted," Miss Busby said. "Someone told me that a woman bid fifty dollars for a table at the Ritz-Carlton and still didn't get it."

"Should we put all of this into our story?" Kitty said.

"I think we should." Miss Busby nodded. "Our slant should be that with Europe ravaged by war, Americans play while they can... I don't know, girls, it might be our turn next. This could be our last new year in the city as we know it; by 1917, we might all be under the kaiser's thumb."

"Do you really believe that, Miss Busby?" Kitty had heard reports that prominent citizens—even Mr. Edison—were calling for preparedness out of fear that the Germans might launch amphibious attacks on America's unprotected eastern seaboard. Mr. Weeks had said that such a scenario seemed highly unlikely; Germany had its hands full battling its immediate foes. It could hardly spare men and resources to wage war in New Jersey.

Sandwiched between Jeannie and Grace, Kitty found herself speeding toward Times Square.

Mr. Weeks had made his own way to the Lanes' hotel, and Rao had driven Kitty and Grace to pick up Jeannie from her boardinghouse. All three were sensibly clad in warm coats, hats, and sturdy boots.

"All the other girls were so envious." Jeannie's cheery smile stretched across her cheeks. "They're bringing in the new year with our landlady in the parlor."

As far as ten blocks away from the intersection of Broadway and Forty-Second Street, which formed the center of the revelries, traffic slowed to a crawl.

"Let's walk from here," Kitty suggested.

Rao parked the car and accompanied the three young women on foot. Merrymakers from nearby hotels and restaurants spilled out into the street in fancy dress. Women laughed as they slung mink stoles around their necks or warmed their hands under gentlemen's jackets. Policemen blew on whistles to keep the swell of humanity in check, and Kitty, Jeannie, and Grace linked arms in fear of being separated. Vendors sold souvenirs including toy cannons, zeppelins that discharged miniature shrapnel, and tiny flags. Horns honked, and young and old alike blew on, banged, or played anything that made a noise, from bagpipes to accordions to tin cans.

Kitty, Jeannie, and Grace didn't speak—they wouldn't have been able to hear one another in any case—so with Rao elbowing a path for them, they simply tried to take it all in and avoid being crushed.

"Out with the old and in with the new!" the crowds chanted.

Joined by hundreds of voices, a chorus sang "Auld Lang Syne" and "We Gather Together."

It was ten minutes to midnight when they finally made it to the Times Building on Broadway. All eyes were on the flagpole from which, at exactly midnight, a ball ablaze with electric lights would be dropped.

The minutes ticked away, then all of a sudden, every building in the vicinity went dark.

"Ten," the crowd roared. "Nine—eight—seven—six."

With each number being called, Kitty felt her blood beat faster.

"Five." Her neck ached from craning upward. "Four—three—two"—it was about to descend—"one."

The ground shook. Times Square was a sea of sound. A globe glowing with the number 1916 appeared in midair.

All the lights in the Times Building and Annex turned back on, and the crowd went mad, blowing horns and banging on anything they could find.

Happy New Year! Happy New Year! Happy New Year! Greetings flew about, and even strangers embraced.

Grace, Rao, and Jeannie beamed, but Kitty felt the slow yet insistent drip of anxiety.

CHAPTER ELEVEN

H er ears still ringing from the previous night, Kitty woke at ten the next morning. She brushed her teeth, slipped into her dressing gown, and joined her father in his study, since he had long ago finished breakfast.

"How was last night?" he said.

"Quite a spectacle."

"When did you get in? I didn't hear you. I must have been fast asleep when you arrived."

"About three. We had to write the story and drop Jeannie home."

"Were the streets still crowded?"

"Not like they had been earlier, but a fair number of people were still out and about."

"Well, I have good news." Mr. Weeks handed her the paper. "The new year has started on an excellent note."

Kitty took a look at the headlines: LUSITANIA SETTLEMENT NOW LIKELY, FOLLOWING AUSTRIA'S COMPLIANCE ON ALL OUR DEMANDS.

"Mr. Musser was right." Kitty smiled to herself as she settled into her chair. Perhaps the country would put all the madness of last year behind it and remain an oasis of calm, even if

Europe continued fighting. "Did you get enough sleep?" she asked Grace as she brought in her tea.

The maid set the tray on a side table. "I'll make up for it tonight, Miss Kitty."

"So what are our plans for today?" Mr. Weeks did his best to appear neutral. "Are we waiting for your beau?"

"He's not my beau." Even as she said the words, Kitty's face grew hot. Soames would be dropping by this afternoon.

She tried not to think of what he could want and to distract herself by sorting through her Christmas cards and correspondence. She showered, changed into one dress, then decided it looked frumpy and selected another that she had bought in London.

The doorbell rang shortly after she and her father finished lunch. They waited in the living room as footsteps sounded in the hallway and Grace brought in their visitor. Kitty wore her hair pulled off her face, the cream-colored dress with lace at the neck, and fleur-de-lis earrings.

"Good afternoon." Soames shook Mr. Weeks's and then Kitty's hand.

Kitty felt relieved to sit back down. Mr. Weeks offered their guest something to drink, and he replied that a glass of water would be fine. The agent looked just as she recalled him: tall but not too tall, kind-eyed, intelligent.

"I was sorry to have missed you the other day, Miss Weeks. I hear you're still with the *Sentinel*?"

"That's right. And you're still with the Service?"

"I am. But I've been reassigned. I'm now part of the squad that protects the president."

"My father mentioned that." Kitty forgot to be shy. "How does it work? You've actually met the president in person? What is he like?"

Soames laughed. "A group of us work in shifts. We're with him all the time."

"Everywhere?" Kitty said.

"Oh yes. At the White House, wherever he travels. This has been my first weekend off in four months."

"You mustn't have a moment to breathe."

"The work is demanding. I'm constantly on my guard. After President McKinley's assassination—well, that's why the Secret Service was put in charge."

"Do you miss the kind of work you used to do?" When she had met him last summer, Soames had been out in the field, solving cases.

"It's a change," he replied. "It's much quieter with Mr. Wilson."

"May I ask you one more question about it?"

Soames took a sip of the water that Grace brought in. "Please do. I always said you're good at your job."

"I feel silly for asking, but…have you met Mrs. Galt?"

"She's Mrs. Wilson now."

"Of course."

"Well, I have met her. I watch her play golf most mornings with the president, and don't tell anyone, but I was at the wedding."

"No!" Kitty's hands flew to her face.

"I was working, but I was there."

"What was it like?"

Mr. Weeks stood. "If you will both excuse me for a moment, I'll be right back."

Kitty had forgotten how much she'd enjoyed speaking to Soames. He treated her like an old friend, an equal, and his unusual profession was fascinating.

"It was a wedding like other weddings." Soames shrugged. "Gifts, flowers, and a beautiful bride. The president is smitten by her. I think I can say this, because everyone knows it—Mr. Wilson is very much in love."

There was an awkward silence, and Kitty tried to think of another question. "How does he run the country with so much on his mind?"

"That I can't tell you. I don't know how he does it. The service trains us to keep our hearts and minds separate."

It occurred to Kitty that he might be trying to send her a message. Perhaps he wanted to let her know that his work precluded the possibility of close relationships. Why come and see her then? Maybe he enjoyed her company just as much as she enjoyed his. Was that so wrong? And was it possible for the two of them, a young man and woman, unconnected by blood or years of familiarity, to be just friends?

"And how about you, Miss Weeks?" Soames said after a moment. "Do you keep busy?"

"I do my best."

"Are there any good stories that you're working on?"

"I'm hoping to interview Mrs. Belmont, and I covered last night's New Year's Eve celebrations in Times Square."

"Now, that is something," he said.

"And there's one other piece of business." She had a feeling Soames would understand. "I met a girl who died under strange circumstances."

"And let me guess…you're not satisfied with the explanation."

Kitty nodded. They had such similar temperaments.

"You should make inquiries if it bothers you. It is part of being a reporter."

Mr. Weeks returned, holding a newspaper. "What do you think of this business about the *Ancona*, Mr. Soames? Does the president think it will spur on a satisfactory end to the *Lusitania* negotiations?"

Soames laughed. "Even if I knew what was on the president's mind, I wouldn't be allowed to say, sir."

"Ah, not fit for civilian consumption. Is that right?" Julian Weeks sat, crossing his legs. "Secretary Daniels has been making all kinds of noises about needing more money for the navy. What did he say recently? That we'll need to spend a billion and a half dollars to be on par with the best fleets in the world."

"That sounds correct." Soames glanced at Kitty.

"They say our army ranks seventeenth in the world in terms of size and capacity. *Seventeenth.*" Julian Weeks shook his head. "The last time we went to war, we had to call for volunteers, but I doubt that Mr. Roosevelt and his Rough Riders would last a minute against the German machine guns."

Kitty cleared her throat. Given the chance, her father would talk about current events all day long.

Soames brushed off his trousers and stood. "I won't keep you any longer. I wanted to say hello since I was in the city. I have a few other calls to make before I leave tomorrow." He turned to Kitty. "I'm visiting Booth and his family." Booth had been Soames's partner in the Service. "You won't believe what he's doing now."

"He runs a boxing club?"

"No." Soames grinned. "He's gone a different route—he owns a grocery store."

Kitty tried to imagine the beefy former agent examining tomatoes and weighing bunches of grapes. "Does he enjoy it?"

"I'm about to find out."

Kitty walked him to the door.

"I'm glad I had a chance to see you." He put on his hat and coat. "I'm not sure when my work will bring me here again. I hope you understand."

"Until next time, Mr. Soames." She watched him leave. The world seemed more alive when they were together. But she had her life in New York, and he had his at the president's side in Washington.

Like a cruel joke, Austria's apology and offer of reparations for the *Ancona* were rendered toothless by the January 2 reports that the *Persia*, a British P&O liner on its way from London to Bombay with 160 passengers and 250 crew on board, had been torpedoed near Crete. Three Americans were on the passenger list: Robert McNeely, who was on his way to Aden to take up his post as U.S. consul; a commercial man from Boston; and a lad from Denver who was to begin his studies at school in Spain.

The fate of the Americans remained unclear, but most of the travelers were believed to have perished. A telegram had been delivered to President Wilson as he honeymooned in Hot Springs, Virginia. Mr. Wilson told reporters that he could not form an opinion until further details became available. Officials in Washington likewise reserved comment on the sinking until the full facts were known. But the U-boat most likely was Austrian, and the international situation looked grim once more.

Kitty calmed her fears by browsing through the advertisements for the Bonwit Teller sale starting on Monday. The Business Pages were optimistic. UNITED STATES ENTERS ERA OF UNLIMITED OPPORTUNITY, one headline proclaimed.

A story about motor cars to mark the opening of the Automobile Salon at the Hotel Astor, which Kitty knew her father would want to attend, noted that in 1901, when New York State became the first in the country to begin registering automobiles, it registered 954 machines, but then, a mere fourteen years later, that number had swelled to 231,000. But record progress and record exports came with record road accidents, many of them fatal. Nothing was ever simple anymore, Kitty thought. It seemed there had to be a dark side to everything.

"What a wonderful story, girls!" Miss Busby rose from behind her desk to welcome her victorious conquerors. "It really conveyed the spirit of the occasion. How was it for the two of you? Did you feel unsafe? Was it too boisterous?"

"We managed, Miss Busby," Kitty replied.

"Well then, perhaps you will work on some more stories together."

"I would like that," Jeannie said.

Kitty kept quiet. She didn't mind having a partner for a story like New Year's Eve, but in situations that weren't so hazardous, she preferred working on her own. Fortunately, Jeannie didn't seem to notice Kitty's silence, or at least, Kitty didn't think she noticed. And then, as was her habit, Miss Busby jumped in with the next matter at hand.

"Any progress on the Alva Belmont interview, Miss Weeks?" She shook her head in disbelief. "I can't believe I'm even considering an interview with a divorcée, but you girls are right. Times are changing."

"I'm waiting to hear from a friend who knows her. In fact, if you don't have anything particular for me to do today, Miss Busby, I'd like to leave early and complete all the arrangements."

Helena Busby pursed her lips. She consulted her calendar and ran a finger down her to-do list. "There's nothing here that Miss Williams can't manage."

They were innocent words but ominous to Kitty, considering that the typist had once briefly taken over her job. Kitty reminded herself that she couldn't have everything. She couldn't have the security of being the Page's features girl as well as the flexibility of chasing down stories that Miss Busby didn't know about. Something would eventually have to give. Either the editor would become more flexible and allow her to investigate and write about whatever she wanted, or, more likely, Kitty would have to make a difficult choice. But that time hadn't come yet. She gathered her things and took a taxi home, since Rao usually didn't wait for her but returned to pick her up later in the day.

Back at the apartment, she asked her father, who was surprised to see her home so early, whether she might have the chauffeur drive her to Westfield Hall.

"I thought that was finished," he said.

"Miss Busby would like me to follow up." If it hadn't been so cold outside, Kitty would have driven herself in her Stutz Bearcat, the sporty, open-topped car that she liked to drive during the spring and summer.

"Is the school open today?"

"Classes resumed this morning."

Mr. Weeks set aside his papers. "This has nothing to do with the Bright girl, does it?"

Kitty didn't answer at once; small fibs of convenience were one thing, but she found it difficult to lie outright.

"Capability." Julian Weeks sounded stern.

"It doesn't have anything to do with her. Not really... I may ask a few questions. I'm curious. I'd just like to put the matter to rest."

"There's nothing there, Capability, or else there's so much more than meets the eye that you shouldn't be involved. My god. A girl frozen to death in the snow. Not a mark on her body. If that turns out to be a crime, I'd hate to meet the criminal behind it."

Kitty wouldn't be deterred. "May I go?"

He shook his head but didn't refuse her.

She called for Rao to drive her to Westfield. It didn't seem fair that a man could follow his inclinations, even put his life in danger if that was where his work led, but a girl had to proceed cautiously, with one hand at all times on the brake.

Mrs. Swartz was in the middle of a class when Kitty arrived. She had gone directly to the science laboratory without checking in at the main building and now watched the schoolmistress through the panel in the classroom door. Mrs. Swartz pointed to a labeled diagram of a flower on the blackboard: "Near the base is a tiny yellow scale covering a small juicy spot, the nectary... Insects visiting the flower, especially those with hairy bodies, often become covered with pollen in their efforts to get at the nectar between the petals and ripest stamens." She spotted Kitty at the window. "Copy this diagram into your journals, girls. I'll be back in a minute."

She came out to the hall, leaving the door slightly ajar so she could mind her students, and spoke in a low voice. "How can I help you, Miss Weeks?"

"I'm here about Elspeth Bright."

Mrs. Swartz's face fell, and her eyes filled with tears. "It's a tragedy. A real tragedy. Such a magnificent student. So much talent... And now it's all gone."

"Did you know that she sleepwalked, Mrs. Swartz?"

"She told me that she used to as a child."

"And did she still?"

Mrs. Swartz tried to recollect. "She never said anything about that," she said finally.

"Do you know what she was working on?" Kitty asked.

The teacher looked over her shoulder and called into the classroom. "No giggling, Belinda." She turned back to Kitty. "We're studying the male and female parts of a flower. You must remember, the androecium and gynoecium."

"Yes," Kitty said. The stigma, style, ovary, and ovules.

She'd learned about all of them, as well as plant and animal classification.

"It makes the girls go silly," Mrs. Swartz said.

Kitty didn't want to be distracted from her question. "Could you tell me what Miss Bright was working on?"

A bell rang, and the girls closed their books.

"That will be all. We'll continue tomorrow," Mrs. Swartz told her pupils.

The Westfield Hall girls glanced at Kitty as they left the science room. One had a question for her teacher. "Let's talk later," Mrs. Swartz said, her voice sharp.

She and Kitty returned to the classroom once the students had vacated it.

"Elspeth didn't discuss her work with me, Miss Weeks. She kept it all under wraps."

"And is that behavior typical of your students, Mrs. Swartz?"

"No, it isn't. But Elspeth was never typical. And to be completely frank, her knowledge of chemistry far exceeded mine. She had all kinds of books in her house, and she heard about the latest developments through her father."

"I know he's a scientist. What exactly does he do?"

"I'm not sure where he worked before, but currently, he serves on the Naval Consulting Board. It's an organization of professional men. I'm not really too familiar with their activities. The only reason I've heard of it is because Elspeth happened to mention it once or twice."

"Was Miss Bright working on something connected with batteries?" Kitty said.

"She may have been, but we'll never know now. Her parents

had men come by this past weekend, and they boxed up all of Elspeth's possessions. Her papers, notebooks, and everything. Miss Howe-Jones felt that it would be best for the other girls that way. We're having a special service for her, but other than that, all traces of her presence will be erased." The teacher blinked away a tear.

"I see," Kitty said, but she didn't see anything. It all seemed innocent enough, but if one attributed a sinister motive to the Brights' and Miss Howe-Jones's actions, then the whole business could seem like a clever effort to cover up...what?

"Well, thank you, Mrs. Swartz. By the way, do you know where I can find Georgina Howell?"

Mrs. Swartz picked up the duster and began to clean the blackboard. "She should be in class. You will have to ask for the principal's permission to remove her."

A man came into the room as Kitty left. He began to converse in German with Mrs. Swartz. "Who was that, Hilde?"

"A girl from the newspapers. She had questions about Elspeth."

Kitty wondered how to proceed. Mrs. Bright had wanted her to speak to Georgina Howell, but she suspected that Miss Howe-Jones wouldn't appreciate her quizzing her students. She walked over to the main building and asked the receptionist whether the principal was available.

"It's good to see you again, Miss Weeks." Miss Howe-Jones's plaid dress reminded Kitty of a picnic napkin. "The teachers and I enjoyed your story. We especially enjoyed the way you compared Westfield to other girls' schools, each run by their own very singular headmistress. I take it as a compliment that you chose to highlight my methods."

"Thank you, madam." Kitty acknowledged the praise with a slight bow of her head. "But I'm here on a different matter, I'm afraid. I wonder if I might ask Miss Howell a few questions?"

"About what, Miss Weeks?"

"The evening of Miss Bright's death." Although she felt sure she would be rebuffed, Kitty spoke matter-of-factly.

The principal of Westfield Hall stiffened. "Really, Miss Weeks. I can't see what business that is of yours. And Miss Bright's death—may she rest in peace—has affected all of us."

"All I want to know," Kitty pushed further, "is whether anything was troubling Miss Bright the night she died. I believe Miss Howell was there. Perhaps she could shed some light on my friend's mental state?"

Miss Howe-Jones drew herself up straight. "You must understand one thing, Miss Weeks. In times such as these, my first thought must be for my students. Miss Howell has no family. She is a scholarship girl, and she has no one except me to protect her. I'm afraid I cannot allow you to speak to her—or to any of my other charges, for that matter."

"Wasn't Elspeth Bright also one of your students?" Kitty countered.

The principal's smile was strained. "I'm sorry you have wasted your time, Miss Weeks. But my decision is final. As a boarding school girl yourself, I'm sure you will understand."

Dismissed, Kitty left the office. A glass-fronted case in the hallway displayed essays and artwork, some marked with first- and second-place ribbons. *Famous Women I Admire. Helping the Poor. My Home, My School, My Days.* There was no way to meet Georgina if Miss Howe-Jones refused to budge. As she walked past the classrooms, Kitty could see that all the girls were busy at their lessons, all except for one—the young girl, Virginia, who Kitty had seen being reprimanded. Virginia came around the corner hefting a canvas sack and disappeared into a room off the main corridor. Kitty waited for a moment, then quietly followed her and peeked inside. Virginia was working in the school's mail room, checking letters one by one and feeding them into small, locked mailboxes.

CHAPTER TWELVE

H elena Busby's spartan alcove spoke volumes about her priorities. While Kitty might have displayed a painting of some natural scene and rolled a colorful carpet on the floor to soften the room's monastic air, Miss Busby contented herself with a giveaway calendar hung from a nail. Last year, the calendar advertised Ace hair oil; this year, the honor went to Mayhew's biscuits ("shortbread to please the most discerning palates"). President Wilson's portrait usually provided the only other relief from the vista of dull, beige paint, but it had been removed, and today, a single hothouse bloom peeked out from a vase.

Kitty sensed the question coming from Miss Busby, so she answered it. "We have the Belmont interview."

"We do?" Helena Busby's expression hovered somewhere between a smile and a frown.

"Cheer up, Miss Busby. It will be wonderful. None of our readers will object." Kitty had telephoned Mrs. Bright the day before, after returning from Westfield, and Elspeth's mother had given her the good news. "And now I feel I ought to prepare. I know nothing about the Congressional Union or Mrs. Belmont's past."

"Of course. You should go to the morgue."

Where else? Kitty thought as she made her way downstairs.

Mr. Musser's eyes twinkled when she posed her question. "First somnambulism, then batteries, and now the Naval Consulting Board? What is on your mind, *fräulein*?"

"You must know about them, Mr. Musser," Kitty said.

"I believe they evaluate proposals from the public."

"What kind of proposals?"

"Inventions that might be useful to the navy. Do you need the files?"

"No thanks. At least, not yet. I told Miss Busby that I would be educating myself about the Women's Congressional Union and Alva Belmont."

"So, you will be interviewing her?"

"How did you know that I might be interviewing her?"

The archivist's face went blank. Then he said, "I guessed. That's what you do, don't you? Interview famous women? Why else would you want to know about Mrs. Belmont?"

Kitty stared at him. Could he and Miss Busby suddenly have started chatting? But that was impossible. Miss Busby never left her alcove, and except for lunch at the cafeteria, Mr. Musser never came upstairs.

She put aside the thought and spent the rest of the morning sifting through articles and familiarizing herself with suffrage acronyms in preparation for the interview—she needed to be familiar with the world in which Mrs. Belmont wielded so much influence.

NAWSA referred to the National American Woman Suffrage Union; CU—the group to which Mrs. Belmont and Mrs. Bright belonged—was the Congressional Union for Woman Suffrage; and WPU was the Women's Political Union. At any rate, the main arc of the suffrage movement that Kitty pieced together was that the NAWSA came into being in 1890, first headed by the seventy-five-year-old suffragist Elizabeth Cady Stanton.

In 1912, two younger suffragists, Alice Paul and Lucy Burns, took charge of NAWSA's congressional committee and decided to shift from winning voting rights for women at the state and local levels to forcing an amendment to the U.S. Constitution so that women everywhere would enjoy the right to vote. They formed the CU in 1913 and then, the following year, parted ways with NAWSA, which disagreed with their objectives and their tactics, fearing that their aggressive approach would antagonize Congress and male voters.

The state-by-state approach had gone slowly. The first state in the Union to grant women the right to vote was Wyoming, followed by Colorado, Utah, and Idaho in the 1890s, then nothing until Washington gave its women the right to vote in 1910. Then came California, Oregon, and Arizona. New York's women still didn't have the right to vote, and the CU urged their supporters in full-suffrage states to force out lawmakers who didn't support a federal amendment.

This was the movement that Mrs. Belmont funded. No wonder people were intimidated by her, Kitty thought. Such fierce political goals combined with her legendary temper made her a force to be reckoned with, and Kitty would soon have the honor of speaking to her in person. She finished her notes, returned the articles to Mr. Musser, and asked Rao to drive her to the Brights' as soon as the day was done.

The butler showed Kitty into a study on the second floor rather than the parlor, which was at ground level. Like the do-gooder Mrs. Jellyby of *Bleak House*, Ephigenia Bright sat at a desk covered with books, papers, pamphlets, and stationery. Her reading glasses slid low on her nose, and her fingers were stained with ink.

"Come in, my dear, and sit down." Mrs. Bright took off her glasses. "As you can see, I'm back at work. I'm not accomplishing much though. More distracting myself."

Kitty had only spoken briefly to Mrs. Bright yesterday, right after she returned from Westfield Hall. Now, she told Elspeth's mother what she had learned—that according to Prudence Marquand, Elspeth had been studying batteries, and, Kitty added, she hadn't been able to speak to Miss Howell, but she had written her a letter asking whether they might meet sometime in private.

"My girl was studying batteries?" Mrs. Bright rubbed her temples. "How odd."

Kitty eyed the papers on the desk. "Perhaps you could look through her schoolbooks."

"Dr. Bright has put all Elspeth's school things into storage at our place in the country." Mrs. Bright sighed. "He doesn't want me upsetting myself any further. He says we will go through them together when we're up there next in the spring."

That was a long time away. "Well," Kitty said, "if I speak to Miss Howell, I will let you know what she tells me. In the meantime, I can't thank you enough for arranging the meeting with Mrs. Belmont."

"Are you ready for it?"

"I've been doing my homework. But there's still more to learn," Kitty said.

"The operetta is her pet project, so I'm sure she will be forthcoming on that score. Are you interested in suffrage yourself, Miss Weeks? I hope you're not a secret member of an antisuffrage league."

"Do such organizations still exist?"

"I've just been reviewing the Massachusetts Anti-Suffrage Committee's *The Case Against Woman Suffrage*." Mrs. Bright fished about among the papers on her desk. "They claim that votes for women will lead to pretty girls buttonholing strange men on the streets on Election Day, listening to shocking testimony in jury trials, running for office—which is sure to encourage girls to remain single and thus take away man's incentive to chivalry—which in turn, will wreak havoc on society." She put away the sheet. "What do you think? Is it convincing or rubbish?"

Before Kitty could reply, a door slammed, and hoots and cries sounded up the stairwell.

"My boys," Mrs. Bright said. "Out to play in any weather…"

A heavy, steady footfall thudded up the steps, the floorboards outside the study creaked, and Mrs. Bright's homely face turned anxious. A man with muttonchop whiskers and a rigid bearing stood in the doorway.

"You have a visitor, Ephigenia?" He glanced at Kitty, and then his eyes returned to the mistress of the house.

"Miss Weeks, please allow me to introduce my husband, Dr. Edgar Bright."

Kitty gave a quick bow of her head. "I am very sorry for your loss, sir."

"You knew Elspeth." It was more a statement than a question.

"Can you believe it, my dear?" Mrs. Bright interjected. "Miss Weeks is a reporter, and she met Elspeth while she was writing that story on Westfield Hall. I asked Miss Weeks to talk to Elspeth's friends as a favor to me, to find out what might have been on her mind that night."

"You did what?" The deliberate restraint in his tone spoke louder than a shriek.

"And she says," Mrs. Bright continued, "that before she died, Elspeth might have been working on something to do with batteries."

Dr. Bright's grip on his briefcase tightened. "You shouldn't have involved a stranger. What Elspeth may or may not have been working on is no one's business but hers and ours."

"I'm sorry, my dear. Miss Weeks is doing me a favor. She won't print her findings in the papers."

"I should be on my way." Kitty looked back and forth between husband and wife. It had been odd of Mrs. Bright to involve her in Elspeth's affairs in the first place, and now it was clear that Dr. Bright didn't approve of her choice.

"Perhaps that's for the best." Elspeth's mother held out her inky hand. "Good luck with the Belmont interview, Miss Weeks. Please let me know if you need any further assistance."

Kitty felt Elspeth's parents' eyes on her as she left.

"President awaits *Persia* details," a newsboy shouted on the morning of January 5 in the distinctive singsong cadence that he and the thousand other newsboys on every corner of the city seemed to share. "Germans send U-boat to Near East waters." The modern-day town crier held up a copy of the *Sentinel*.

"No, thanks," Kitty said. Kitty pushed through the revolving doors, checked in with Miss Busby, who seemed to be in an ebullient mood, and raced downstairs to the morgue.

"I have news for you." A grin lurked behind Mr. Musser's walrus mustache. "Of course, I forgot to mention the most obvious fact when we spoke last. It is Mr. Edison who runs the Naval Consulting Board. But you were aware of that, correct?"

"Excuse me?" Kitty put down her pen and pad.

"The board was set up this past July by Secretary of the Navy Daniels to evaluate civilian inventions and proposals that might be of use during wartime. Mr. Thomas Edison chairs it, and it is composed of civilian members—scientists and so on."

Kitty's thoughts spun so fast they almost made her ill. Could Elspeth have submitted a proposal to the board that Mr. Edison chaired and her father served on? One for her own battery? Could that be why she and Dr. Bright fought?

"But that's not why you're here, I presume?"

"No, no." Kitty needed to focus. "Mr. Musser, can you give me whatever you have on Mrs. Belmont?"

Once again, Kitty spent the morning piecing together a story, but this time, it had to do with the society matron, and when she was finished, Kitty realized that she might be in over her head. Alva Erskine Smith was born in Mobile, Alabama, in 1853, the seventh of nine children. By her own reckoning, she was a tempestuous child. Her brother, Murray Forbes Smith Jr., died when she was four, and when visitors said that her father would never recover from the blow and that no other child would take his place, little Alva became furious at the thought that a living daughter couldn't substitute for a dead son. When she no longer wanted to sleep in the nursery and her mother wouldn't allow her to move to a different room, she smashed the china figurines on the shelves and attacked a picture hanging on the wall. She was whipped—but allowed to move into her own room, as she had planned.

Miss Smith met new-money William K. Vanderbilt at a popular vacation spot, and they married in a grand wedding in 1875. Their daughter, Consuelo, was born a few years later. When William K.'s grandfather, "Commodore" Vanderbilt, founder of the New York Central Railroad, died, he left a fortune of one hundred million dollars, of which three million dollars went to his grandson, Alva's husband. Alva built herself a home, Idle Hour, on Long Island and invited reporters to write about it. When William K.'s father died in 1885, he left Alva's husband the mind-boggling sum of sixty-five million dollars. She began work on her home in Newport, inspired by the Parthenon and the Petit Trianon in Versailles.

But this was only the beginning. She engineered a great match between her daughter and the Duke of Marlborough. The two were married in a sumptuous wedding at Saint Thomas Episcopal Church on Fifth Avenue just a few months after Alva divorced William K. on grounds of adultery in "the most sensational divorce case in America." She kept her house in Newport and, reporters guessed, a lump sum of over two million dollars, as well as an annual income of a hundred thousand dollars.

Kitty could only marvel at the then–Mrs. Vanderbilt's boldness and self-assurance in throwing over one of the richest men in America. At the time, she had said that "society was by turns stunned, horrified, and then savage in its opposition and criticism."

"After the divorce, not a single one of my friends would recognize me," Alva told a reporter before setting off for Europe with five maids, a male servant, and seventy pieces of baggage.

Mrs. Belmont must be over sixty now, Kitty thought, calculating quickly. She married Oliver Hazard Perry Belmont, the son of Jewish banker August Belmont and also a divorcé, in a civil ceremony in 1896. He died twelve years later, in 1908, after which the widowed Mrs. Belmont threw her considerable energies and wealth into the suffrage cause. "It is a mistake to believe that any woman, no matter what her financial condition of life, can lead an idle existence," Mrs. Belmont told reporters. "It is merely a question of the worthiness of her activities."

And this was the woman whom Kitty would be interviewing.

"You will listen more than ask questions," Miss Busby said when Kitty came back upstairs and confessed to being apprehensive. "Talk about the operetta. Don't get drawn into personal matters, and everything will work out."

"I suppose so."

"The interview is next week, so you will have plenty of time to prepare yourself."

Plenty of time to become more nervous was more likely the case. But Kitty took some consolation from the thought that Mrs. Belmont relied on the press to relay her message. "The American woman has been brought up to shun publicity, but we must forget our personal inclinations for the sake of a great cause," she declared in one of the stories Kitty had just read. "To be successful in any phase of politics, one must give one's life more or less to the public, and that is the lesson the American suffragist must learn."

A typist poked her head into the alcove. "Telephone call for you, Miss Weeks."

Kitty took it on the instrument on the third floor landing, between the coop and the cafeteria. She had to stick a finger into one ear so she could hear above the din from the kitchen and the relentless click-clacking of typewriters.

"Miss Weeks?" The man's voice was unfamiliar. "This is Dr. Edgar Bright. May I speak to you at the *Sentinel* tomorrow? This concerns my daughter."

CHAPTER THIRTEEN

"Let's go to the movies, Grace," Kitty suggested over lunch in the pantry. When she felt in need of company at home, she would join the maid and Mrs. Codd for lunch. Right now, she needed distraction, and the pictures would provide the perfect antidote to her sense that something she might not like was about to happen. Dr. Bright hadn't told her with any specificity why he wanted to talk to her. And he wasn't the most personable individual. She doubted that he just wanted to chat.

"Can I, Mrs. Codd?" Grace turned to the cook. Although Kitty was her employer, Mrs. Codd supervised her work, and she often needed Grace to help peel potatoes or do other chores in the afternoon.

"'May I,' child. 'May,' not 'can,'" the cook said.

"It's the same thing," Grace protested.

"No, it's not. Of course you *can* go to the pictures. Will I let you—that's the question." She wiped her hands on her apron. "Of course I will."

Grace polished off her lunch and washed the dishes, and an hour later, she and Kitty walked down to the cinema on Broadway. There were no set start or finish times like there were for stage performances—the reels of film played in an endless loop. One could arrive whenever one wanted and pick up in the middle of the program.

Kitty and Grace had to sit through only a few colored slides advertising hair tonic and hosiery before the pianist changed her music to a rousing tune that signaled the start of the final episode of *The Romance of Elaine*, featuring Kitty's favorite heroine, Pearl White.

Miss White was sensational. Her first series, *The Perils of Pauline*, had exploded on the screen last year, and Kitty and Grace had watched every episode. It was followed by more: *The Exploits of Elaine*, *The New Exploits of Elaine*, and now *The Romance of Elaine*. A glass slide had announced Pearl's new series, *The Iron Claw*, which would begin next month.

Kitty thought it uncanny that the pictures reflected current concerns. In *Perils*, Pearl fought a treacherous secretary; in *Exploits*, a shadowy scientific force; in *New Exploits*, a cunning Chinaman; and in *Romance*, a German spy by the name of Marcus del Mar. His mission: to steal plans for a wireless torpedo, the latest in scientific warfare. And today's episode revealed that he had hidden a getaway submarine in a secret harbor.

So, perhaps fears of amphibious forces storming the East Coast weren't unfounded—or perhaps pictures like this magnified concerns that wouldn't otherwise have picked up much traction.

The action on the screen swept Kitty away. The episode ended with a column of water shooting in the air as del Mar and his accomplices were blown up in their submarine by the very torpedo whose plans he had been trying to steal.

The theater audience stomped and cheered their approval. If only she were allowed to interview Pearl White someday, the actress would have so much to tell the Ladies' Page readers, Kitty thought. What it was like to do her job, how they selected stories to film and how she performed her daring stunts…but of course Miss Busby wouldn't permit that kind of interview to be printed, not at the moment.

Kitty would have to take it one step at a time. First, the divorcée, Alva Belmont.

At ten o'clock the next morning, a messenger came to the hen coop to tell Kitty that someone was waiting for her down below.

"Anyone important?" Jeannie said as Kitty pushed back her chair.

"No." The blood pounded in Kitty's ears. "Just a friend of my father's."

Dr. Bright was waiting for her in the lobby, checking the time on his pocket watch against the time on the *Sentinel*'s three-faced clock. The muttonchop whiskers gave him the air of a confederate general. Kitty almost expected to see medals on his chest and a sword dangling from his side.

"Miss Weeks." He clicked his watch shut and slipped it into his pocket. "Thank you for taking the time. If it's not too cold for you, perhaps we could take a walk."

Kitty had left her coat upstairs but was wearing a light jacket over her blouse. "I have permission to be away from my desk for ten or fifteen minutes, no more."

"That should be more than enough."

Enough for what? Kitty wondered.

They pushed their way through the paper's heavy brass revolving doors and stepped outside.

"Which way?" she said.

He didn't reply and started to walk. "My wife tells me you met my daughter a few days before she died, Miss Weeks?"

Kitty felt a sudden wave of panic. Was he trying to suggest that she might have had something to do with Elspeth's death? She steadied herself. "I did meet Miss Bright. At Tipton's."

"And may I ask what the two of you discussed?"

"Oh, this and that," Kitty said. "We spoke about school, Miss Howe-Jones, and so on."

"Nothing else?"

"Not that I recall, Dr. Bright." Why did he want to know? The details of their conversation were none of his business.

"And yet..." They crossed the street; midtown on a week-day had no shortage of traffic, but Dr. Bright seemed to be one of those fearless pedestrians who walked right into it, assuming the cars would stop for him. "And yet," he went on, "you seem to know that Elspeth was involved in something to do with batteries."

"That information came from Miss Marquand."

Dr. Bright looked at her strangely. "What does Miss Marquand have to do with this?"

A driver honked at them. "Get out of the way!"

Dr. Bright didn't bat an eyelid.

Kitty felt more than frazzled. She wanted to scream. Why were they discussing this in a place where a millimeter's movement back or forward might result in death or dismemberment for either one?

To her relief, a few moments later, they were back onto the safety of the sidewalk.

"Miss Bright's friend Prudence Marquand mentioned batteries to me," Kitty said. "She also told me that your daughter kept a photograph of Mr. Edison pinned above her desk. Does that sound correct?"

Dr. Bright paused. His expression seemed to soften for just an instant. "My daughter's tastes in decor are hardly my concern. What else did Miss Marquand tell you about Elspeth's work?"

Kitty looked up at him. "May I ask why you'd like to know?"

He swung around to face her, eyes narrowed with fury. "How dare you? She is my daughter. I have the right to ask whatever I want."

Shaken by his outburst, Kitty wondered how long their conversation would last. Perhaps she should tell him that it was time for her to return to the *Sentinel*.

Dr. Bright paused at the corner of the block and then began to cross a street with two-way traffic. "If you would like me to believe that you want to help my family, that you cared about Elspeth, you will tell me everything you know."

"Dr. Bright." Kitty hoped he would believe her; she spoke loudly so as to be heard over the roar of motors. "I don't know anything more than what I've already told you."

"You're hiding something from me." He turned to look at her in the middle of the street. A car careered toward them.

"Watch out," Kitty yelled, pulling him out of the way while

she took a step back. Brakes squealed, and she felt a thud as another vehicle, traveling in the opposite direction, barreled into her.

CHAPTER FOURTEEN

S he's coming to," a woman's voice said.
   "Capability."

Kitty heard her father's voice.

"Capability?"

"What happened?" She tried to speak, but her voice came out a croak. Her eyes wouldn't open.

"You were hurt. A car ran into you."

"Not too much talking, sir," the woman's voice said.

Without warning, Kitty threw up. Distant voices said, "You should leave, Mr. Weeks. We'll take care of her."

Kitty awoke in darkness. "Where am I?" She couldn't see anything.

"You're in the hospital, miss," a soothing voice said. "Not to worry. You're being looked after."

Kitty felt a pinch on her arm, then she faded away. When she opened her eyes again, it was morning.

A cheery nurse wheeled in a tray of breakfast. Kitty shuddered at the sound of the trolley scraping against the floor.

"Come along, Miss Weeks." The woman fluffed Kitty's

pillow. She wore a white cap and white starched apron held up by pins. "It's time to eat now."

"I feel foggy," Kitty said. "What happened to me?"

"You were in an accident, I believe." The nurse handed Kitty a glass of juice. "I've been working here for thirty years, and ever since there have been motor cars on the roads, we've seen the number of road accidents increase. You're one of the lucky ones. Just badly bruised but no bones broken. I've seen much worse."

"How long have I been here?"

"They brought you in late yesterday morning," the nurse said.

There was a knock at the door, and a man in a white coat came in. "How is our patient today?"

"Doing well, Dr. Stevens," the nurse replied.

He perched on the edge of Kitty's bed. "May I?" He checked the pulse on her wrist.

"She did cry out at night a few times," the nurse went on.

"Really?" The doctor held on to Kitty's wrist. "About what?"

"Batteries," the nurse said. "And dead girls in the snow."

"Really?" Dr. Stevens sounded bemused as he put Kitty's hand down. "Nice strong pulse. Follow my hand with your eyes." He moved his finger from side to side.

"What does a young lady like you have to do with batteries?"

"Not much."

"Perhaps," he said, feeling the glands on her neck, "you were hit by an electric car. Say ah." He checked her throat. "No fever?" he asked the nurse.

"No, Doctor."

"Perfect. This injury aside, you're in good health. You'll notice we've bandaged the shoulder, and you should rest it for the next five days. The skin on your face is badly grazed, but it will heal in time. No visitors until two o'clock today. No reading, no writing, and no close work until next week."

"I beg your pardon?" Kitty tried to sit up straight and winced.

"You hit your head, Miss Weeks, and the brain is a sensitive organ. We must give it time to recover." He began to fill a hypodermic syringe. "This will help ease the pain and allow you to sleep better."

"No!" Kitty said.

"Come now, Miss Weeks." The nurse held her arm.

"No!" Kitty repeated with all the strength she could muster. The last thing she needed was to become reliant on morphine. It brought back memories of Dr. Flagg, Mrs. Vanderwell's nerve man. "Dr. Stevens?" The needle hovered in midair, and Kitty took a deep breath. "Do you believe that girls who work too much can damage their bodies for life?"

The doctor lowered the syringe. "Some people think that's the case, but I'm of the opinion those theories don't hold water. If you're concerned about your health, there's no need to worry. Only the healthiest specimens come away from vehicular collisions as unscathed as you have."

Kitty relaxed into a smile. "No needle, please." She needed to economize on words.

"It won't hurt."

"I'm all right," she said as clearly as she could manage.

He handed the injection back to the nurse. "All right, we'll wait and see. But you must rest. Do you understand?"

Kitty dozed off until lunchtime. When she awoke, she asked the nurse to telephone her father, but the woman was firm. Mr.

Weeks had been here this morning, and she would now have to wait to see him until after lunch was finished at two o'clock.

At any event, it was Jeannie and Miss Busby who graced the clinical hospital room with their presence as Kitty spooned up the last bite of her tapioca pudding.

"We brought you flowers." Jeannie set the stems on the table beside Kitty.

"I'll find a vase," the nurse offered.

"What happened, if you don't mind my asking?" Miss Busby pulled up a chair. "Why did you leave the office in the first place, and who was that man with you?"

"He's the father of a friend. He wanted to talk to me."

"Luckily, he sent word about what happened. Otherwise, I would have had no idea where you had disappeared to."

Kitty stared at the editor. She couldn't pinpoint what it was exactly, but something about Miss Busby looked different.

"Motor vehicles ought to be banned," the editor continued. "They're a menace. Perhaps..."

She tilted her head, and Kitty realized what it was. She hadn't ever seen Helena Busby beyond the confines of the *Sentinel*. She seemed out of place in the normal civilian world—but of course, Miss Busby must have a life outside the newspaper.

"When you are better, we can write a story about it," Miss Busby went on. "Not about your accident, of course, but the phenomenon of deaths caused by automobiles. Although, come to think of it, perhaps a personal touch would be nice—'My Experience as an Injured Pedestrian' or something of the sort."

Jeannie looked embarrassed and said to Kitty, "We really came to wish you a speedy recovery."

Miss Busby nodded. "And Mrs. Belmont's secretary rang this morning to discuss details of the interview. I'd like to check with the doctor that you will be ready by next week. Otherwise, I'll need a contingency plan."

"Miss Busby!" Jeannie said.

"It's all right," Kitty said. "I understand."

Miss Busby shot a look at Jeannie. "You see, I told you she wouldn't mind."

The nurse returned with the flowers arranged in a vase.

"Give Miss Weeks the file, Jeannie."

Jeannie Williams reached into a bag she was carrying and brought out a manila folder.

"Mr. Musser was reluctant to part with it, but we convinced him, didn't we, Jeannie? By the way, he sends his best wishes."

"Miss Weeks isn't allowed to read." The nurse handed the folder back to Jeannie. "Doctor's orders."

Miss Busby folded her arms across her chest.

"Now, please," the nurse commanded.

Medicine won. Jeannie put the file away.

"I'll be fine by Wednesday," Kitty said. "And besides, I've already done my research on Mrs. Belmont."

"Do you think those grazes on her face will disappear soon?" Miss Busby asked the nurse.

"It should take a month or so, madam."

"Oh my." Miss Busby's shoulders sagged with disappointment. "Well, Mrs. Belmont will have to put up with it."

"Do I look so bad?" Kitty asked.

"Nothing that a little powder won't fix," Jeannie said.

The two women left shortly afterward.

"She's quite something, the old lady," the nurse said, straightening the blankets around Kitty's bed.

"Miss Busby? She says strange things, but she's all right once you get to know her."

Julian Weeks arrived at three. He apologized for being late but said that he had spent the past hour convincing the doctor to allow Kitty to return home. "I'm sure you'd like to spend tonight in your own bed." He patted her leg through the blankets.

Dr. Stevens returned to check Kitty again. "I'm allowing you to leave," he said, "but only if you promise me to do the same things as you would here. Rest. Drink plenty of liquids. No sudden movements, no music, no reading and writing, as I've said before. And then on Monday, I'd like you to come back and see us."

Despite her protests, Kitty was taken downstairs in a wheelchair and then transferred into the car. Every bump of the Packard made her bones ache, but she survived the drive home and walked into the apartment leaning on her father's arm. Grace and Mrs. Codd were thrilled to see her, and Grace had run a warm bath with salts.

Kitty felt relieved to be back, and after she bathed and washed her hair, she lay under the sheets, ready for a nap before dinner.

Her father knocked and came in. "How are you feeling?"

"Not too bad."

He hovered near the foot of her bed. "Capability, I know who you were with when the accident happened."

Kitty's chest tightened.

"The Brights have been calling, asking about you."

"How is he?" Now that her father knew, she may as well inquire after Dr. Bright.

"Dr. Bright is fine, thanks to your quick thinking. It was he who called the ambulance." Julian Weeks clasped and unclasped his hands. "I told you not to become involved with that family."

Kitty looked away. "He asked to see me."

"Why?"

She sighed. "To find out what I know about his daughter."

"You do know something about his daughter then." Mr. Weeks turned on his heel and paced about the room. "Look, Capability, I will admit that there's something unexplained there. But while they may have lost their child, I am not about to lose mine. Give it up." He couldn't keep the emotion from his voice. "For me."

Kitty thought long and hard. "You know I can't."

He stopped and turned to face her. "Dr. Bright told me what happened. He was talking to you—"

"In the middle of the street," she interjected.

"—and a car came up from behind him."

"I thought he might be run over."

"And in helping him, you were injured. You see, you don't have to be doing anything wrong in order to put your own life in jeopardy."

Grace knocked at the door. "Do you need anything, Miss Kitty?"

"I'm fine, Grace."

The maid didn't seem convinced, but she backed out and closed the door.

"I've heard that Dr. Bright serves on the Naval Consulting

Board," Mr. Weeks continued. "He's probably evaluating proposals that, should they be approved, would be worth millions of dollars to someone."

Kitty saw the black car hurtling toward Mr. Bright. His argument with his daughter. "Do you think someone might have been trying to run him over?"

"I don't know," Mr. Weeks said forcefully. "And I don't want to know. Can't you see that there may be larger issues at stake than just some boarding-school girl who sleepwalked? That this could involve our government and the military?"

Chapter Fifteen

K itty felt a bit better on Saturday, but her father still wouldn't let her get out of bed. Grace brought in her breakfast and fussed over her until she felt desperate to be left alone.

Mrs. Vanderwell telephoned that afternoon, but Mr. Weeks took the message, which he relayed to Kitty in her room. "Amanda Vanderwell is on her way back to New York. She'll be here soon." He named the day.

"That's wonderful!" The news already made Kitty feel less achy. It was something to look forward to. Her best friend in the city would be back in town. She tugged at the bandages around her shoulder. They had begun to irritate more than they helped. Tomorrow, she would take them off and return to normal.

"I told Mrs. Vanderwell about your accident, and she's very worried," Mr. Weeks went on. "She thinks you might have your head in the clouds because of the Bright girl... Anyhow, she's going to send you some of her very own bread pudding."

"You mean her cook's very own bread pudding." As far as Kitty was aware, Mrs. Vanderwell never set foot inside her kitchen, let alone prepared a dish with her own hands.

Mr. Weeks smiled. "I'm sure that, to her, it's the same thing. By the way, the Brights telephoned again. They'd like to see you and thank you in person for your help. I said I'd let you know."

"And that's all?"

"The Lanes sent flowers… If you're feeling better, I might go out for a bit, join them at their hotel for dinner."

"You shouldn't stay here cooped up," Kitty said. Her father seemed to be seeing a lot of the Lanes, but better that than him bored at home and monitoring her every move.

Sunday morning brought even more improvement. Kitty got out of bed and walked around the apartment. She took a look in the mirror. Her face was still a mess—she had a red graze running down her cheek. She would have to do something about it before she went to see Mrs. Belmont.

Although Mrs. Vanderwell didn't approve of telephone calls on Sunday, Kitty called her at eleven.

"I hear Amanda's coming back. Can I visit as soon as she arrives?"

"Of course, Capability. But first, have you recovered? You must promise me you will be more careful in future."

"Of course, Mrs. Vanderwell."

Kitty waited until her father went to take his bath. Then she picked up the instrument again and asked the operator to connect her.

"How are you, Miss Weeks?" Mrs. Bright came on the line. "Dr. Bright and I have been worried sick about you. And my husband owes you his thanks and his gratitude. If you hadn't acted so decisively, he might have been killed. As it is, you paid the price."

"I'm feeling better every day, Mrs. Bright," Kitty said. "I'm young, and I'll recover fast."

"Young bones do recover quickly. But all of this is my fault," Mrs. Bright went on. "Miss Weeks…"

"Yes?"

"Your father doesn't want us speaking to you anymore, and I can't say I blame him. I'd feel the same if you were my daughter. This should be our final conversation. Elspeth is gone, and I must come to terms with that." Kitty pictured Dr. Bright hovering in the background while Mrs. Bright spoke. "And you must get on with your life."

"Yes, Mrs. Bright." Kitty replaced the receiver.

The message was clear: Elspeth's mother would no longer help her. She was on her own.

"Don't even try to read." Mr. Weeks snatched the paper from Kitty's place at the table on Monday morning. "Now that you're up, I take it that you will go see the doctor at the hospital as he asked?"

Kitty unfolded her napkin and spread it on her lap. "I think I'm better off resting at home."

"Why are you so stubborn?"

"I don't like hospitals."

"Capability—"

"I promise that if I start to feel worse, I will pay him a visit. Don't worry about me," she insisted. "Please carry on with your day."

Mr. Weeks left for his club at eleven, and Kitty telephoned Miss Busby at the *Sentinel*. She again reassured the editor that she would be fit to interview Mrs. Belmont on Wednesday.

"Are you certain, Miss Weeks?" Miss Busby's voice crackled

down the line. "This is extremely important, and if we have to cancel, I'd prefer to do so in advance."

"We won't have to cancel. I'll come in tomorrow for a short day. You'll see, I'm fine."

The operator transferred Kitty to Mr. Musser. When he came on, she asked him a favor.

"You're all better, Miss Weeks?" he said. "I heard about the accident."

"Word spreads fast."

"Yes." He cleared his throat. "I suppose it does… Take care of yourself, and I will be waiting."

❧

On Tuesday, Kitty went to the *Sentinel,* having promised her father that she wouldn't stay long and that she would return home at the first sign of fatigue or discomfort.

"Ah, Miss Weeks," Miss Busby exclaimed when Kitty came in. "You look much better. A little worse for wear, but quite within the realm of acceptable." Kitty had followed Jeannie's suggestion and covered her grazed cheek with face powder.

"I'm not planning to stay long, Miss Busby," she said. "I just wanted to take care of a bit of last-minute research before tomorrow."

"Quite right, Miss Weeks. You must do whatever is necessary to make this a success. God speed, my dear."

As promised, Mr. Musser was ready, but first, Kitty had to interrupt the ditty he was humming to himself. "*When the grown-up ladies act like babies, I've got to love 'em, that's all... I want to be the popper. When they walk like babies, talk like babies, that's the time I fall. Though they may be forty-three, I want to bounce them on my knee.*"

Kitty knocked on the counter, and he looked up, a smile plastered on his face.

"Ah, Miss Weeks. What do you think of my musical abilities?"

"They're excellent, Mr. Musser."

"Let's take our seats." He gestured to the tables at the morgue, which were usually empty when Kitty came in but today were occupied by four other reporters sifting through papers.

"So," he said, carting a file under his arm, "I found nothing for 'batteries' as they pertain to the navy. So then I thought and thought."

"Yes." Kitty couldn't wait for him to get to the point.

"I knew I had read something, and then I remembered—it had to do with submarines and batteries that *didn't* work."

"Say more," Kitty urged.

Musser opened the file. "This is one from last March." Kitty had told him when they spoke on the telephone that she wasn't allowed to read and had asked if he would read to her. "A United States Navy submarine, the F-4, sank during routine maneuvers near the coast of Honolulu. The probable cause was seawater leaking into the submarine's lead-acid batteries, which produced chlorine gas that asphyxiated the crew. All twenty-one men aboard perished."

He flipped to a different page. "This story, printed a few days after the accident, explains that the battery is the heart of a submarine, like the periscope is its eye. When running on the surface, a submarine can use gasoline engines or even steam turbines as in the case of some French ones, but once submerged, the boat must be sealed, and there can be no outlet for the exhaust. Hence the need for exhaust-free power in the form of energy stored within batteries." He looked up. "Needless to say, the issue of seawater leakage is a major problem for the lead-acid submarine batteries currently in use."

Mr. Musser went on. "Secretary Daniels tells us that 'submarines have given us more trouble than anything else in the navy... We have yet to find a successful type of battery and engine. The lead casings around the batteries are liable to be eaten out by the sulfuric acid in the batteries. Then the steel surrounding the lead is eaten through, and the salt water from the submerging tanks gets in, and chlorine gas is generated, which is very dangerous to the crew.'"

"Excuse me—" A reporter at the next table spoke up.

"Ach, I am too loud," Musser said. "I will speak softly."

"No, not at all. I couldn't help overhearing though. I've been writing stories about chlorine. The Germans used it at Ypres, but of course the British had tried it out first on their enemies."

Kitty had heard that men started frothing at the mouth before their lungs were eaten away. Their bodies had been found twisted in agony on the battlefield.

"That's why Mr. Edison has devised an entirely different kind of battery for our submarines—"

"Excuse me." Kitty interrupted him. "Did you say Mr. Edison has devised a new battery?"

"Yes. One that works on a solution of potash so its parts don't corrode or destroy one another."

"Why isn't it being used?"

"It still has to be tested."

"And when will that be?"

"This Saturday, as a matter of fact. Right here in New York City." The reporter noticed the puzzled look on Kitty's face. "At the navy yard in Brooklyn."

"And if the batteries work?"

"They will turn our submarines into the world's safest and most powerful fighting force. Simply put, they will transform our fleet."

CHAPTER SIXTEEN

I sn't it strange," Kitty said to her father as he poured drinks in his study before dinner, "that Mr. Edison chairs a committee to which he himself might have to send a proposal for evaluation?"

"Which committee?"

"The Naval Consulting Board that Dr. Bright serves on."

"Are you still thinking about that business, Capability?"

"Just thinking."

"It's known as a conflict of interest." He handed Kitty her glass.

"Well, if Secretary Daniels knows that Mr. Edison is such a prolific inventor, why appoint him to the post? It's hardly fair to ask a man to rule on the fitness of his own product."

"Normally, I would agree with you, Capability, but in this case, Mr. Edison is a patriotic citizen. I doubt he would propose anything that he thought was of less than one hundred percent value to our country."

"I suppose."

"And besides, who else could Daniels have chosen to fill that seat? Someone who knows less than Edison does about these kinds of things?"

Kitty tried to get as much sleep as she could that night in preparation for the next day's interview with Mrs. Belmont, but her dreams were filled with car accidents, Thomas Edison aiming chewing tobacco into a spittoon, and Elspeth laughing and laughing as the half-deaf old inventor struggled to hear her through an old-fashioned hearing horn. Had Elspeth invented a battery that competed with Mr. Edison's—had she admired him and hoped to emulate his achievements in some small measure—could he, or someone in his team, have stolen her ideas?

Kitty woke feeling uneasy, whether from the dreams or the prospect of the interview, she couldn't tell. She chose a green dress, applied extra ointment and powder to her cheek, and arrived with some trepidation at the building unofficially known as the Belmont Suffrage Headquarters at 13–15 East Forty-Second Street. Mrs. Belmont's personal residence wasn't far away at 477 Madison Avenue, but she met all business callers at her place of work. When Kitty rang the bell, Mrs. Belmont's secretary, Miss Baehr, escorted her to a private office on the second floor.

"Mrs. Belmont only sees visitors by appointment," Miss Baehr said in hushed tones. "She plans to speak with you today and expects you will return next week to observe rehearsals and meet Miss Maxwell, the composer, and the rest of the cast."

"If that's what Mrs. Belmont wishes, then of course." Kitty half expected to be provided with a list of dos and don'ts and a suit of body armor before she went inside.

A small but redoubtable woman with chubby cheeks and a determined chin came out from behind her desk to shake Kitty's hand when the secretary knocked.

"Finally." Mrs. Belmont's rasping laugh scraped Kitty like sandpaper. "Miss Busby of the *Sentinel*'s Ladies' Page deigns to send someone to see me. I've enjoyed—and not enjoyed—forty years of relentless publicity, but this is the first time with someone from your paper. What do you say to that, Miss Weeks?"

"I don't believe the Ladies' Page has been in existence for forty years, Mrs. Belmont."

"It hasn't." Mrs. Belmont took a seat on an armchair and gestured to an empty one opposite her. "But you know what I mean."

The room was filled with books and papers and filing cabinets, and young women knocking softly came in and out to retrieve papers or check something in a folder.

"So tell me, what has piqued your editor's interest in my activities all of a sudden?"

"Miss Busby believes our readers will be interested in your suffrage operetta. It's such a novel idea." Kitty felt she must hold her ground or risk being run over for the second time.

"Ah, I see. Safe enough for the Ladies' Page." Mrs. Belmont nodded. "I thought so. You can bury it amid society tableaux for charity or the black-and-white ball at Sherry's sponsored by the Ladies' Auxiliary of the Lying-In Hospital."

"No. It will be a feature article."

"My, my, I'm flattered. Is this your doing, young lady?"

"Ah." Kitty didn't know what to say. She was spared by someone coming in with a letter for Mrs. Belmont to sign.

The older woman put on reading glasses and scanned the document for a moment. "*Women should have a voice in deciding what is and what is not obscene in regards to motherhood.* Nicely written. I like it."

Her assistant, a competent young lady, college-educated by

the looks of it, handed her a pen, and Mrs. Belmont signed. The assistant blotted the paper and took it away.

Alva Belmont looked up at Kitty. "That was a petition to say that Mrs. Sanger can't have a fair trial unless women are allowed to serve on the jury... You do know of Margaret Sanger and her *Family Limitation* pamphlet?"

"I've heard about her, yes. Hasn't she been charged with criminal activities?" Kitty didn't really keep track of such matters.

"By the post office," Mrs. Belmont said drily. "For distributing information on birth control by mail. Her friends have organized a dinner for her at the Hotel Brevoort on Monday before she goes to trial. She and other prominent activists will be speaking. Would you like me to arrange a ticket for you?"

Kitty tried not to be derailed. "I was hoping you could tell me about your plans for the operetta, Mrs. Belmont. And Miss Baehr said I could come see a rehearsal next week."

"That you certainly must, Miss Weeks." Mrs. Belmont hunted through a pile of papers on her desk. "Here is a copy of *Melinda and Her Sisters*. Miss Elsa Maxwell has written the music and lyrics. You might care to read it in advance." She handed Kitty a typewritten, bound copy of the manuscript.

"May I ask what inspired you to join the suffrage movement, Mrs. Belmont?"

"Well..." The older woman adjusted her collar. "My daughter Consuelo, the Duchess of Marlborough, first opened my eyes to the cause. But here's the thing. My interest stems from my own history. I divorced Mr. Vanderbilt in 1895—almost thirty years ago now. The practice is slightly more common these days, but when I did it, I created a furor. My own lawyer warned me that I might be undermining the foundation of our society by showing up the shortcomings of the rich. But why should I have to put up with my husband's affairs when I wouldn't have been allowed the same conduct?

"Men of a certain class feel they can do whatever they like," she went on. "Keep that in mind when you start thinking of marriage, Miss Weeks. Society never let me forget that I had the temerity to walk away—and the women who were most savage in their opposition were the ones with the most unhappy marriages."

Kitty reminded herself to breathe. Mrs. Belmont wasn't known for her reticence. She would say what she had to say, and Kitty would have to remember it—but the philanthropist's strong views gave Kitty a better appreciation for Miss Busby's hesitation.

"I've been a rebel my entire life." Mrs. Belmont's eyes blazed. "And after my second husband died—I knew no happiness like I knew with Oliver—I realized that I could no longer remain idle.

"I believe that if you want a thing well done, you must do it yourself. I spared no effort in raising my children and designing my home, and now I spare no effort in promoting the cause of suffrage. Something needs to be done, Miss Weeks." She banged her fist against the glass-topped coffee table so that it rattled. "We must convert the multitudes. Half of our population cannot be treated as less than the other. The cause requires publicity as well as a definite program. My program is to champion a federal amendment to the constitution and to use my wealth and my position in society—for in the end, no one turns their back on money—to create news, to create publicity for us all. The operetta is just one of my many activities. Do you find it hard to speak?" She looked at Kitty.

"I'm not sure what to say," Kitty replied, overwhelmed by the older woman's vigor and passion and swayed by her words.

"I'm not surprised that you're silenced—so much of what we have been taught to say is what men think is fitting for a woman to say."

Kitty found her voice. "How did you break the habit?"

"Thankfully, I never had the habit. But I'm getting old, while you, Miss Weeks, are the next generation. And it pains me to see so many girls your age *not* jumping on the bandwagon. *Not* realizing that if change has to come, they must be part of it."

"Are you suggesting that I'm shirking my responsibilities?" Kitty knew full well that she wasn't involved in the fight for suffrage, but she was also certain that her father would have a fit if she took on another set of commitments in addition to her job.

"Absolutely," Mrs. Belmont replied. She smiled. "But don't look so worried. Your coming here, your speaking to me is a first-rate beginning. Give my girl your address, and she'll have a ticket sent over to you for the Sanger dinner. And you will be back next week to watch the rehearsals?"

"Yes, Mrs. Belmont."

"Don't forget the manuscript. Tell me what you think when you've read it." And Mrs. Belmont dismissed Kitty with a wave of the hand.

Miss Busby didn't expect Kitty back at the *Sentinel*, and Kitty needed to burn off her excess energy, the tension that had built up over the course of the interview. If it had been warmer, she would have walked home. Instead, she asked Rao to drive her to the Vanderwells.

Mrs. Vanderwell greeted Kitty warmly but with some surprise. "I'm so pleased to see you looking well." She wore a dress with an S-shaped silhouette from the nineties, which made her look her age, and a bracelet of Amanda's baby hair wired with silver around her wrist.

The older woman patted the seat beside her on the couch. "That scar on your cheek—"

Kitty touched her face. "It will take a few weeks to disappear… So Amanda will be here soon?"

"Oh yes, I couldn't be happier. By the way, you never told me how your appointment with Dr. Flagg went. Did he reassure you about Elspeth's somnambulism?"

"In a manner of speaking. He made me worry about my own health. But things have happened since then that have made me wonder."

"About what?"

"Whether there's more to it than just sleepwalking."

"Oh dear." Mrs. Vanderwell fidgeted with her bracelet. "I take it you've heard about Mr. Emerson then."

"No." Kitty sat up straight. "I haven't."

"He used to be Dr. Bright's assistant. Then he was fired, but from what I gather, he continues to be a regular visitor. You wouldn't forget him if you saw him. He's the handsome, chiseled type. I, for one, would never have hired a young man like that with a daughter in the house, even if she only came home on holidays."

"You think he and Elspeth—?"

Mrs. Vanderwell knitted her lips together. "People talk. I don't know if any of it is true."

"What do they say?"

"The usual things. I leave it to your imagination."

"And he's handsome." Kitty recalled the young man by the fireplace when she and her father visited.

"Like a Greek god." Mrs. Vanderwell glanced toward the heavens. "In my younger days, I might have swooned. But of course, he's entirely unsuitable. And from all accounts, a very volatile fellow."

"I see." This Mr. Emerson added a new angle to Kitty's picture of Elspeth. She had briefly considered the idea of a secret beau during her conversation with Prudence Marquand but had given it up in part because she had no insight into Elspeth's private affairs.

"There is one other matter." Kitty filled Amanda's mother in on her meeting with Alva Belmont and the tickets she'd been offered.

"Oh my goodness." Mrs. Vanderwell's hand flew to her heart. "You're considering attending a talk by the *family limitation* woman? Mr. Vanderwell would have me out on the streets in a second. I had no idea you knew about such things, Capability. You can't be seen there. You have your reputation to consider." She took Kitty's hands in her own. "Promise me you won't go."

"I thought it was time I learned more about what's really

happening in the world," Kitty said. "Not just wars and such, but other things."

"You can't cross that line." Mrs. Vanderwell's usually placid face hardened. "I'm speaking to you like the mother you don't have, Capability. You must consider your future. It's all right for the Alva Belmonts of the world to say and do what they want. But you don't have her clout. You won't be able to withstand the repercussions."

Kitty left the brownstone, pondering Amanda's mother's advice. The sun had come out, and although it was chilly, she decided to take a walk to clear her thoughts. Central Park was only a few blocks away.

She asked Rao to wait and then headed toward Fifth Avenue, which ran alongside the park. A stone wall, no more than about four feet high, bordered the perimeter of Olmsted and Vaux's magnificent creation. Beyond it, the ground sloped downward and was planted with now leafless shrubbery and trees to obscure views of the surrounding buildings and dull the relentless sound of traffic.

Kitty stopped at the pedestrian entrance on Sixty-Ninth Street. That must have been where Elspeth walked in. Kitty could see the Brights' home halfway down the street, which dead-ended into the park. The automobile lane through the greenery ran a few blocks farther north. A cold gust of wind made Kitty shiver. She walked to where she imagined Elspeth had died. The snow had melted, and stalks of grass poked their way up through damp soil. Kitty closed her eyes and tried to channel the dead girl to ask her what had happened that night, but all she heard was the sputtering of a motor car and the thin chirp of a bird foolish enough to be out in winter.

She crossed Fifth Avenue and headed toward the Brights' home. The butler ushered her in.

Dr. Bright looked out of the window, his hands clasped behind his back. He turned when she entered.

"My wife is resting, Miss Weeks," he said, "or else I'm sure she'd want to thank you in person. But frankly, I'm surprised to see you here. Your father let us know in no uncertain terms that he didn't care for us telephoning or making contact in any other way and that he didn't want you to continue this relationship. And I must say, I think he is correct."

If Elspeth's father was grateful that Kitty had pulled him away from the oncoming motorcar, he hardly showed it.

"I'm a bit worn out," Kitty said. "Do you mind if I sit?"

"Please." He gestured toward a chair.

"I wonder if you would talk to me about a few matters that have occurred to me."

"Given all you've done, I suppose I can hardly refuse you." He remained on his feet.

Kitty didn't allow his guardedness to deter her. In fact, it spurred her on. If he had been kinder or more gracious, she might have considered that she ought to be more sensitive to his feelings. Instead, she came straight to the point. "I know that Mr. Edison is working on new batteries for the submarine fleet," she said, taking note of his look of surprise. "I was wondering whether he submitted a proposal to the Naval Consulting Board, and whether Miss Bright knew about it."

Dr. Bright backed up to a chair and dropped down. "For

a Ladies' Page reporter, you do have unusual interests," he said finally.

Kitty saw no need to justify herself. "Did Miss Bright know about Mr. Edison's work? Had she read his proposal?"

He reacted strongly. "That is no concern of yours."

Kitty gaped at him. "You asked to meet me to speak about Miss Bright's work, sir. You wanted to know what I knew about her investigations into batteries. At first, I thought it was just some scientific hobby. Something she was tinkering with in the laboratory. But to be honest, your questions have made me doubt that."

"In what way, Miss Weeks?" He didn't bother to conceal his anger.

"In a way that involves Mr. Edison and submarines and navy contracts. Is it a coincidence that Miss Bright, who was working on batteries herself, died three weeks before Mr. Edison's batteries were about to be tested?"

"How do you know about the tests?" Dr. Bright said.

Kitty ignored him. "What really happened, sir? What did the two of you argue over that night?"

Dr. Bright hung his head. "It was such a waste. Such terrible timing."

"What was a waste, sir?" Kitty felt she must get him to tell her more.

"Elspeth's death of course. So unnecessary. She was such a clever girl. Too clever perhaps. She thought she understood…"

"What did she understand?" Kitty persisted.

"There's nothing more to it!" He jumped to his feet. "We fought. She walked out in her sleep." His voice wavered. "Do you think I don't feel it? She wasn't yet eighteen, my firstborn, my only daughter. Do you think I don't miss her with all my heart?"

Kitty was touched by his pain but plowed on. "So you don't believe her death has anything to do with the Naval Consulting Board or Mr. Edison?" There, she had come out and said it.

"I am certain that Mr. Thomas Alva Edison, the greatest inventor of our times, did not lure Elspeth to the edge of Central Park."

"You're right." Kitty rose. Either the man was willfully misunderstanding her or he couldn't bear to admit that his daughter's death might be connected to his professional affairs.

"Edgar—" Mrs. Bright entered the room in her robe and stopped when she saw their visitor. "Miss Weeks, I didn't expect to see you here."

"I was about to leave," Kitty said.

"Why did you come?"

"Miss Weeks had some questions," her husband replied.

"I wanted to learn more about Mr. Edison and his batteries and Miss Bright and her work," Kitty replied. "But Dr. Bright seems to know as little about it all as I do."

"Is that true?" Mrs. Bright turned to her husband, who didn't answer. "You owe her something, Edgar. After all, we involved her—"

"You involved her," he corrected.

"—and she saved your life." Mrs. Bright completed her sentence. "What can we do for you, Miss Weeks? We'd like to thank you properly."

"Oh, there's no need—" Kitty began. And then she had an idea. "Can I... I'd like to visit the navy yard this Saturday."

From the look of annoyance that flashed across his face, Kitty could tell that Dr. Bright wasn't pleased.

"I'm sure Edgar can arrange it, can't you, my dear?" his wife said. "You used to love to bring Elspeth and show her around."

"That's the day of the tests, but you knew that, didn't you?" Dr. Bright frowned at Kitty.

"Now, now, Edgar. You will do it for me." Mrs. Bright reached out and squeezed her husband's hand. "Come on Saturday, Miss Weeks, and my husband will take you."

The conversation had produced far better results than Kitty could have anticipated. From nothing concrete, just questions and speculation, she would now have the opportunity to see the new batteries being tested, perhaps even catch a glimpse of a real submarine. For the duration of the trip, she would be immersed in Elspeth's world, and who knew what she might learn.

CHAPTER SEVENTEEN

S o how was the interview?" Glowing with anticipation, Miss Busby welcomed Kitty back to work the following morning.

Kitty handed the editor two sheets of paper. "It went well, I think. Mrs. Belmont did most of the talking. Here is my summary."

"Wonderful," Miss Busby said. "I'll take a look, and we can discuss when I've finished."

"She wants me to come in next week to watch rehearsals."

"Next week?" Miss Busby's voice went up an octave. "That means I won't have anything to print until"—she peered at her calendar—"January 22 at the earliest. Can't you squeeze in another visit sometime today or tomorrow?"

"If you'd like to speak to her secretary, Miss Busby, please go ahead. I, for one, would prefer to leave plans as they are." Kitty had no intention of getting on Mrs. Belmont's wrong side.

Evidently, neither did the editor, because she relented. "Fine, but you must be prepared to write quickly in that case. The Saturday after is the twenty-ninth, and we can't have a January feature that runs at the end of the month."

"Not to worry, Miss Busby."

Helena Busby sighed. "And any thoughts for February?"

"I'm working on it." Perhaps, Kitty thought, if the trip to the navy yard went smoothly, she might suggest some sort of naval theme—a tribute to "Our Men in Uniform." But first things first. She hadn't yet completed the January story.

"Rumor has it," Miss Busby said, "that the president may be coming to New York to promote his preparedness plan. If that's true, we could try to work it up from a woman's angle."

Kitty couldn't resist a little dig. "Will Mrs. Wilson be accompanying him?"

Miss Busby didn't appreciate the humor. "I've told you before, Miss Weeks, and I hope never to have to repeat myself. As far as the Ladies' Page is concerned, Mrs. Galt is no one. Do I make myself clear?"

"Yes, Miss Busby." Kitty realized that if the president was visiting, that meant Soames might be in town as well. Would he come to see her? She tried not to raise her hopes. He was sure to be busy with no less a personage than the president of the United States to protect. And New York City demanded all one's attention under the best of circumstances.

꧁꧂

Two letters waited for Kitty on the silver tray in the foyer. One was from Mrs. Belmont's suffrage headquarters and included two tickets to the Sanger dinner, along with a covering note signed by her secretary, Miss Baehr. The other came from Westfield Hall. Kitty took it to her rooms and slit the envelope open. It contained a short note from Georgina Howell, saying that she had received Kitty's letter and that she planned to be in

Manhattan on Monday or Tuesday. She asked if she might drop in at the *Sentinel* so that they could speak in person.

Kitty wrote a reply to say yes and included her home address in case she wasn't at work. She folded the letter paper into thirds, slipped it into an envelope, and ran down to the post office on Broadway to stamp and send it off herself. Soon, she'd have some answers.

She may have gone down the rabbit hole on this Elspeth Bright business, but she reassured herself that in the next few days, she would be back on solid ground.

For the moment, however, domestic matters beckoned. Mrs. Codd wanted to sit down and tabulate grocery bills, which they did every two weeks, and the linens had been returned from the laundry. Kitty and Grace checked the delivery, counting every pillowcase and napkin and marking each off in the household ledger. Then Kitty went through the cabinets and put together the list of staples that needed to be ordered: flour, salt, sugar, tea, coffee, and so on.

The Misses Dancey had been all for creating lists, and Kitty had adopted the habit with gusto. She wrote everything in her cloth-bound ledger and found that it helped her to keep track of expenses and also not forget anything, which she was apt to do when the Page was foremost in her mind.

She performed exercises in her room, jumping jacks and stretches, then tired, she lay in bed and skimmed through Arnold Bennett's chapters on writing. She particularly appreciated his observation that "we may no more choose our styles than our character" and his advice never to pass judgment on one's own writing until it was a week old, because "until a reasonable interval has elapsed, it is impossible for you to distinguish between what you had in your mind and what is actually on the paper."

She had dozed off in the midst of his suggestions on how to avoid trite expressions when Grace knocked on the door.

"Miss Kitty." Her face shone. "Mrs. Tate has arrived."

Kitty hurriedly closed her book. "Really?"

"She's waiting in the hall. She has your dresses."

Kitty stood up at once. "Don't make her wait, Grace. Bring her right in."

Mrs. Tate was Kitty's seamstress and one of the most in-demand women in the city. She would take her clients' orders, promise left and right to be back at a certain time, and then miss the given date. Instead, she would breeze back at a moment of her choosing. If Kitty was out, Mrs. Tate would leave the clothes, and Kitty would have to telephone and try to set a time to meet for any necessary alterations. If she was home, well, she would drop whatever she happened to be doing. Everyone understood that that was the price of doing business with the seamstress.

"Ah, Miss Weeks." Mrs. Tate bustled into Kitty's sitting room, her canvas bag bursting. "I have your skirts." She opened the bag and removed one of tartan wool and another that was dark green. "Do try them on."

Kitty and Grace hurried off behind the changing screen.

"Sorry I'm late." She always apologized, but her apologies didn't mean anything. "Just recovering from the new year's rush."

Kitty had selected the materials and decided on the patterns way back in November.

"Some of these ladies, not you of course, but some others insisted that I come back for two or three fittings."

Kitty came out wearing the tartan. Grace offered Mrs. Tate tea, which she accepted.

"Please turn, Miss Weeks." She inspected the skirt. "I think it may need to be pinned right here." She tugged excess fabric near the hips.

"Can you do it while I wait?" Kitty asked.

"You and so many others. Why don't you let me take it home? I'll have it back to you in a few days."

She'd have it back by next season, Kitty thought, by which time it would be too late. "It's just a few stitches. Please, Mrs. Tate."

The seamstress conceded, and Kitty joined her father for dinner later that evening in a cheerful mood with two more items to wear in her closet.

"What are your plans for the weekend?" Julian Weeks wanted to know.

"I may help Mrs. Vanderwell prepare Amanda's room for her tomorrow." Kitty had never lied outright to her father before.

He held up his wine glass so that it caught the light from the electric chandelier. The cut-glass facets scattered the ray into dazzling patterns on the white tablecloth.

"Do you feel you would have benefitted from a woman's touch these past few years, Capability?"

"No. I have Amanda, Mrs. Vanderwell, Miss Busby. I think I'm quite well looked after. Why do you ask?"

"No reason. I'm just curious."

Kitty changed the subject, hating having deceived her father but equally angry that she didn't feel like she had another choice. A confrontation with him over her true whereabouts on Saturday would lead to a conflagration. He'd told her quite clearly that he didn't want her looking into Elspeth's death, even though he gave her plenty of leeway in other matters. At some point, they would have to have it out. But not at the moment.

"Terrible business in Mexico," she said. The papers had reported the death of nineteen Americans, murdered by Pancho Villa's marauding bandits.

"It is indeed," Mr. Weeks said. They lapsed into silence.

"Are you busy on Monday?" Kitty asked after a while. She hadn't decided what to do about the Margaret Sanger dinner.

"I'm afraid so."

"Mrs. Belmont gave me a ticket to an event that I might like to attend—"

"Would you go by yourself?"

"Yes."

He seemed distracted. "Capability, there are some things we should talk about."

"What kind of things?" The question hung between them.

He wiped his forehead with a napkin. "Let's leave it for a different evening."

Kitty needed time to wrap up her investigation into Elspeth's death, so she didn't argue.

Kitty left the apartment giddy with excitement but also flush with a sense of disbelief. It didn't seem possible that she, Ladies'

Page reporter Capability Weeks, was on her way to the United States Navy Yard, where she would observe tests that would transform the American fleet. In terms of the work she wanted to do, the kind of stories she wanted to write, she was finally headed in the right direction.

Rao drove her in the Packard to the East Side. As she requested, he dropped her off at the Vanderwells. Kitty pretended to look for something in her purse and waited until he turned the corner before she made her way by foot to the Brights' home. She rang the bell to their door a few minutes before noon. The butler opened it and asked her to wait just as Dr. Bright, buttoning his gloves, came down the front stairs.

"You're here," he said without preamble. He sounded as though he hoped she might not come.

"I'm looking forward to the excursion, Dr. Bright."

"And your father knows your whereabouts?"

In for a penny, in for a pound, Kitty thought as she answered, "Yes."

The butler helped Dr. Bright with his coat, and they climbed into his waiting motor car.

Kitty glanced over at Dr. Bright as the car turned toward Fifth Avenue and then veered southward. Like her father, he rode sitting upright and stared straight ahead. She distracted herself with the view from the window as the car made its way toward Brooklyn. On its own, Manhattan was a tiny island, but with its boroughs, Brooklyn, Queens, the Bronx, and Staten Island, it formed a vast metropolis surrounded on all sides by water. Piers and bridges sprouted everywhere like grass.

Smaller islands dotted the waterways around Manhattan:

Blackwell's Island with its Home for the Aged and Infirm; Randall's Island with a School for the Feeble Minded and a Custodial Asylum for Idiots; Governors Island, now a military prison; Ellis Island, where millions of immigrants had arrived in the United States; and Bedloe's Island, with the Statue of Liberty, holding her torch over three hundred feet into the air.

Dr. Bright's chauffeur drove down Canal Street toward the triumphal arch and colonnade laid out in a horseshoe shape that formed the entryway to the double-decker Manhattan Bridge, which *King's Views* said had the greatest traffic-carrying capacity in the world. As they motored up the incline leading to the bridge and crossed the East River, barges and ferries puffing along beneath it, Kitty could make out the elegant Brooklyn Bridge suspended like a necklace above the waters to the south and the utilitarian Williamsburg Bridge through Dr. Bright's window. Beyond it stretched another testament to the city's progress, the Queensboro Bridge, resting on six enormous masonry piers.

The navy yard was located in the Wallabout Bay on the Brooklyn side of the East River, between the Brooklyn and Manhattan Bridges. Kitty had looked it up in *King's*, which described it as the most important and best-equipped of the nine navy yards in the country. It had two and a half miles of waterfront and four dry docks. Machine, boiler, and plumbing shops; painting, blacksmithing, and cooperage works; and storehouses, foundries, and marine barracks occupied its 144 acres, nineteen of which were reclaimed from the sea.

A uniformed guard stopped the car as it approached the entrance gate. "Visitors only allowed on weekdays, and you will need a pass from the captain of the yard."

Dr. Bright's chauffeur showed him some papers, which he checked. He peered into the vehicle.

"We're going to the E-2, dry dock 2," Dr. Bright said.

The guard waved them on.

They drove through the complex, past stately buildings and long, low sheds. Everywhere, men were busy at work, some in naval uniforms and others wearing grease-stained overalls.

"You should feel honored," Dr. Bright said as they climbed out of the car. "This is a once-in-a-lifetime chance to witness a historic breakthrough, one that will strike the fear of God into the naval world and preserve our sailors' lives."

"How exactly, sir?" Kitty picked up her skirts and followed him toward the ships and the activity near the water. "Would you be able to explain it to me in laymen's terms?"

"Our navy is everything, Miss Weeks. It's our best source of defense, and the submarines are its most sophisticated weapon. Great sums of money have been spent to come up with a solution to make them safer to inhabit, and Mr. Edison's new battery will both prevent asphyxiation of the crew in the event of a prolonged submersion and will extend the underwater cruising range of the craft from less than one hundred to one hundred and fifty miles. That may not sound like much to you, but the craft's increasing range makes it twice as lethal."

"Thank you for putting it so clearly, Dr. Bright." Kitty looked around her. There were fewer people here and no sign of any submarine. "It's pretty quiet, isn't it?"

"Lunchtime on a Saturday," Dr. Bright said. "And we aren't advertising the tests." He walked on.

"Where is the vessel, Dr. Bright?"

"Not far. Come along... Elspeth never wanted to leave when she came to this place." His mustachioed face didn't give anything away.

"Is that so?" Fear curled tightly in Kitty's stomach. There was no evidence of life in the vicinity. No sailors strolling by. No sound of people working. She was alone in a strange place with a strange man whose motives she didn't fully comprehend. If she called for help now, no one would be able to hear her. "Where are we going?"

"Dry dock number 2." He pointed.

Kitty saw nothing. Just some sheds and the masts of ships in the distance. "What is a dry dock?" She must keep him talking.

"It's a dock that can be filled with water so a vessel floats in, and then drained, in order for repairs to be made on the hull. You remind me of Elspeth... She was always curious, ever since she was little. Always asking questions."

Kitty felt sick. Curiosity killed the cat. The next life on the line might be hers.

"She would have gone far if she had been a boy," Dr. Bright said.

"I think she intended to go far as a girl."

"Here we are." He stopped suddenly.

About fifty yards away, a gigantic U-shaped depression had been carved deep into the ground. Steps on the side allowed visitors to climb down, like in a steeply inclined amphitheater. A chain-link railing bordered the edge to prevent accidental falls.

Kitty quickened her pace and looked over. At the base of the amphitheater, sitting on what looked like wooden railway tracks, with ladders reaching up to it and ropes lashed to its sides, was an ominous, windowless, metal beast, narrow and streamlined so that it could prowl unseen through the depths and destroy ships sailing above it. A bridge had been constructed over the vessel, and a couple of workmen stood there casually talking.

Dr. Bright came up to Kitty. "The E-2 submerges several hundred feet and carries a crew of twenty-five. The batteries are being tested inside this very minute."

Kitty's heart beat faster.

"When they're not underwater, the submarine comes to the surface, and the men can stand on top to get some fresh air."

Kitty clutched the flimsy chain rail, nervous about toppling over. She was frightened by heights and tight spaces. Not for a thousand dollars would she have entered that metal tube, and not for ten thousand would she stand on top of it as it bobbed around in the Atlantic.

"Would you like to take a closer look? No one will mind if we descend."

"I'm all right here," Kitty said, watching the men beneath her.

Out of nowhere, a boom like a thunderclap ripped through the air. Kitty found herself stumbling backward. A plume of smoke shot from the submarine's hatch. Something dark landed with a thump on the hull. All was quiet for a minute, then men emerged from the shadows, yelling and looking around in wild confusion.

"Get back to the car." Dr. Bright stood in front of Kitty, blocking her view. "Now!"

Kitty hesitated. She had no idea what was going on, what had caused the blast.

"Now," he repeated. There was no mistaking his command-
ing tone. He stayed in place, making sure Kitty obeyed, while
sailors and workmen raced toward the vessel. An acrid smell
began to make her feel ill, and Kitty pulled a handkerchief from
her purse to cover her nose and mouth.

Several paces ahead, a man in a suit strode along. Kitty
couldn't tell why she thought he looked suspicious, and then
she realized—he was the only person other than her walking
away from the scene of the incident.

"Hey, you," Kitty called.

He turned for an instant, just long enough for her to see
his face.

"Stop," she yelled, but he broke into a run. Kitty followed.
Dr. Bright's former assistant was too fast for her until, in the
distance, he must have seen the guard at the gate barring the
way, because he slowed down and she was able to catch up
with him.

"Mr. Emerson." She gasped for breath.

"How do you know my name?"

"We met in passing at the Brights' home. I'm Capability
Weeks, a friend of Elspeth's."

"Oh yes?" His eyes darted around. There was no way out
except past the watchman.

"I believe you used to work for Dr. Bright? What are you
doing here?"

"What am *I* doing here? I might ask you the same question."

"I came to observe the tests."

His lips parted into a smug smile that unnerved her.

"Were you invited?" Kitty said.

"None of your business." He lifted his hat, smoothed down his hair, and, cool as could be, strolled over to the guard. "There's been an explosion at the E-2. They need your help."

The guard rushed off. Emerson tipped his hat to Kitty. Her hands clenched into fists, furious that she couldn't clock him one. She could only watch as he sauntered away.

Dr. Bright returned to the car about half an hour later, muttering and shaking his head.

"Is everything all right?" Kitty asked.

"No, it's not," he said tightly.

"Is anyone injured?"

"I'm sure you'll read all about it in the papers tomorrow, Miss Weeks. It goes without saying that this is not for you to report." He tapped the glass partition between them and the driver. "Let's go."

The chauffeur started the engine.

Kitty's head throbbed as the vehicle lurched forward. "Mr. Emerson was here. He seemed in a hurry to make himself scarce after the blast."

Dr. Bright turned to her. "Phillip Emerson—who used to work for me?"

"I don't know his first name, but yes."

Dr. Bright didn't ask how Kitty was acquainted with him.

"Should we tell someone?"

His jaw clenched. "That won't be necessary."

She waited a moment and then broached a question that had

crossed her mind from the moment she laid eyes on his former assistant. "Dr. Bright, do you think the explosion might have been deliberately caused?"

"You mean sabotage?"

"I suppose so, yes."

Dr. Bright started to reply, then thought better of it. He didn't say anything for the rest of the drive back to Manhattan.

Chapter Eighteen

"Well, well, well." Julian Weeks picked up his copy of Sunday's paper. "There seems to have been an incident at the navy yard in Brooklyn."

Kitty's face burned as she hunched over her bowl of Kellogg's cornflakes. She had woken early and scoured the entire article.

Her father dropped into his chair and started to read, shaking his head in amazement from time to time. "Four men were killed, and ten were injured while tests were underway on a new battery. They're blaming Thomas Edison and his engineers."

"Is that so?" Kitty hoped her words didn't sound too forced.

"This submarine, the E-2, was the only one on which the new battery was being tested, and if it passed, it would have been used across the fleet."

"Um-hmm." She kept her voice neutral.

"Apparently, a great column of smoke shot out of the hatch. It had something to do with the hydrogen the batteries produced. Combined with the oxygen in the air, it formed steam, and the force of the explosion was so great," he went on, scanning the page, "that it wrecked the entire interior of the craft. And pushed out the body of the chief engineer, which fell onto the hull. The fumes were dense and pungent enough—"

"They were." Kitty recalled the acrid odor.

"I beg your pardon?"

"I mean," she corrected herself, "were they?"

"Oh yes. Enough to make extrication extremely challenging. Rescuers went in with oxygen masks but were still forced to operate electric fume blowers for several hours before they could remove the bodies, many of which were severely mangled."

Kitty covered her face with her hands. Had she and Dr. Bright been any closer to the boat, had they gone below as he had suggested...

"What's the matter, Capability? You look pale all of a sudden. Are your injuries from the accident still bothering you?"

"I think I might need to lie down," Kitty replied.

"I think you should. The doctor prescribed rest, but you've been rushing around as though nothing happened. It was bound to catch up with you." He put aside his paper. "Have you given any further thought to what you told me? That you might quit the Page?"

"No!" Kitty sat up straight. "That was in the heat of the moment. Right after Elspeth died."

"You were concerned about your health."

"Dr. Stevens said I'm perfectly fine."

"Dr. Stevens also said you shouldn't strain yourself."

Kitty pushed back her chair. "I may have overdone it a bit yesterday. I'm going to lie down now."

On her way to her rooms, Kitty whispered to Grace, "Please bring me a copy of the newspaper when my father isn't looking." She added, by way of explanation, "He thinks I need to take a nap."

As she lay in bed, Grace knocked on the door. "Here you go, Miss Kitty. Would you like me to close the curtains?"

"No thanks, Grace. I'll relax like this for a bit."

The papers blamed the Edison battery and ruled out sabotage, but Kitty wasn't so sure. What had Dr. Bright's assistant been doing there? He had seemed so shifty at first, and then he had smiled that self-satisfied smile, the memory of which still made her skin crawl.

She scanned the stories, which examined the incident at the navy yard from various angles. One said that there had been over two hundred deaths due to collisions, explosions, and chlorine gas in submarines even before the vessels were first used in combat. Most of those casualties had been borne by the navies of France, Great Britain, and Russia. The United States Navy remained notably free of losses until the sinking of the F-4 due to a corroded battery lining the previous March.

Still, the E-2 had the reputation of being an unlucky craft, and the lead-acid batteries that it normally used had caused problems, which the new batteries were supposed to solve. Once, the paper said, while practicing maneuvers, a crewman noticed chlorine gas gathering in the boat. It was hurried to the surface and the hatch opened to give the crew fresh air, but still, every crewman started bleeding from the nose and mouth, and one suffered irreparable damage to his lungs.

Another article, BLOW TO EDISON BATTERY, reported that "upon the results of investigation into the cause of the E-2 explosion will depend on whether the Edison battery is used or discarded by the United States Navy..." It speculated that the accident had occurred under the battery deck most likely while the battery was being discharged, "that is, while the electrical energy that had been stored in the battery was being removed by means of a rheostat." If subsequent investigation confirmed that the explosion occurred while the battery was being discharged rather than charged, it would mean the end of the battery as far as the navy was concerned.

Previous tests of the Edison battery had shown only infinitesimal amounts of hydrogen being produced while the batteries were in use.

So either those tests had been wrong, or this time, something different had occurred.

Kitty looked away from the jungle of words printed on the page. She couldn't see her way through it. She couldn't begin to understand why Mr. Emerson had been at the navy yard, and whether his presence there had anything to do with Dr. Bright and what happened to Elspeth.

CHAPTER NINETEEN

K itty reminded Mr. Weeks over breakfast that she would be attending Mrs. Belmont's "charity event" that evening.

"I have been meaning to ask. What is it?" he said. "One of those suffragist shindigs?"

"Not exactly." Kitty felt pretty certain that in his book, Mrs. Sanger would be worse than any suffragist shindig. "It's just a cause she supports."

"A group for brow-beaten husbands?" He chuckled. "Will you be late?"

"I should be back by ten."

"Keep Rao with you. I'll be out at a meeting, but be sure that you give Mrs. Codd the order for my dinner."

To avoid being scolded for straining herself, Kitty brought the paper along with her to the car.

The news of the explosion had taken a bizarre turn: A FOREIGN NAVY USES EDISON BATTERY TOO... HYDROGEN GAS NO DEFECT.

In the course of defending the Edison battery tests on the E-2, Dr. Miller Reese Hutchison, Mr. Edison's "personal representative and chief engineer," had let slip that the Edison battery was already in use in the war in Europe. "Up to that moment," the story said, "it had been supposed that the United States had an option on the exclusive use of the device if the tests to which it was to be subjected proved satisfactory."

Dr. Hutchison was quoted as saying, "The Edison cells have been in use on submarines for a long time, although this is not generally known. Mr. Edison is not in the munitions business, and he has not sold any since the war, but before that, three submarines of a certain European power were fitted with these batteries. They have not met with any accident."

A large number of visitors, including women and girls—all of whom were kept back by a squad of marines—had gathered to watch the hauling away of the E-2's twisted interior. "Rumors that the explosion Saturday afternoon was deliberately caused were denounced as falsehoods yesterday by Commander Frank B. Upham, second in command of the navy yard," the story went on.

That would seem to exonerate Dr. Bright's assistant, but the question of why he had been wandering about in the vicinity of the dry dock remained unanswered.

Dry dock. Kitty had just learned the term, but it already felt like second nature.

She turned to the following article. A Denver automobile manufacturer, working with Edison batteries similar to those used in the E-2, had said that they had caused "frequent and sometimes dangerous explosions."

"Only a few weeks ago," the manufacturer told reporters, "a navy official and I were discussing these new batteries, and I then warned him of the danger I had discovered. The new Edison batteries constantly generate hydrogen and oxygen."

Kitty thought it strange that the navy had allowed the tests to proceed regardless.

What with the event at the navy yard and her nervous

anticipation about attending the Sanger talk that evening, Mrs. Belmont's theatrical production had slipped Kitty's mind, and she only recalled it when Miss Busby asked about the *Melinda and Her Sisters* rehearsals.

"You are going tomorrow, aren't you? Make sure you take down all the debutantes' names. I want our readers to know who will be playing whom. And get them to tell you how they feel about acting in a play. Did Mrs. Belmont's secretary give you a copy of the script?"

"Yes," Kitty replied.

"Have you read it yet? Is it any good?"

"I was planning to read it today, Miss Busby," Kitty improvised.

"Well, please do it now. There's no time to lose."

Kitty turned to leave, but Helena Busby hadn't finished. "I'd like to be able to include a summary of the piece, since most of our readers won't be able to afford seats at the Waldorf. I hear they'll be going for as much as one hundred and twenty-five dollars for a box. We must give them the feeling of what it would be like to be there. The operetta on the one hand, the society scene on the other. Do you see what I'm aiming for?"

"I do, Miss Busby."

"All right then. Why don't you go somewhere quiet and begin? How about down to the morgue? Tell Mr. Musser I sent you."

Kitty stopped by her desk and picked up her copy of the theatrical.

"Where are you going?" Jeannie asked.

"Downstairs to read."

"Really?"

"Miss Busby wants me in the morgue so I can concentrate."

"Is that so?" Jeannie grinned. "R-r-romance." She rolled the *r*.

"You think?"

"I'm sure."

Kitty wrinkled her nose. "Those two? They've both been here forever."

"Exactly." Jeannie looked at Kitty with meaning. "Rekindling old sparks."

"Where do they meet?" That question still baffled Kitty.

Jeannie thought for a moment, then she laughed. "I don't know."

Downstairs, Mr. Musser was busy with his boys at the back, so Kitty picked an empty seat and opened her typewritten copy of *Melinda and Her Sisters* by Mrs. O. H. P. Belmont and Elsa Maxwell, with music and lyrics by Elsa Maxwell.

The play began at the villa of the nouveau riche couple, Mr. and Mrs. Pepper of "Oshkosh out West," where preparations were underway for a coming-out party for seven of their daughters. Kitty had no idea what to expect but suspected she would be in for a good time.

Two gossips, Mrs. Malaprop and Mrs. Grundy, set the scene. "Have they enough money to move east and buy a villa at Newport?" Mrs. Malaprop asked, regarding the Peppers.

"It doesn't take *money* to get a villa at Newport. It takes brains," Mrs. Grundy replied.

Mr. and Mrs. Pepper made their appearance. "Today is the day of which I have always dreamed," Mrs. Pepper declared. Today, their beautiful girls would be coming home with new accomplishments that would be sure to get them all good husbands.

"I am going to see to it that our girls get all the advertising that the morning paper can print," Mrs. Pepper continued. "That will get them good husbands, if anything will. Publicity is the very keynote of life nowadays."

Kitty suspected that Mrs. Belmont had contributed that line. Alva Belmont understood the importance of publicity to the success of her endeavors, which was no doubt why she had invited Kitty to observe the rehearsals in the first place.

Mrs. Pepper explained why she educated her daughters: "So far as knowledge goes, we don't send our girls to school to learn anything, for a perfect lady should know absolutely nothing. It creates an atmosphere of mystery and elusive charm. That's what men like in a woman. She should know nothing, think nothing, say nothing, but dress well, look well, and dance."

Kitty smiled. She could think of a couple of girls who fit that description. Later, the Peppers' youngest daughter, Melinda, arrived onstage, "dressed very plainly but attractively and carrying a suffrage flag with children of the poor holding onto her skirt and men and women in every walk of life following her in the procession."

The town's mayor, Mayor Dooless, took Melinda to task for her beliefs, and while Kitty agreed with most of Melinda's arguments, one gave her pause: "But by denying women the political right to vote and by allowing old black Joe that same right, you place old black Joe mentally and economically in a position superior to that of the late Mrs. Dooless, your capable and very good wife."

Fortunately, Melinda had other tricks up her sleeve. "Mayor, what exactly constitutes a citizen of a country?"

The mayor replied, "A man who pays his taxes."

"But women pay taxes just the same as men, and yet they have no rights."

The mayor pointed out that it was the idea of women holding office that men objected to. "What would happen to the country with a pack of women howling in the Senate and giving pink teas at the White House? Why, the whole country would go to the dogs!"

And Melinda replied undaunted, "The country has been going to the dogs for quite a while now. Why not give it to the cats for a change? Statistics teach us the women make just as good surgeons, lawyers, architects, and in fact excel in all the practical arts... When a woman tightens the rein and puts the bit on intellect and instinct, she will be unconquerable."

The play ended abruptly, to Kitty's dismay—she had been enjoying it thoroughly—with Mrs. Pepper convinced by her daughter and ordering her other children, "Girls, girls, put away your curls! If the men won't be prepared, we'll show them that the women are for preparedness anyhow!" The entire party then burst into a song called "Girls, Girls, Put Away Your Curls," followed by another rousing number, "Carry On!"

Kitty tried to think how best to summarize the play without giving away key lines, which she was sure Mrs. Belmont wouldn't want, when she heard a voice say her name.

"Is it Miss Weeks?"

Kitty put down her pencil.

"I'm Phineas Mills. You came to see me about the somnambulist who died."

"That's right." Kitty remembered the curly-haired reporter from the sixth floor.

"They send Ladies' Page girls down here?" He didn't hide his surprise.

"Sometimes. We all need to look into things. Speaking of which"—Kitty realized he might have further information she could use—"did you happen to meet a man by the name of Emerson when you went to the Brights'? You couldn't miss him; he's a handsome fellow."

"Why do you ask?"

Kitty blushed. "No real reason."

"You're still bothered by her death."

"I suppose I am."

"Well." He scratched his head with the back of his pencil. "I'd need to check my notes. I'd be happy to...if you like."

"I would, thank you."

"Let me finish here first, and then I'll see what I can find."

Kitty wrote her summary and handed it to Miss Busby.

The editor read through it quickly. "Nicely done, Miss Weeks. I'll look forward to seeing what you have to report on tomorrow's rehearsal." She paused. "I must say, I'm rather glad I pushed us down this course."

Rao drove Kitty to the Hotel Brevoort on Fifth Avenue and Eighth Street in Greenwich Village that evening. Since her favorite no-nonsense brown suit had been sent to be mended after its outing to the navy yard, she wore a plain navy-blue one without any jewelry or trimmings so as not to attract attention. She arrived late in the hope that she would be seated in the back and would be able to leave early if necessary. A woman beneath a suffrage banner took her ticket, and another seated her at a table in the hotel's spacious ballroom, which was already crowded with at least a hundred diners. More than half were women in smart attire. Later, Kitty would learn that people of influence, like the writer Charlotte Perkins Gilman and Walter Lippmann, the youthful editor of the *New Republic*, had been present, but since she didn't move in their circles, even had she known, it wouldn't have mattered. She had gone out on a limb by being there. She would turn twenty soon, marriage and motherhood would be in the cards someday, and bit by bit, she had to understand the choices that other women faced, whether or not her father or anyone else approved.

Mrs. Sanger came to the podium. She had a sweet, pretty face and kindly eyes with a downward cast. She didn't appear in the least threatening to Kitty, more like someone who one might meet for tea or at a millinery shop than a powerful women's advocate. Mrs. Sanger thanked her friends for supporting her on the eve of her trial and acknowledged that her pamphlets might have been too hysterical or too radical for some. But, she declared, they were the only way she could get attention for the subject of family limitation.

Kitty looked around her. No one seemed shocked by the subject. Mrs. Sanger held her audience rapt. For the poor, she said, "birth control does not mean what it does to us. To them, it has meant the most barbaric methods. It has meant the killing of babies—infanticide, abortions—in one crude way or another."

Kitty dreaded to imagine what Miss Busby or Mrs. Vanderwell would say if they knew she was listening to this. The Danceys would have fainted—but not before they pulled her from the hall first. Mrs. Sanger went on to discuss "the tribe of professional abortionists" who profited from others' misfortunes, and she spoke feelingly of foundling asylums.

"How," she asked, "could I awaken public opinion to this terrible problem?" She could have taken a more conservative path, but would anyone have listened? This very gathering, she concluded, was proof that her words had been heard, and she exhorted the social workers present to gather the interest that had been roused and direct it.

The crowd rose to its feet in applause, and as it died down, Kitty slipped away. Family limitation, abortion, infanticide… It was both fascinating and gruesome, but she had heard enough for the present. The next time she decided to attend such a talk, she would inform her father and have it out with him in advance.

She had been lucky not to bump into anyone she knew, Kitty thought as she handed her token to the coat-check girl.

"Miss Weeks!"

Kitty dropped her purse.

Sylvia Lane smiled and picked it up for her. "What brings you to the Brevoort this evening? Is Julian here as well?"

"I came by myself." Kitty could barely trust herself to speak. "And you?"

"Mr. Lane and I are staying here."

Kitty could have kicked herself. Her father had mentioned it, but she hadn't been paying attention.

"Did you attend the Sanger dinner?" Miss Lane's smile didn't budge an inch, while Kitty's face, already hot, felt like it would burst into flames.

"I'm sorry, I'm running late." She grabbed her coat from the attendant. "If you will excuse me, Miss Lane." Of all people, how could she have run into that woman?

She hurried out and searched the avenue for Rao. Touring cars were parked on both sides of the street, and in the darkness, they all looked identical. Fortunately, the chauffeur spotted Kitty and drove over.

She climbed in, and they set off for home. There was no doubt about it, she was wading into murkier and murkier waters. Unwanted pregnancies...foundling homes...a sickening possibility occurred to her. She wanted to shrink away, but she willed herself to face facts. Elspeth Bright could have wandered lightly clad into the dark, cold night because she was pregnant. Kitty felt the full force of the Misses Dancey prohibition against so much as pronouncing the word and recalled their habit of skirting around it with euphemisms. If Elspeth had found herself in such a situation, she may well have decided to end her life. She would have known that her somnambulism would provide the perfect cover. No one would ask any further questions.

Even the most particular girls from the finest homes made mistakes. Hadn't Mrs. Vanderwell said that there had been talk about her and the dashing, yet shifty Mr. Emerson?

CHAPTER TWENTY

T he curtain rings slid across the wooden rod with a drawn-
out swish, and light poured in as Grace opened the drapes
in Kitty's room.

Kitty blinked in the brightness. Her navy-blue suit had been
brushed and hung on its hook, ready to be returned to the
closet. No, she hadn't dreamt it. She had gone to the Brevoort
last night, bumped into Sylvia Lane, and conjured up all kinds
of scurrilous scenarios about a dead schoolgirl with whom she
had a very tenuous relationship.

Kitty sighed. She was finished. There was no way around it.
Once her father found out where she'd been, he'd probably
pack her off to a convent.

"How was last night?" Mr. Weeks said when Kitty came in
to breakfast.

It was now or never—and she wasn't ready. "It was fine."

"What are your plans for the day?" Her father nodded absently.

So he hadn't yet spoken to Miss Lane. "Workwise, you
mean?" Butter scraped against toast. "I'm to observe the
rehearsals for Mrs. Belmont's operetta."

"You're moving in exalted circles."

She forced a smile.

"On a more mundane note, I've invited the Lanes for dinner."

The room started to spin. "When?"

"This evening." He folded his newspaper. "I'm hoping that Miss Lane... I was thinking that you and I, we might like another woman's presence in the house."

Kitty pushed back her chair. She couldn't stay here anymore. "I really can't afford to be late today. I should be off."

"Oh." Julian Weeks sounded both hurt and baffled. "Well, see you later then." His voice followed Kitty as she left the room.

She couldn't believe it. For twenty years, he hadn't bothered to remarry—and she could have used a mother when she was a child. Now, when she no longer needed one, when she was forging her own path to independence, making a life for herself, he was springing Sylvia Lane on her.

"Court of Inquiry for E-2!" a newsboy cried.

"Could you stop for a minute, please?" Kitty asked Rao. She beckoned to the newsboy and bought a copy of the paper through the window. In her eagerness to leave the house and blot out her father's words, Kitty hadn't even stopped to glance at the headlines.

There had been another casualty as a result of the weekend's submarine disaster, and Secretary Daniels had convened a special court to conduct a sweeping investigation "to cover all matters pertaining to the explosion or cause thereof."

He also announced that henceforth, all batteries, engines, and other vital parts would be subjected to more rigorous laboratory tests before being installed in submarines, with a view toward preventing future accidents. Currently, due to the lack of adequate laboratories and research facilities, there had been no other way to test Mr. Edison's invention.

And all the while, Mr. Edison's representative, Dr. Miller Reese Hutchison, continued to insist to the press that the batteries were flawless.

The story had become more and more perplexing. Why would Hutchison tell a deliberate falsehood when the facts were stacked against him and the truth was about to be determined once and for all? Despite all evidence to the contrary, Kitty wondered whether Mr. Edison's man might not be as wrong as he seemed. Phillip Emerson could have been hired by some outside party to create trouble.

The car pulled up in front of Alva Belmont's offices, and once again, Miss Baehr brought Kitty to see her employer.

"Come in." Mrs. Belmont stopped frowning at her papers, and for a moment, she stared at her visitor blankly, then recalled who Kitty was.

"Oh, you're here to cover the rehearsals, Miss Weeks. Well, you're in good luck. Our two professional actresses, Miss Marie Dressler and Miss Marie Doro—I'm sure you've heard of them both—who are to play Mrs. Pepper and Melinda, are in, as well as the debutantes. And our boxes at the Waldorf are selling like hotcakes."

"And individual seats, madam?"

"Those are flying away for a mere ten dollars."

There was nothing mere about the sum to Kitty, although it might have been pocket change to Mrs. Belmont.

"I'd like you to convey the spirit behind this performance,"

Alva Belmont instructed. "The importance of suffrage. Talk to the actresses and debutantes, and allow the public to learn their views as well."

"I'll do my best," Kitty said.

Mrs. Belmont's eyes narrowed, and Kitty thought she might be in for it. Had that been a weak response? Was she about to witness Mrs. Belmont's legendary temper?

But instead, the suffragist simply said, "Women in this country suffer under unjust conditions against which they have no means of protection. And all about us, we have evidence of the futility of attempting to get results without the ballot to enforce our demands. As Miss Laura Clay of Kentucky has said, 'the forward movement of either sex is possible only when the other moves also.' Do you understand what that means?"

"I think so." Mrs. Belmont waited, so Kitty clarified. "Men can't improve their lot until women's lot improves."

"Exactly," Alva Belmont said. "There is no more pernicious form of slavery in the world than the subjection of women to men, Miss Weeks. It's all the more degrading because women don't understand the extent of their subjection." She shifted gears. "Who sent you to me?"

"Do you mean the *Sentinel* or Miss Busby, my editor?" Kitty still felt as though she were walking on hot coals and that she couldn't afford to put one step wrong.

"No, no. You came to me somehow. You were recommended."

"By Mrs. Bright."

"That's it. How is Effie Bright holding up? That daughter of hers was quite a firecracker. I like girls of that sort. One day, she would have been quite an asset to our cause…" The suffragist glanced at her papers. "Ask Miss Baehr to give you the cast list for your story, would you?"

"Yes, Mrs. Belmont. Will that be all?"

Kitty went to find Miss Baehr, who escorted her to the room being used for rehearsals. The playwright, Elsa Maxwell, a buoyantly large woman who looked like she could have been whipped up by a jolly French pâtissier, was in the midst of directing a group of young women in song:

"For a thousand years or so,
Since many moons ago,
Men have ruled us women East and West.
From the caveman in his lair,
To the flyer in the air,
To keep us women down, they thought was best."

Miss Baehr whispered, "Miss Maxwell tells a funny joke—she said that Prince Christian of Hesse saw her swimming off the coast of Eden Roc and mistook her for a rubber mattress!"

"But turned now is the tide,
And we cannot be denied—"

"No, no, no," Miss Maxwell interrupted. "*C'est terrible.* Let's take a break. Everyone, go get a drink of water before we start from the top."

"I can't believe we have to do this for the whole day," one of the young ladies in Kitty's earshot said to a cast mate.

"And every day," the other complained. "I thought it was all supposed to be good fun."

Miss Baehr introduced Kitty to Elsa Maxwell.

"A pleasure to meet you, Miss Weeks." She had a slight British accent.

"Are you from England, Miss Maxwell?"

"Oh no! I'm just a piano player from Keokuk, Iowa, who found fame and fortune in England." Elsa Maxwell chuckled. "And now I've crossed the Atlantic to come home and work on *Melinda*."

She excused herself, explaining she had to check on music to help the cast hit the notes right.

Kitty approached the two professional actresses, who would be playing Mrs. Pepper and Melinda Pepper. She had seen them both in the movies but never in the flesh. Not surprisingly, she had the disorienting sensation that she knew both ladies intimately and, at the same time, not at all.

She first spoke to Marie Dressler, the big-boned comedienne whose performance she'd thoroughly enjoyed alongside the funnyman Charlie Chaplin in *Tillie's Punctured Romance*.

"I'm giving six weeks of my time to the cause," Miss Dressler said. "Time that I wouldn't sell to anyone. I'm making my own costume. Green train and all."

"I didn't know suffrage meant all that," the dainty Marie Doro told Kitty, describing how she felt after she first read her libretto. "It appeals to the very highest and best there is in me. I love the part of Melinda."

The debutantes, who seemed excited to be questioned by a reporter, giggled and said that suffrage was "just the thing."

Kitty watched the women rehearse their songs and lines for another half an hour and jotted down her notes. It occurred to her how strange it was to hear Miss Dressler and Miss Doro speak. On screen, she saw their lips move and read snippets of their dialogue, but until today, she had never heard their voices.

"A young man came looking for you," Jeannie said to Kitty when she returned to the office. "Do you have a new beau I should know about?"

"I have no idea what you mean, Jeannie." It was one thing to speculate about Miss Busby's affairs, but when it came to her personal life, Kitty preferred to nip all teasing in the bud.

"Don't tell me you don't know. Six foot tall"—Jeannie threw Kitty a sidelong glance—"curly haired, a little nervous. Walks like a friendly giraffe."

"How does a friendly giraffe walk, Jeannie?" Kitty said, but Jeannie's description did the trick. "Do you mean Mr. Mills?"

"Ooh, Mr. *Mills*."

"Come on, Jeannie. What did he have to say?"

"He wants you to speak to him. Up at the newsroom."

Kitty turned to leave.

"Don't do anything I wouldn't," Jeannie said.

Kitty didn't look back, so Jeannie couldn't see her laughing. Jeannie Williams was unstoppable. What she would say if and when Kitty had a *real* beau—now that would be hard to imagine.

The whole rigmarole of knocking on the glass partition and waiting to be noticed was becoming tedious, but Kitty still hadn't reached the point when she was ready to barge right in. She sometimes wondered what would happen if she did. Surely, all hell wouldn't break loose.

Mills emerged from the smoke-filled enclave. There was something nervous and shambling about him. She had to give Jeannie credit for being observant.

"Miss Weeks."

"You were looking for me, Mr. Mills?"

"I went over my notes like you asked." He held a worn notepad in his hands. "There's no mention of a Mr. Emerson being at the Brights' home the day I was there, the day they found her body. But would you know, he seems to have been present at the dinner."

"With her friends, the night before?"

"That's right."

Kitty was astounded. Why hadn't Mrs. Bright said something? She'd only mentioned the Marquands and Georgina Howell. "Do you have the names of everyone who was at the house the night Elspeth died?"

Mills found the correct page. "Here it is... At dinner on Christmas Eve: Dr. Bright, Mrs. Bright, Elspeth Bright, the Bright twins, Miss Georgina Howell, Miss Prudence Marquand, Mr. and Mrs. Marquand, and Mr. Phillip Emerson. Does this mean something to you?"

"It does, but I'm not sure exactly what at the moment."

"If you're planning to write something," the young man said, "you will tell me?" It was half statement, half question.

"I'm not writing anything yet, Mr. Mills. I still have to finish my assignment for the Ladies' Page."

Kitty would have loved to have been a fly on the wall at dinner the night Elspeth wandered out into the snow. She needed a complete picture of the evening in order to make sense of it.

Georgina. Georgina Howell would be able to tell her, and she was supposed to be in town yesterday or today.

Kitty raced down the stairwell. She hoped with all her gadding about she hadn't missed the schoolgirl.

"Sorry, Miss Weeks." The guard in the main lobby shook his head. "No one has come by asking for you these past two days. And not a young lady. I'm sure of that."

Kitty slowly made her way back upstairs to the hen coop.

"How is Mr. Mills?" Jeannie smiled at her, unwilling to let the joke die.

"He's fine," Kitty replied drily. "By the way, has a girl by the name of Georgina Howell stopped in or telephoned?"

"No need to get uppity… But no, not that I know of."

Kitty sat at her desk, agitated, then got back up.

"Something the matter?" Jeannie looked up from her work.

"I should speak to Miss Busby." Kitty made her way down the hall.

The Ladies' Page editor had just finished reading Kitty's notes from the rehearsal. "Lovely, so colorful. The mattress bit is a nice touch, but we can't put it in."

"Why not?" Kitty thought it sounded perfectly fine.

"Well"—Helena Busby scrambled for an explanation— "a woman mistaken for a piece of furniture? That's most unorthodox."

"I thought we were aiming for a new Page in the new year and so on."

"Not so new, Miss Weeks. I have my limits."

Reluctant to go home and face the prospect of dinner with the Lanes, Kitty hung about at work until four in the afternoon. But to her dismay, Georgina Howell didn't make an appearance.

Chapter Twenty-One

B e careful. It's hot, Miss Kitty." Mrs. Codd opened the cast-iron pot herself. A marbled cut of meat garnished with herbs simmered inside, quashing Kitty's hopes that dinner would have to be canceled. Instead, the inevitable would happen: Mr. Weeks would propose to Miss Lane, Miss Lane would reveal her sighting of Kitty at the Hotel Brevoort, and any trust Kitty and her father had established between them would be ruined.

Four or five years ago, Kitty had come across Mrs. Gaskell's *Wives and Daughters* at her school library. In it, the well-meaning widower Mr. Gibson remarried with devastating consequences for his only daughter. His second wife, Miss Clare, was kind but thoughtless and self-centered. And like Sylvia Lane, she was a member of the teaching profession: Miss Clare had been a former governess to aristocracy.

Kitty groaned and flung herself onto her bed. She had devoured the novel, drawn to it by the parallels between Molly Gibson's situation and her own. But unlike Molly Gibson, Kitty was now an independent young woman of the twentieth century who held down her own job. Her life didn't have to be turned topsy-turvy by the wind of her father's affections.

It wasn't long before the Lanes arrived, and after some small talk between all four, Sylvia Lane took a seat beside Kitty on the couch.

Any moment now, Kitty thought, the woman would plunge the dagger.

"That's a very pretty dress," Miss Lane said quietly.

"Thank you." Kitty braced herself. *Here it comes.*

"I don't pretend to know you." Miss Lane spoke softly so the men couldn't overhear. "But I believe I understand your predicament."

Kitty colored despite herself.

"The world is changing rapidly," Sylvia Lane continued. "We're living in a modern age whether we want to or not, and you like to be in the thick of things. I'm similar to you in that regard."

Kitty backed away. Nothing was worse than Sylvia Lane cozying up to her, suggesting they had interests in common.

"We won't tell Julian that you went to hear Mrs. Sanger speak." Miss Lane patted the cushion between them. "That will be our little secret."

The nerve of the woman. Kitty jumped to her feet. "My father and I tell each other exactly what we need to know. Now, if you will excuse me, I must check on dinner." Kitty rushed to the kitchen and held a glass of ice water to her forehead. She waited until she felt calmer before returning to the living room, where Sylvia Lane regaled the men with stories of the overzealous saleswomen at Bergdorf Goodman.

"Capability prefers B. Altman," Mr. Weeks said.

Miss Lane turned to Kitty. "I've never been. Perhaps we could go together?"

The buttons on Kitty's dress felt tight, constricting her chest. "Miss Busby keeps me very busy. I must check my schedule."

"I understand, you're a working girl," Miss Lane said as Mr. Weeks frowned.

"Capability will take you one day. She knows the place like Livingstone knew Africa."

Kitty didn't reply. She couldn't help herself. She didn't see why she must go out of her way to be nice to this woman. Miss Lane might marry her father, and she, Kitty, would be polite. That was all.

Dinner went on and on and on. Kitty wished she hadn't ordered so much and so well. Hugo and Sylvia Lane and Julian Weeks looked happy and at ease in one another's company, while Kitty felt like the odd one out. She could tell her father wasn't pleased with her. He didn't do much to include her in the conversation or even glance her way, and she couldn't say she blamed him.

The Lanes left after eleven, without a word mentioned about the Brevoort.

"You still don't approve of Sylvia," Mr. Weeks said when the door closed behind their guests.

Kitty was too tired to argue.

"I asked you a question, Capability. Do you not like Miss Lane?"

"I don't know her," she said finally.

"Why don't you get to know her?"

"I don't want to. Not right now."

"And that's just the problem," he burst out. "You're predisposed against Miss Lane, because you don't want me to share my affections with anyone. But Sylvia is well-educated and well-traveled. She's not as old as I am but not as young as you are. She should be a perfect match for both of us. You don't see that, because you don't want to see it."

"That's not true." Kitty felt like a child.

"Why aren't you giving her a chance then? You can't let your hopes color your vision, Capability. There's a world out there, and it doesn't take too kindly to motherless young women, particularly ones who hold down jobs. You need someone to show you the way, and I'm no use in that regard."

"And she is?"

"She's worked. She's a teacher."

Kitty opened her mouth to speak and closed it again.

"Would you prefer that I picked some society lady—"

"To be honest," Kitty said, "I'd prefer it if you picked no one."

"I have a life to lead, Capability." He looked undone by her behavior. But he had no idea how he had torn her world apart.

⁂

"What is it like living at the women's boardinghouse?" Kitty asked Jeannie as soon as she arrived at the *Sentinel* the next morning. "Do you have your own bedroom?"

"Just about. It fits a bed, a bureau, and me. Anything else and one of the three would have to be booted out." Jeannie's pencil hovered over proofs. "Why do you want to know? Are you thinking of writing a story about it?"

"Perhaps. That's an idea."

"We sit together in the parlor every evening, and the food is terrible. We have to keep to rules. Our landlady doesn't like us walking out with young men. And she charges five dollars a month."

"But you're free. You're independent."

Jeannie looked doubtful. "I'd take my own apartment, a car, and a maid over independence any day."

"Yes," Kitty said. The point was that with Miss Lane living there, it wouldn't be her apartment anymore. "Who would want to give up all that?"

Five dollars a month, she thought as she went to speak to Miss Busby. Mr. Weeks hadn't wanted her to take a salary for her position at the Ladies' Page; he thought no self-respecting girl from a good family needed one, and that taking cash in exchange for her services would make her beholden to the paper. Kitty had argued that by not taking a salary, girls who could manage without one did a grave disservice to those who needed to be paid. (She had read that in *Vocations for Girls*, her career guide.) But she also felt, although she hadn't said it, that not taking a salary would do *her* a disservice. It would turn her into a dilettante, an amateur, and devalue her efforts. In the end, Kitty won. She was paid a salary—not much, since she only worked half days—and used it as pocket money. The amount felt trivial in comparison to the sums she had at her disposal through her father, but she was glad she had taken a stand. Now, it might enable her to buy her freedom.

"Mrs. Belmont's secretary telephoned," Miss Busby said. "She'd like to review your article before it comes out."

"Miss Baehr wants to review my piece?"

"No, Mrs. Belmont does."

"Doesn't that go against the rules of journalistic freedom, Miss Busby?" Kitty asked.

Helena Busby shrugged. "What Mrs. Belmont wants, Mrs. Belmont gets. And besides, we're not really journalists, are we? Miss Baehr said that Mrs. Belmont would like to make sure you didn't give away too much of the plot. She sounds very hands-on."

The remark stung. Kitty considered herself a newswoman even if the editor didn't. Miss Busby's words reminded her that she must quit the Ladies' Page as soon as something better came along.

"On to the next order of business." Helena Busby changed the subject. "As I mentioned, the president will be in the city next week. Whether he will be traveling with"—she caught herself just in time—"Mrs. Galt is immaterial."

Miss Busby's antagonism toward the new Mrs. Wilson seemed to match Kitty's aversion to Miss Lane.

"I'm beginning to feel," she continued, "that we can work it up into a story by focusing on him. Where he stays, what he eats, who he meets, and such."

"A day with the president?" Kitty said.

"Exactly." Miss Busby sniffed. "It's something to think about. In the meantime, I've marked a few items for correction on your Belmont piece." She handed Kitty her pages. "Please have them typed and then send a copy across."

Kitty ran her eyes over the corrections, which were minor— Miss Busby had removed the mattress comment—and headed for the hen coop, where she took a seat at one of the empty typewriting machines and slowly pecked out a fresh copy. The keys were so stiff and heavy, it was difficult to understand how the typists were able to work for hours.

She put the article in an envelope and went to look for one of the *Sentinel*'s messenger boys.

The little fellow tucked her envelope in his satchel and pulled out a letter. "This just came for you, miss."

Kitty checked the return address: Westfield Hall.

She brought the letter to the women's restroom. The facilities were a much-appreciated innovation by the paper's founder's son, Mr. Eichendorff. Miss Busby had told Kitty that when she first began working here, there weren't enough women on staff to warrant a separate females-only toilet. Now, fortunately, there was one right on the third floor.

My dear Miss Weeks,

I understand that you recently wrote to our head girl, Miss Georgina Howell, requesting a conversation. I must say I am most displeased by your conduct.

As you are aware, we do not as a rule permit our pupils to meet outsiders during the school term. Now, events have taken a disturbing turn: Miss Howell has been missing for the past twenty-four hours. I am sure that you can imagine how serious this is and that you would not wish to be held responsible should any misfortune befall her.

I trust that you will inform me at once, should you hear from her. Any detail, no matter how trivial, could prove useful in determining her whereabouts. The other students believe that she is out sick. I believe I can count on your complete discretion in this matter.

In the future, please refrain from communicating with any of Westfield Hall students—whether in person or in writing. My girls are still young, and do not fully appreciate the consequences of their actions.

Sincerely, Miss Howe-Jones. Principal

Kitty rushed from the restroom. Georgina Howell was missing. She hadn't meant to encourage her to come to Manhattan. She had thought about including all her questions about Elspeth's death in the letter but had finally decided to leave it open-ended, fearing that specific inquiries might set off alarm bells—and now the schoolgirl was gone.

She checked the time on her watch: a few minutes past twelve o'clock. She told Miss Busby she wasn't feeling well—still suffering from the aftereffects of her accident—and asked if she might leave early.

"Rao," she said to the chauffeur when she climbed into the car. "Does Mr. Weeks need you this afternoon?"

"He wants me at the club."

Kitty didn't want to wait until the following day. She grabbed a biscuit from the tin at home and bundled up into her warmest coat, gloves, and hat.

A group of chauffeurs interrupted their card game as she entered the New Century's two-story garage. Usually, owners told the doorman, who would call for the drivers, and they, in turn, would bring the cars out front.

"Do you need some help, Miss Weeks?" one of the chauffeurs said.

"Can you help me take the cover off?" Kitty pointed to her car.

With its open top and sides, Kitty's Stutz Bearcat gave her no protection in winter and was currently covered in canvas.

"If you don't mind my saying so, miss, you'll freeze. Where is it you'd like to go? If it's not far, I can take you in the Williamses' auto."

"I'm going to be a while," Kitty replied.

"Are you sure, miss?" The man looked worried.

"I'll be fine," she assured him.

He removed the protective cover and watched while she tested the engine. Kitty tightened her scarf, strapped on her goggles, and held on to the wheel as the machine roared.

She pulled out of the garage, her foot on the gas. There wasn't much that matched her sense of exhilaration at being in control of so much speed and power. Luckily, the snow had melted, and there wasn't too much on the streets. If she got stuck out of town... She didn't want to think of that. She had no contingency plan.

The road became quieter as she left Manhattan. Trees edged the way, their skeletal branches silhouetted against a forbidding sky. Any minute now, she might come across a headless horseman charging toward her. Kitty giggled nervously. Forget Elspeth—it would be her body that would be found frozen in an open car.

Another vehicle followed her. At first, Kitty didn't mind—she enjoyed the company—but then, when the automobile didn't pull away on any of the side roads and maintained a steady distance behind the Bearcat, she began to feel anxious. Anyone could see she was on her own, just a girl driving her roadster in a deserted part of the country. Kitty sped up. The car behind her matched her pace.

Her eyes started to water behind her motoring goggles, her cheeks and hands turned numb from the cold, and the silent trees flashed by.

She caught sight of a gasoline station in the distance. She maintained her speed, then pulled in suddenly. The car behind her kept going.

"Can I help you, miss?" A fellow in overalls emerged from the small shack behind a single pump.

Relief flooded over her. "I'd like to fill up, please."

He inserted the hose into her gas tank and pumped a crank.

"Pretty old system you have here." Kitty's breath came out in white puffs.

"My pa invented it." He grinned wolfishly, a wad of chewing tobacco stuck in his jaw.

"How far is Westfield Hall from here?"

"Fifteen minutes, thataway. You a student?"

"I'm on my way to meet the headmistress." Kitty put on a haughty manner.

"How now, Howe-Jones?" He laughed.

"Excuse me?"

"That's what my pa used to say: How now, Miss Howe-Jones? I call her How-Now-Howe-Jones. You get it?"

He waved as Kitty drove away, her heart thumping. "Give her my regards!"

Why hadn't she noticed that Westfield was in the middle of nowhere, Kitty asked herself as she embarked on the final leg of her journey. Perhaps because the previous two times she had made the trip, she'd been safe in the Packard with Rao. It occurred to her that, like the founders of her own boarding school, Miss Howe-Jones had selected this out-of-the-way location to keep her charges out of trouble. But the Misses Dancey seemed to have been luckier on that score.

Kitty arrived at the school without incident and parked beside the low stone walls.

She warmed herself by the fire in the reception room, sinking into the floral-print sofa. On the coffee table in front of her, a vase had been set with an assortment of red and white buds. Having offered Kitty a cup of tea, Miss Howe-Jones's bespectacled secretary informed her that the headmistress would see her shortly and resumed typing.

"Did you telephone this morning, Miss Weeks?" she asked a moment later.

"No," Kitty replied, face flushed from the warmth of the nearby flames. "No, I did not."

The door to the principal's office opened, and little Virginia appeared.

"Hello," Kitty said. She'd seen her so many times, she felt she knew the girl.

"Hello." Virginia adjusted her belt.

"I'm Capability Weeks, the reporter from the *Sentinel*."

"I remember."

"Are you still reading *Automobile Girls*?"

"Yes, I am. I love the series."

"Enough chattering, Virginia." The typing stopped again. "Run along. I'm sure they're waiting for you in class."

In her office, the normally stone-faced principal looked shattered. "Did you receive my letter, Miss Weeks? Is that what brings you here? Do you have news for me about Georgina?"

"I'm afraid I don't, Miss Howe-Jones. I came because I'm concerned. You see, Miss Howell wrote to me and said she would come visit me at the *Sentinel* on Monday or Tuesday, but she never arrived."

The headmistress brought a handkerchief to her lips.

"You must be mad with worry."

"I try to do my best for all my girls. They're everything I have. And Georgina was special." The headmistress took a deep breath. "She was my all-around girl. Bright, athletic, a good speaker. Everyone loved her. It wasn't difficult to gather contributions so that she could attend Bryn Mawr in the fall."

Kitty noticed with dismay the headmistress's use of the past tense. "You don't think—"

"I don't know what to think. Sunday evening was the last time anyone saw her." It was Wednesday. "She didn't attend class on Monday, but the teacher didn't think much of it. Georgina had other responsibilities as head girl and editor of our yearbook."

"When did you realize she was missing?"

"One of the girls reported that she wasn't at Vespers on Monday evening—that's when I went to look."

"Have you spoken to the police?"

"No!" Miss Howe-Jones shook her head. "A girl missing from the school? That would cause a scandal. I wrote to you because I found your letter and thought that perhaps you knew where Georgina had gone."

The headmistress rose and went to stand by the window, hands clasped behind her back.

Kitty followed her gaze through the panes to the wintry grounds, powdered with snow. There were no girls outside today. "I'm concerned, Miss Howe-Jones," she said finally. "I'm concerned Georgina's disappearance might have something to do with what happened to Miss Bright."

"That's impossible." The headmistress swung around.

"Please hear me out, madam. Miss Howell was at the Brights' home—"

"That's just a coincidence." The headmistress snapped out each word. "Mrs. Bright took pity on her. That's why she was there, although I've said plenty of times that Georgina and I enjoyed our Christmases together."

Miss Howe-Jones took a step toward Kitty. "Please listen to me carefully, Miss Weeks. This school and decades of service, all for the benefit of others, will come crashing to the ground if even a hint of Georgina's disappearance gets out. I *must* find her, and I hope you will let me know if she surfaces. And in the meantime, you will promise not to contact my students ever again, and you will not repeat our conversation to anyone.

"I'm waiting, Miss Weeks," the principal said when Kitty didn't reply. "Georgina will come back to school. But I cannot risk jeopardizing Westfield Hall's reputation."

"I understand, Miss Howe-Jones."

"Do I have your word?" Miss Howe-Jones's tone carried the ring of someone who didn't expect to be disobeyed.

"I won't say anything until the end of this week." Kitty couldn't manage to put up better resistance, and in any case, she had no intention of tarnishing the school's good name. "If Miss Howell doesn't return by then—"

"Your interference in my school must end, Miss Weeks. You can see how much damage it has already caused."

Chastened, Kitty gathered her things and left the principal's office as a bell rang and joking and chattering girls poured out of classrooms, unaware that one of their own was unaccounted for.

"Miss Weeks." A voice called her name. It was Virginia. "Here you go, Miss Weeks." The schoolgirl handed her a brown paper bag. "You must read it. I think you will enjoy it." Then she ran off to join her classmates.

Kitty reached in and pulled out a book. Virginia had given her a copy of *The Automobile Girls Along the Hudson.*

CHAPTER TWENTY-TWO

R esting in bed after a hot bath and something to eat, glad that nothing untoward had happened on the ride back to Manhattan, Kitty picked up Virginia's gift. She'd seen the novel before, but they were for younger readers, and she wondered whether Virginia thought she might like it because she drove her own car. But then, Virginia didn't know she drove her own car, did she? Hoping she wasn't the recipient of stolen goods, Kitty opened the volume to a random page:

> The travelers lunched at Allaire, as usual, in the little open-air French restaurant... But they did not linger after lunch. Ruth was hoping to make Tarrytown in time for dinner that evening, instead of stopping for the night in New York, which, she said, appeared to be suffering from the heat like a human being. "The poor, tired city is all fagged out and fairly panting from the humidity. If all goes well, I think we should get to New York by four o'clock, have tea at the Waldorf, and start for Tarrytown at five."

She flipped through the pages, and a note fell out, written in a neat schoolgirl script.

Dear Miss Weeks,

I know you are a reporter and that it's your job to find the truth. So please tell us this: Who are Georgina Howell's parents? Don't you wonder why Miss Howe-Jones chose her to be the head girl? Howe-Jones and Howell—I think those names sound similar. What is your opinion?

Kitty stared at the words. Virginia must have written this. Seeing her come out of the principal's office a second time suggested that she was a girl who regularly got into trouble. If so, perhaps she was trying to fan the flames of mischief and pay back the headmistress for humiliating her in front of Kitty before the holidays. Schoolgirls loved to make a mountain out of a molehill, loved intrigues, loved to make up stories. And as much as Kitty's teachers, the Misses Dancey, had tried to maintain a calm atmosphere, they couldn't keep envy, jealousy, or rumors at bay. How much harder that would be at Westfield Hall, where girls were openly punished and allowed to take nasty jabs at one another in the yearbook.

She telephoned Mrs. Bright while Mr. Weeks dressed for dinner in his rooms.

"You really shouldn't be calling, Miss Weeks," Mrs. Bright said.

"I was wondering whether Georgina Howell was staying with you."

"Why would Georgina be here?"

"Well, she mentioned she would be in town, so I thought perhaps, since she doesn't have any family…"

"She isn't with us," Mrs. Bright said stiffly. "I don't know what's going on with that school, letting its students roam about."

"Would you happen to know anything about Georgina's parents, Mrs. Bright?"

"Oh." The line went quiet. "I believe they died years ago in a boating accident."

Lieutenant Charles Cooke, commander of the E-2 submarine, testified before the Naval Board of Inquiry that on September 9, 1915, he had requested, in writing, hydrogen-detecting apparatus for the E-2 because he believed that "the possible danger to be apprehended in the use of the Edison battery is an explosion of hydrogen." His letter was never answered.

Kitty read the morning papers in bed, feeling sniffly and slightly feverish after yesterday's open-air drive.

Lieutenant Cooke also testified that he had requested individual voltmeters to be installed on each one of the cells of the E-2's batteries. The recommendation was turned down by the department and by the Edison Storage Battery Company. In fact, Mr. Hutchison, Mr. Edison's chief engineer, told him those safety measures weren't required. Lieutenant Cooke also said that the tests underway at the time of the E-2's explosion had been made at the request of the Edison staff.

"Lieutenant Cooke, youthful in appearance, alert, and expert in matters pertaining to submarines, was the only witness appearing before the court yesterday afternoon," the article said. "He answered all questions in carefully measured words. It is doubtful if a clearer-speaking witness ever appeared before a naval court. Not once was he at a loss for an answer for any question."

Kitty sipped her tea and took a bite of Mrs. Codd's home-made scone. She couldn't understand how the commander of the submarine, who was not a scientist, had suspected the possibility of danger when no one else appeared to have been worried by it. The story didn't provide an explanation for his suspicions. And in light of all the death and destruction the explosion had caused, it was alarming to think that when Cooke alerted the authorities, no one paid attention.

She dragged herself out of bed and dressed for work. The graze on her cheek had almost faded.

"Not feeling well enough to take breakfast with me but well enough to go to the *Sentinel*?" Mr. Weeks said as she passed him on her way out.

Kitty inclined her head and said, with what she hoped sounded like regret, "Nothing like that. I just woke up late." She sucked on a lozenge.

He nodded and returned to his coffee while she left for the day, not enjoying the tension between them but believing that avoidance would be better than a quarrel. They hadn't spoken much over dinner the previous night.

As Rao drove her downtown, Kitty fingered Virginia's note in her pocketbook. She still didn't know what to make of it. Kitty closed her eyes and pictured Miss Howe-Jones and Miss Howell side by side. She was struck by the similarity of their names, but it was hard to judge the similarity of their looks: Georgina's youthful face was sweet and open; Miss Howe-Jones's mouth seemed perpetually puckered in disapproval. If there was a family resemblance, it wasn't readily apparent.

"We should have a room coming available at the boarding-house next month." Jeannie and Kitty sat side by side at their desks in the front of the hen coop. "If you want it, you should hand in a deposit soon."

"I'm not certain that I'm ready to take the leap quite yet," Kitty replied. "But I will keep it in mind."

"Is something the matter at home?"

Kitty picked up her files. "No, no." She made her way to Miss Busby's alcove.

"Mrs. Belmont read your story yesterday," the editor said. "And I'm pleased to tell you that it passed muster."

"So it will print in Saturday's Page?"

"That's correct." Miss Busby flipped through the papers on her desk. "Along with a photograph of Mrs. Belmont, Miss Maxwell, the actresses, and the debutantes. It's going to be quite a departure for us."

Kitty smiled. "Actresses on the Ladies' Page—"

Miss Busby finished the sentence for her. "What is the world coming to? By the way, Mrs. Belmont informs me that the ladies of the Congressional Union plan to meet the president when he's in Manhattan, and they'd like us to join the press that will cover the event."

"It's an event?" Kitty pulled up a chair. "Where does it take place?"

"At the Waldorf Hotel. Mrs. Belmont and her friends from the Woman's Congressional Union plan to press him on the urgency of a constitutional amendment giving women the right to vote."

"And you approve of this, Miss Busby?"

"We've stayed out of politics for all these years... Quite frankly, I'm of two minds, Miss Weeks. But Mrs. Belmont isn't an easy person to say no to."

Kitty was dying to write the story. Finally, she'd be treated like a member of the press corps, but she didn't want to do it just because her editor hadn't been able to resist Alva Belmont's influence.

"Would it be good for the Page?" she said.

Miss Busby bit her lip. "Mrs. Belmont is persuasive."

"Mrs. Belmont doesn't run the Ladies' Page, Miss Busby. You do."

"You're right, Miss Weeks." The editor sighed. "It's just that I used to feel I could exert my will over what we print, but nowadays, it seems the world exerts its will over me. Mark the day in your calendar in any case. It's the twenty-seventh. Kaiser Wilhelm's birthday."

"I will, Miss Busby." Kitty hid her smile. Only Herman Musser could have supplied Helena Busby with a fact like that.

※

Although she was exhausted, Kitty asked Rao to drive her to see Amanda—she had been so busy, she hadn't had time to think about her friend's return, something she had longed for from the day Amanda kissed her on both cheeks and sailed for England. New York would be a better place now that Amanda Vanderwell was back in town. Even a small dose of her breezy social commentary could lift Kitty's spirits. The buildings' shadows would seem shorter, the days brighter with Miss Vanderwell's contagious smile and charming—but astute—observations. In a different time and place, Amanda could have made something of herself. She could have been a general leading troops into battle, Kitty thought, or a prime minister charting her nation's course through stormy seas. She had a knack for drawing people to her, and somehow, they ended up doing what she wanted.

"Capability," Mrs. Vanderwell called from the parlor as soon as Kitty set foot inside the brownstone. "I'm so glad you're here."

"Is everything all right?" Kitty said, surprised that mother and daughter weren't together.

"Amanda's upstairs in her room." Mrs. Vanderwell's soft features quivered. "She has changed so much. I barely recognized her. Go see for yourself. Maybe you can cheer her up." She dabbed her eyes with a handkerchief.

Kitty dashed to the second floor and knocked on the second door down the darkened landing—another instance of the Vanderwells saving on electric bills.

"Come in," a voice called.

Amanda sat curled in an antique slipper chair beside the fireplace, a silk blanket over her knees.

Kitty rushed over to give her friend a hug. Amanda, one of the prettiest girls in the city, had lost about ten pounds, her face was gaunt, and her eyes had lost their luster.

"I look a mess, don't I?" Amanda summoned a smile. "While you look radiant. In the very pink of health."

Kitty laughed. "That makes me seem like a ruddy farm girl."

"Not anymore. Good health is all the rage. Ask the men who have lost arms or legs or eyes... They're never going to be what they once were. They just settle for being alive... What a life."

"Was it so bad?" Kitty pulled a chair up beside her.

"Bad? It was awful! I can't begin to tell you, Capability. That's why I didn't write." She ran both hands through her hair. "Men falling like flies—and those were the ones who hadn't already died on the battlefield. I've seen so many men injured. So many maimed. The nurse said I would grow accustomed to it, but I never did."

Kitty had never heard Amanda talk like this.

"I can't tell you what I saw, Capability. Skin charred like a crackled pig. Bleeding lungs. Dark hollows where eyes should be. Ears blown off. And then I come home, and I hear that the president wants us to prepare. For what?" She held Kitty's arm so tightly that Kitty thought her sleeve might rip. "To see all our young men shot to pieces?"

"I'm so sorry, Amanda."

"Don't feel sorry for me. You made the right decision not to attend the training." Amanda had tried to convince Kitty to leave the *Sentinel* and join her as a nurse last summer.

"Only because I'm a reporter at heart," Kitty replied. "I don't have any special powers of intuition."

"Well, I wish I had been something at heart and never gone. What I've seen and heard can't be undone. I will never stop having nightmares."

Kitty clasped her friend's hand, and the two girls sat together for a few minutes in silence.

"So distract me, Miss Weeks. What have you been working on lately?" Amanda said presently.

Kitty told her about Mrs. Belmont.

"Ah, Alva, Alva, Alva." Amanda's lips curled upward.

"Have you met her often?"

"Not so much. She's been busy with her suffrage work ever since I've come of age, but I feel as though I know her well. One reads about her constantly."

Hearing the hint of lightness in Amanda's tone gave Kitty hope. "There's something else," she said. "Something mysterious. At least, I think it's mysterious; no one else seems bothered."

Amanda slowly rose and took a turn about the room. "I don't think I can hear it. I don't have the stomach for any more horrors."

At that moment, Kitty felt as though she'd lost both her best friend and a trusted confidante.

"I'm sorry, Capability." Amanda turned to the window and looked out.

"No, I'm sorry that I brought it up. In your condition—it was very thoughtless of me."

The fire crackled in the hearth. Kitty wracked her memory for some diverting anecdote. Amanda might be amused by stories of Miss Lane, but Kitty wasn't ready to joke about her yet.

Amanda looked over her shoulder. "Is it very important to you?"

"Oh no, not at all."

"I may not be myself"—Amanda managed a grin—"but I can still tell when you're lying."

Kitty didn't deny it.

"All right, tell me about this mysterious case."

"Are you sure? There's sleepwalking and a death. Schoolgirls and submarines."

"Now I am intrigued." Amanda settled into her chair as Kitty launched into her account of Elspeth Bright.

"Where to begin," Amanda said when Kitty finished. "First, Westfield Hall—my aunt Felicia went there. And she always said Miss Howe-Jones was an excellent headmistress but kept her students on a very short leash, which is why Mummy never sent me. She thought I wouldn't survive. And she was probably right. You know me. I'm a wreck without home-cooked meals."

Now she was beginning to sound like the Amanda of old. Kitty pictured Mrs. Vanderwell sending daily hampers to Amanda at the boarding school—Miss Howe-Jones would throw a fit.

"Second, I'm sorry to hear about Elspeth. I knew her when she was younger. She used to come around sometimes. I'm not surprised to hear she had a scientific bent... Lastly, I have some experience with sleepwalkers."

"You have? When?"

"Half of the men at the convalescent home had some form of disturbed rest. Some cried out; others muttered in their dreams. The ones with legs walked around. Once, when I was on night duty, one of the fellows opened the door and went outside. I had to bring him back, but I wasn't allowed to wake him—that would have been too distressing in his fragile condition."

"So what did you do?"

"I lightly placed my hand on his shoulder and led him in the direction that I wanted him to go."

"That's all?"

"That's all."

"You just led him along, and he went where you wanted?"

"That's right." Amanda nodded.

"And he didn't wake up?" Kitty felt the flickering of an idea.

"No."

"Do you think it could work in reverse? I mean, could someone who was prone to sleepwalking somehow be urged into getting up and going out without being aware of it?"

"Oh. I haven't given that any thought... I suppose it might be possible. But you said she was wearing a coat and boots. That would be harder to orchestrate, I think, without waking her up. It's a very trancelike state, you know. There's almost something mystical about it."

Kitty took a deep breath. "There's something else. One of the girls who was there that evening has gone missing." While Kitty described the details surrounding Georgina Howell's disappearance, Gilbert the maid brought tea and muffins and waited, nodding with approval as Amanda took a bite. Kitty sensed that Amanda hadn't been eating well, so she told the story with care, being sure not to leave out a single detail, and kept one eye on the tray, watching Amanda slowly make her way through two of the little cakes.

"You must find her," Amanda said after Kitty had completed her account. "It's clear she admires you and that she wants to become a newswoman. You should help her."

"And you don't think I'm meddling?"

"Of course you are meddling, but that's your job. If you don't want to meddle, you should go back to judging contests and reporting on who was wearing what, when, and where. But as far as I can tell, if you want to write something that counts, you're going to have to be prepared to ruffle some feathers."

"I suppose you're right."

"I know I'm right. You can't make omelets without breaking eggs."

"I have to get my hands dirty."

"What's good for the goose is good for the gander." Amanda laughed.

Kitty hugged her friend. "I've missed you. I'm so glad you're back."

CHAPTER TWENTY-THREE

K itty telephoned Westfield Hall from home that afternoon, but Miss Howe-Jones, sounding tense, told her
that there was still no news of the missing head girl. Kitty then
called the *Sentinel* and asked to speak to Mr. Mills.

"Would you do me another favor?" she said. "Would you
speak to your contacts at the police department and find out if
a young woman, about seventeen or eighteen years old with
dark hair, has been brought in or"—Kitty hated to say it—"a
body matching that description has been found?"

"Sooner or later, you're going to have to tell me what this is
for," the reporter replied. "And I think you should tell me now."

"I promise, I will, Mr. Mills. As soon as I understand it myself."

"The Ladies' Page won't print this, Miss Weeks. It's going to
have to be a news story—and in that case, I'm sharing the credit."

"Absolutely. Thank you, Mr. Mills." Kitty hung up the line.
She didn't care about credit. All she wanted to know was where
Georgina was—and why.

She needed to start looking for the Westfield Hall girl at
once. A young, friendless girl in Manhattan would probably
seek shelter in a boardinghouse.

In a burst, Kitty's recent exertions caught up with her. Her
throat felt sore and her head hot. Sucking lozenges all day had

kept her going, but now, she lay in bed—for just a minute—
and woke up, still fully dressed, the next morning.

Grace brought her breakfast and the newspaper. "Mr. Weeks
said you must be tired, Miss Kitty. You slept for fifteen hours."

"I feel refreshed." Kitty had showered, spritzed some eau de
cologne on her wrists, and changed into a clean set of clothes,
but she didn't say no to eating in her room so that she could
pore over the latest E-2 stories without being asked questions.

The Naval Board of Inquiry had warned Mr. Edison's representative, Miller Reese Hutchison, that the Edison Company
was an "interested party" in the inquiries and that he must
not make any statements to the press that might prejudice the
public's opinion as to why the explosion occurred.

A second article confirmed that the E-2's commander had
indeed informed the navy in writing about the need for hydrogen detectors on board the submarine. The detectors had not
been provided, because the navy had been unable to find any
such instrument that would be reliable. Instead, at some earlier
date, they had sent an air expert who asserted that the amount
of hydrogen developed while the battery was being discharged
was only infinitesimal.

Despite her lingering doubts about Mr. Emerson, Kitty had
to agree with the paper's conclusion that the catastrophe on the
E-2 had most likely been caused by a combination of the navy's
lack of suitable instrumentation and the Edison company's
overconfidence in its own product.

She finished her scrambled eggs and toast, brought the cutlery
together, and untucked her napkin. There was nothing she
could have done to prevent the deaths at the navy yard, but she

would do everything in her power to find Georgina. She would begin her search of boardinghouses today. The Westfield Hall student couldn't have vanished into thin air.

"Are you feeling better, Capability?" Mr. Weeks called as Kitty passed by the dining room.

"Somewhat, thanks."

"I'm worried about you." They hadn't spoken much since their last altercation.

"I'm just a bit tired, but I feel revived now."

Kitty hurried from the apartment before she burst into tears or said something she would regret. He was right; she should grow up. His romantic life was none of her concern. She had more pressing matters—matters in which she could actually make a difference—clamoring for her attention.

Kitty found Miss Busby in a should-I-should-I-not mood. She was tempted to find her boss a dandelion and let her blow until fate and the wind decided whether she should cover Mrs. Belmont and the Congressional Union's meeting with the president.

While the Ladies' Page editor dithered, Kitty went to speak to Jeannie.

"Would you help me make a list of boardinghouses in the city, preferably ones that are cheap and would allow a girl to stay on a short-term basis?"

Jeannie looked concerned. "Are things so bad for you, Miss Weeks?"

"Oh no, not for me," Kitty clarified. Although, she thought, never say never—she might have to consider the possibility. "I'm searching for a friend."

"That's good to hear, because you won't like those places. Roaches, bedbugs, unwashed sheets." Jeannie shivered. "They make mine look like the Ritz."

"So can you help me?"

"I have to finish proofreading for Miss B. If you can start putting a list together from the directory, I'll look through it and tell you which ones are cheaper."

Kitty went to the morgue, found a copy of *Trow's General Directory of the Boroughs of Manhattan and Bronx*, and began leafing through it page by page, jotting down the names and addresses of boardinghouses for women.

"Working hard, *fräulein*?" Mr. Musser called from behind his counter.

"A girl has to earn her living," Kitty said.

She was on her twenty-second entry when one of the mail boys came looking for her. "There's someone waiting to see you by the clock, miss."

"Who is it?" Kitty asked.

"She didn't give a name."

Kitty wondered whether her luck had finally turned.

"Don't forget to put away the book before you leave," Musser said.

She hurriedly replaced the volume, stuffed her papers into her pocket, and ran upstairs. There, amid the mail boys, the reporters, and the advertising men rushing in and out, stood a solitary figure in a dark cloak. Kitty took a step nearer. It was Georgina Howell.

CHAPTER TWENTY-FOUR

M iss Howell." Kitty reached for her hand. "Are you all right? You've had us all worried sick."

"*All?*" The Westfield Hall student moved toward the exit.

"I spoke to Miss Howe-Jones. She was very concerned about you."

"I don't want to go back." She may have been just a schoolgirl, but Georgina sounded sure of herself.

"Where have you been sleeping these past few nights? Would you like to come upstairs and have something to eat?"

She nodded, and Kitty brought her up to the cafeteria, where they ordered tea and, since it was between breakfast and lunch, made do with boiled eggs, cheese, and crackers.

"I've been staying at a boardinghouse." Miss Howell devoured the food. "But I don't have much money, so this is much appreciated."

"Which boardinghouse?" Kitty felt pleased she had been on the right track and glad she had been spared the trouble of knocking on doors.

Georgina Howell sprinkled a peeled egg with salt. "For the moment, I'll keep that to myself."

"Fair enough. What brings you to Manhattan? And why didn't you come see me earlier?"

"I needed a few days to be by myself and think about my future. I would have sent word, but I didn't want anyone looking for me. If you're not too upset, I hope you will help me, Miss Weeks. I'd like to become a reporter, just like you are."

"You must finish school first."

"Did you finish school?"

"I did, and I think it's stood me in good stead."

"The trouble for me is that if I stay on, Miss Howe-Jones will trap me in her web. She holds me too close," Georgina cried. "I must escape while I can. I have no desire to become a charity case at Bryn Mawr."

"The two of you aren't related, by any chance?"

"Who? Miss Howe-Jones and I? No. What makes you ask that?"

"I was just wondering. Your names sound so similar."

Georgina shook her head. "She's my guardian, that's all." Georgina Howell pointed to her cloak and smart dress. "Look at my clothes, Miss Weeks. These are all hand-me-downs from former students. I want to earn my own way. I don't need any benefactors or fancy scholarships."

Kitty understood how she felt. Not about the benefactors, but about needing to be free.

"Did you go to college, Miss Weeks?"

"I considered applying to Columbia University's School of Journalism. But it's a four-year course, and to be honest, I didn't think I would get in. Besides, I wanted to start working right away."

"So do I. Is that so wrong?"

"Well, you know I can't tell you that it is." Kitty leaned

across the table. "But I had to convince my father, and you will need to convince your headmistress."

"She will *never* be convinced." Georgina sounded frustrated. "Miss Howe-Jones thinks she knows what's best for everyone. Can you imagine what that's like, Miss Weeks, having your life mapped out for you in advance? She would have me wind up a spinster, teaching English literature at some New England girls' college, then return to take her place at Westfield. I've told her several times that I want to live in New York, but she won't hear of it. You must know how desperate I feel."

Kitty shared Georgina's sense of urgency. Yet she could barely take care of herself, so how could she help another young woman?

"Miss Howell—" Kitty touched her cheek.

"Were you hurt?" Georgina noticed the redness.

"I was in a car accident. And that's another reason—if something happens to you, who will look after you? Who will pay your bills? I have my father. You need your guardian."

Georgina remained silent. "Was it painful?" she asked after a while.

"The accident?" What a strange question. "Not at the moment it occurred, no. I was knocked unconscious, but afterward, it hurt like mad... Miss Howell, I must ask you something." Kitty changed the subject. "This has to do with the night Elspeth Bright died. Were you aware that she fought with her father?"

The young woman's eyes narrowed, and Kitty sensed her disappointment but didn't know what Georgina expected of her. She was sure of one thing though: a young, decent girl couldn't survive in New York alone. Even Jeannie and the other typists had families, no matter how far away, that they could rely on.

"Miss Howell," Kitty prompted. "Elspeth and Dr. Bright—did they have an altercation?"

"Yes they did, and Elspeth told me about it," Georgina said finally. "She had discovered something about some new Edison batteries not working and informed Dr. Bright, but he wouldn't believe her. He insisted her findings must be in error."

With a sharp intake of breath, Kitty realized that her imaginings had been misguided. Elspeth hadn't invented her own storage battery—at least not that anyone knew of—but she had figured out that the Edison ones were defective.

"She felt sure she was right," Georgina continued, gathering steam, "and she told Dr. Bright that if he chose not to, she would notify the Naval Consulting Board herself."

"And did she—did she send a letter or message?"

"Where was the time? Mrs. Bright called her to help, then the guests arrived, and not more than a few hours later…" Georgina shivered.

Weighed down by what she had learned, Kitty finished the sentence for her. "Yes. Not more than a few hours later, Elspeth was dead."

CHAPTER TWENTY-FIVE

Georgina left, telling Kitty she was determined to make a clean break with Miss Howe-Jones, even though Kitty begged her not to rush into something she might regret. Afterward, she couldn't concentrate on her work. All she could think about were Dr. Bright and his daughter. Elspeth had known that the batteries were imperfect. Like that personable captain of the E-2 who testified in front of the Board of Inquiry, she may have suspected that the batteries were dangerous despite the navy and Mr. Edison's experts' insistence that they weren't. She had told her father she would go to the Naval Consulting Board herself if he didn't.

"Leaving early, Miss Weeks?" Jeannie asked as Kitty collected her things.

"Yes, have a good weekend." Kitty had become fed up with pushing papers around.

"Thanks. You too. Do you still need my help with the boardinghouse?"

"That matter seems to be resolved for the moment. Thanks, Jeannie." She had to face the suspicion that had troubled her intermittently since the day of her own accident. Could Dr. Bright have engineered Elspeth's death? Could a father turn on his own daughter in such a vicious manner?

"No!" She stepped into the elevator.

"I beg your pardon?" The operator turned to Kitty.

"Sorry. I'm just talking to myself."

Dr. Bright couldn't have been threatened by his daughter. He had been certain of the batteries' safety. He wouldn't have brought Kitty, a reporter, to the naval yard if he suspected that she might witness a disaster. It would have been an embarrassment to him if Elspeth went over his head and contacted his colleagues at the board, but that would have been all. Not reason enough—if there ever could be enough reason—to wish for the death of his own child.

He must have wanted to speak to Kitty to make sure that Elspeth hadn't told anyone else about her suspicions. It wouldn't look good for the navy, the board, and the Edison company if the news came out that a board member's daughter doubted its chairman's prized invention.

Elspeth had died after a heated argument. That might seem suspicious, but it could also be a perfectly reasonable explanation for what triggered her final, fatal instance of somnambulism.

Shaken, Kitty telephoned Miss Howe-Jones from the apartment. The headmistress deserved to know that her pupil was alive and well even though Georgina wanted to keep her address secret.

"Miss Weeks." Miss Howe-Jones picked up the line.

"Good afternoon, Miss Howe-Jones. I wanted to let you know Miss Howell came to see me today."

"Where is she?" The headmistress sounded frantic. "Is she with you? Keep her there. I will send a car."

"As far as I can tell, she doesn't want to return to Westfield."

"Impossible. Where is she staying?"

"She didn't say, Miss Howe-Jones."

"You just let her go? You didn't ask?"

"I couldn't prevent her."

"I didn't expect you to be so callous, Miss Weeks. Miss Howell is all alone. She has no one else in the world."

"I couldn't detain her by force, madam," Kitty said. "Besides, she seemed to want to take care of herself. In fact, she seemed eager to take care of herself."

"That is not for you to judge." The headmistress slammed down the receiver.

Kitty slowly hung up her end of the line. Later that evening, Julian Weeks invited Kitty to the Lanes' for dinner, but she declined, blaming a headache.

"You are going to have to give in at some point, you know," he said as he left. "You can't have a headache forever."

Kitty's *Melinda and Her Sisters* story appeared on Saturday below an attractive photograph of Miss Maxwell directing Miss Dressler, Miss Doro, and the debutantes. The news section of the paper reported that the author Henry James was very ill in England and that in the article AWAKE AND PREPARE, printed in the *Metropolitan Magazine*, former President Theodore Roosevelt had called for a navy that would be second in size and efficiency only to that of Great Britain.

"We do not need to make it the first," Mr. Roosevelt wrote, "because Great Britain is not a military power, and our relations

with Canada are on a basis of such permanent friendliness that
hostile relations need not be considered." He also proposed that
the regular army should be increased to a quarter of a million
men and wrote that "Neither of these needs is in any way met
by the administration's proposals... During the last three years,
our navy has fallen off appallingly in relative position among
the nations."

Kitty kept reading in her rooms, since Grace told her that
her father had already eaten breakfast. "Our government should
make provision this year which will insure the regaining of
our naval place at the earliest possible moment." All the more
reason for Edison's batteries to work. "On paper, our present
strength is 100,000 men," President Roosevelt went on, "and
we have in the United States a mobile army of 20,000 men...
We should have a mobile army of 150,000 men to guarantee
us against having New York or San Francisco at once seized by
any big military nation which went to war with us."

Kitty couldn't think who might want to attack the United
States. Mr. Roosevelt had already eliminated Canada as a possibility. Perhaps Mexico then?

At any rate, it was clear that war clouds had gathered.
President Wilson's preparedness tour was just the next step.

She folded the paper, brushed her teeth, and dressed. It
was odd that life-and-death matters on an international scale
were so often decided by families. Not just the obvious ones:
Kaiser Wilhelm of Germany was first cousin to King George
of England, who was the cousin of Tsar Nicholas of Russia.
But here in America as well: Treasury Secretary McAdoo was
President Wilson's son-in-law, and Theodore Roosevelt's

distant cousin, Franklin Delano Roosevelt, was Naval Secretary Daniels's second-in-command.

And women were supposed to be gossips who made everything personal. How would things be *impersonal* between these men? Did wearing trousers give them some special abilities that those who wore skirts didn't possess? As far as Kitty could tell, men were just as petty as women, but when they didn't get their way, they didn't resort to intrigues—they started wars. Everyone said that the kaiser had demanded that Germany's navy be strengthened, in part because his uncle Edward, the previous king of England, had snubbed him at the royal family's annual regattas.

Julian Weeks knocked at Kitty's door. "What are your plans for today?"

"I thought I'd take a walk."

"May I join you?" He was trying to make amends.

"Of course."

They dressed warmly and walked up Riverside Drive in silence. The crisp breeze from the water chilled Kitty's cheeks, but it was nothing compared to the icy wind during her drive to Georgina's boarding school.

"Aside from your feelings about Miss Lane," Julian Weeks said presently, "you don't seem to be yourself. Is something else troubling you?"

Kitty sighed, wondering whether to tell him. Not everything perhaps, but some part of what had been gnawing at her. "A girl from Westfield Hall ran away from school. She wants to become a reporter and came to find me at work, asking for my help."

He blinked. "And what did you say?"

"The headmistress is her guardian. She has no family, no friends, no money. I told her not to act too fast."

"Where are her parents?"

"I believe they died in an automobile accident."

"Where is she staying?" Mr. Weeks slowed his usual brisk pace.

"She didn't tell me."

"Does she seem like a sensible girl?"

"Oh yes. She's sensible and intelligent. She's the school's head girl."

"We should help her then."

Kitty turn to face him. "*We* should help?"

"You forget that I'm an orphan myself." Julian Weeks had been raised by nuns and had escaped as a boy, eventually making his fortune abroad. "If she wants her freedom, she should have it."

"I don't believe this," Kitty retorted angrily. "You support Miss Howell but leave me in the lurch."

"What *haven't* I allowed you to do, Capability?" Mr. Weeks turned on her. "You're one of the fortunate ones. You have money and independence and a parent who dotes on you. This poor young woman has nothing. If she makes contact again, I'd like to speak to her."

Kitty shook her head. "She wants to work. She doesn't want to continue receiving handouts."

"I understand that too. That's exactly how I felt."

Kitty gritted her teeth. By virtue of being parentless, it seemed that Georgina Howell was more deserving of his sympathy than his own daughter. She didn't hear him standing up for *her* rights very often. She couldn't deny it. She was jealous.

Everyone and everything seemed to take precedence over her. First, his work; then, Miss Lane; now, a girl they barely knew. It was too ridiculous.

Fortunately, they didn't discuss Georgina any further, and the next morning, Mr. Weeks was back in form.

"It seems Mr. Edison's man, Hutchison, has gone and hoisted himself by his own petard." He sat in his study, enjoying a lazy Sunday, and chuckled. "It says here that he's placed the blame for the E-2 explosion not on the fact that his batteries generated hydrogen but on the shoulders of the vessel's commander, who he believes neglected to have the blowers going at full speed during the test."

In an attempt to be productive, Kitty had started knitting a scarf, but she hadn't made much progress.

"You see, the Board of Inquiry asked Hutchison whether he had ordered the discharge of the batteries on the day of the explosion," her father said. "Edison's man replied yes. They asked whether any other representative of the company had been present during the process, and he said no. Then they inquired whether he had informed Lieutenant Cooke, the commander, that the batteries discharged at different rates. And do you know what Mr. Hutchison answered? He said"—Mr. Weeks peered at the newspaper—"'I would no longer think of giving such information to men like Lieutenant Cooke, who know their business, than I would of telling an engineer that he must keep water in his boilers while his fires are going.'"

"What does that mean?" Kitty put down her needles.

"It means that Edison's man is accusing Lieutenant Cooke of incompetence. The navy will never stand for it. It's one thing to make a mistake, even kill men for the sake of progress. It's quite another for a civilian to blame one of the navy's own for an error the civilian caused. However promising this new battery might be—and it seems to have promise—I'll bet you this is the last we hear of it."

"So that's the end?" Kitty said. "Because of one man's foolishness, we'll turn our backs on an invention that in the long run could save sailors' lives?"

Mr. Weeks shrugged. "That's what I predict. I hope I'm wrong."

The telephone rang, and Grace answered the line in the foyer. She looked into the study. "It's a Miss Howell for you, Miss Kitty."

Georgina sounded distraught. "I need your help, Miss Weeks. Miss Howe-Jones has discovered my whereabouts."

Chapter Twenty-Six

K itty and Georgina decided to meet at a café that wasn't far from the *Sentinel* and, as it turned out, Georgina's boardinghouse. The place had tiled walls and was usually filled with workers from nearby offices, but it was quiet on a Sunday. Mr. Weeks held the door open, and Kitty went in first, shook hands with Georgina Howell, and then introduced Miss Howell to her father.

"I hope you don't mind my coming along," Mr. Weeks said, pulling back his chair. "My daughter told me about you. I was abandoned by my parents when I was an infant, so I understand your position."

Kitty was still taken aback by how easily he said those words to a complete stranger, when it had taken him years to reveal the truth to her.

"Did you feel trapped?" Georgina said.

"All the time. I ran away when I was younger than you."

A glimmer of hope came into Georgina's eyes.

"I wanted to make my own way in the world," Mr. Weeks said, "but I believe that your headmistress has plans for you."

"She wants me to go to Bryn Mawr on a scholarship."

"That doesn't sound too bad."

"It is for me. It's not what I want."

Julian Weeks raised his hand to catch the waitress's attention
and ordered three cups of coffee. "She's been good to you
generally?"

"I can't complain."

"Hmm. And you want to become a reporter, like my daughter, is that correct?"

"Yes." Georgina nodded.

"We'll help you out, Miss Howell. But you should finish the
school year and part on good terms with your headmistress.
Don't make this about you being a runaway. You'll ruin your
prospects and her reputation in the process."

A rattletrap of a car jolted down the street.

"My father will speak to Miss Howe-Jones," Kitty said.
"He'll plead your case and offer to be your guarantor when you
come to New York. But he can't do it if you leave without
her permission."

Georgina's lower lip trembled. "You don't understand, do
you? She makes her own rules. In Miss Howe-Jones's world,
she is the law."

The rickety motor car pulled up outside the café, and the
man from the gas station near Westfield climbed out.

Georgina gasped. "She's here. I didn't think she'd be so fast."

Through the window, Kitty saw the gas station fellow open
the back door, and Miss Howe-Jones emerged, brooch clasped
to her neck, head held high. She looked up and down the street
with disdain and made her stately way toward the restaurant.

"She'll never let me leave." Georgina stood.

"Please, Miss Howell, take a seat," Kitty said. "We'll talk to
her together. The three of us."

"You think you know everything. Well, you don't!" Georgina sneered. "You don't know what it's like to be in my shoes, and you don't know the first thing about Elspeth. Do you really believe that she died because of her somnambulism? She was awake, and she went to meet someone."

"How do you know?" Kitty looked up at her in shock.

"I'm not here to argue."

"You didn't tell the police?"

"And get the Brights worked up into a lather over nothing?"

"Georgina, their daughter died," Kitty said, aghast.

"There was no sign of foul play," Georgina said. "She never told me who she would be meeting, and to be honest, Elspeth used her sleepwalking as a cover to do whatever she pleased."

Miss Howe-Jones had her hand on the glass door to the restaurant. She pushed it open. "Georgina. Come with me." Her words carried the ring of unmistakable authority. She threw a scornful glance at Kitty. "Shame on you, Miss Weeks. You knew she was here all along."

Georgina didn't reply but edged away, crossing the room to the door.

"Where do you think you're going?" the headmistress said as the handful of other patrons turned to watch.

Julian Weeks tossed a few coins on the table, and he, Kitty, and Miss Howe-Jones followed the student onto the sidewalk.

Traffic streamed along in both directions, but the girl from Westfield Hall didn't care; she looked for an opening and started to cross.

"Don't be silly, Georgina." The headmistress's voice rose. "You're all alone. You have nowhere to go."

"Come back," Kitty called. "We'll help you."

"Too late." Georgina looked over her shoulder.

Too late. The words reverberated in Kitty's mind days later. She had been too late. She had been too cautious. She hadn't given Georgina enough encouragement. But what should she have said—that the life of the working girl was a bed of roses, that she would find a job, earn enough to be able to afford a decent place to sleep, that she would have been able to write whatever she wanted?

It was no excuse.

Georgina remained still, her head turned. *Too late.* She took a step into the traffic. Brakes screeched and horns blared as a speeding motorist mowed down the schoolgirl.

CHAPTER TWENTY-SEVEN

That poor, unfortunate child." With unsteady hands, Julian Weeks poured himself a measure of whiskey while Kitty huddled in the corner of the sofa. "I feel guilty. We let her down."

They had spent half an hour at the scene, waiting for the police to arrive. Miss Howe-Jones wouldn't speak to them or allow them to approach Georgina's body. She stood guard over it, her arms outstretched, protecting her student from the crowd of gawking onlookers. Kitty and her father gave their statements to a portly officer, and since there didn't seem to be anything else they could do, they hailed a cab and drove away.

"What do you think Miss Howe-Jones will tell the girls at school?" Kitty said finally. She pictured the headmistress addressing a stunned assembly—girls in tears, teachers distraught.

"I don't know... But Georgina's death has hit her hard."

"If I were her, I'd say that Georgina met with an accident on a trip to Manhattan to visit the doctor."

"The poor girl seemed frozen in the middle of the street. We should never have allowed her to try to cross."

"I wonder whether she did it on purpose," Kitty said slowly. "It's the way she walked into the traffic... She had asked me about my accident earlier. I didn't make too much of it at the time, but now…"

"What are you suggesting, Capability?" Mr. Weeks drew himself up. "That she would rather kill herself than return to school?"

"Not necessarily kill—perhaps just shock Miss Howe-Jones into paying attention."

"That's most extreme." He looked at Kitty. "If you want my attention, promise me that you will ask."

Kitty managed a halfhearted smile. "I was struck by what Georgina said about Elspeth right before she left the restaurant— that Elspeth went out to meet someone."

Julian Weeks banged down his glass. "Enough about Elspeth."

"I have to finish," Kitty said. "I have to find out what really happened."

"For whose sake, Capability?"

"I beg your pardon?"

"For whose sake? Yours? I doubt the Brights want you poking about."

Kitty could hear the pain in his voice.

"Two girls have died," he went on. "What more has to happen for you to leave it alone? Do you want to wind up like them?"

"Of course I don't." Kitty put down her glass. "You're right that two girls have died. I don't want them to have died in vain. I don't want Georgina's death on my conscience."

"You're looking for a reason." Each word carried the force of anger. "And sometimes, there isn't a reason. Sometimes, accidents are just accidents. Sometimes, people—the best people, the most talented people—do unexpected things like walk in their sleep. You're trying to make sense of a world that makes no sense most of the time. Some idiot in Sarajevo shot another idiot from a dynasty that probably shouldn't exist any longer—and what happens? All of us, all of Europe, half of Asia, all of us are paying the price."

"I can't speak for the idiot in Sarajevo." Kitty chose her words with care. She knew she was on the brink of something important. "But I can speak for myself, and I know what I want. I want to try to make sense of what's happening around me. You may be able to manage by laughing at absurdity, but I can't. Not yet."

For once, her father was silenced.

"There's one more thing I'd like to add," Kitty said. "I'm sorry that I've been behaving like a spoiled child lately. You should go ahead with your plans with Miss Lane. I will adjust."

"I hoped you would do more than just adjust," he said. "I hoped you would be happy, not only for my sake but for your own."

"That," Kitty said, "will come. It may take some time."

"Do you mean it?"

"I meant everything I said right now."

Helena Busby was in no mood to be trifled with when Kitty reported for work the next day. "Imagine my surprise, Miss Weeks, to open this morning's paper and find *your* name mentioned in connection with the vehicular collision death of a Westfield Hall girl, Georgina Howell."

Kitty and Mr. Weeks had spent the rest of Sunday quietly at home, and she was caught off guard by the onslaught. "My father and I happened to be there, Miss Busby. When the police arrived, they wanted to speak to us. One of the City reporters—"

"I know how we make news, Miss Weeks. I wasn't asking you for a tutorial."

"Miss Howell wanted to become a reporter," Kitty continued. "I told her she should finish school. She telephoned me at home, and my father accompanied me to meet her. We hoped to persuade her to return to Westfield Hall."

"I see." Miss Busby wrapped her arms around her thin chest. "You do understand that your behavior might have ramifications for the Page? Future interview subjects, when they hear your name, will put two and two together."

"I didn't push her under the car, madam."

"You must understand this, Miss Weeks. Whenever any interview is complete, your involvement with the subject ends. That's *it*. An interview is a window into someone else's life. But then that window closes. No one will speak to us if they think that they might have to put up with your interference afterward."

"It won't happen again, Miss Busby."

"I feel I've heard those words from you before, Miss Weeks. I've a good mind to deny you the opportunity to cover the Congressional Union's meeting with the president."

"You've made your decision? The Page will run a story?"

"It is our civic duty, yes."

Civic duty had never before been a motivating factor for the editor. "If I don't go, who will?"

"I've a good mind to do it myself. Jeannie Williams is hardly prepared."

"Please, Miss Busby, it was an honest mistake." Kitty couldn't let this chance slip through her fingers.

"I certainly hope so." The arms unfolded. "Mrs. Belmont did ask for you by name... Now go on and do your homework before I regret my decision."

Phineas Mills bumped into Kitty as he stepped from the elevator. "Miss Weeks, just the person I was looking for."

"Well, that's a nice coincidence." She was on her way to the morgue.

"I spoke to my contacts at the police department. They haven't brought in any girls matching the description of the girl. The young ones are all beggars or"—he cleared his throat—"streetwalkers. Unless she's putting on an act?"

Kitty had forgotten about her request to the news reporter. "Thank you, Mr. Mills." No point in telling him that the girl had been found. And was dead now.

"So what is all this about? Can we have a cup of tea in the cafeteria?"

Kitty checked her watch. She had promised Miss Busby that she would behave. "I'm sorry, I have some work to do downstairs."

"Maybe we could meet afterward?"

Kitty thought for a moment. "That's not a bad idea." There still remained one other individual she wanted to question with regard to Elspeth's death, and she was afraid to face him alone. "If you can find out where the Brights' dinner guest, Mr. Phillip Emerson, lives, we could go speak to him together."

❦

"Here you go." Mr. Musser thumped a stack of papers in front of Kitty. "Mr. Woodrow Wilson and woman suffrage. I'm behind today, so can you read for yourself?"

"I feel much better, Mr. Musser. I'll be fine." The scores of articles seemed daunting, so Kitty began with the simplest task—arranging them in chronological order.

"I can tell you that Mr. Wilson doesn't approve of women in public life." Mr. Musser hovered over her. "He prefers them ornamental. Seen but not heard, except for behind closed doors. He's a Southern gentleman after all."

In that case, Kitty thought with amusement, he must have really enjoyed his stint on the faculty at women-only Bryn Mawr College. Mr. Wilson had taught there and at Wesleyan University, followed by Princeton University, where he served as president. He was said to detest newspaper women and women in business generally, and glancing at an early article, Kitty saw that he had once maintained that universal suffrage lay "at the foundation of every evil in this country."

"Suffrage is not a national issue, so far," he had said in 1911, the year before he was elected president of the United States. "It is a local issue for each state to settle for itself."

Then, in 1915, on the eve of the suffrage referendum in New Jersey and on the day he announced his engagement to Mrs. Galt, he told reporters, "I intend to vote for woman suffrage in

New Jersey because I believe that the time has come to extend that privilege and responsibility to women of the state, but I shall vote not as the leader of my party but only upon my private conviction as a citizen of New Jersey, called upon by the legislature of the state to express his convictions at the polls."

The article went on to report that the president would not encourage the Susan B. Anthony amendment to the constitution and that he disapproved of any attempt to "fasten woman suffrage" on states, like the Democratic South, which weren't ready to vote on it themselves.

Kitty looked for Mr. Musser. He was behind his desk. "The suffrage referendum in New Jersey lost, didn't it?" she said.

"Oh yes, *fräulein*. By more than forty thousand votes. What do you think of Mr. Wilson so far?"

"I think he seems like a very cautious man"—Kitty kept headstrong Mrs. Belmont in mind—"and that I should be ready for fireworks."

CHAPTER TWENTY-EIGHT

The telephone in the foyer rang as Kitty returned home and was peeling off her gloves. "That's all right, Grace." She reached for the receiver. "I'll take it."

It was Phineas Mills. "I've found Mr. Emerson's address. Can you meet me back at the *Sentinel*?"

Kitty peeked around the door into her father's study. He was sitting with Miss Lane, and both looked pleased with themselves. He beckoned her in. She gestured for him to wait.

"Could you give me half an hour, Mr. Mills?" She joined her father and, for the first time, appraised his friend without clouded eyes. Sylvia Lane was lively and attractive, and she didn't simper. He could have done much worse. Kitty decided she might as well try to get to know her.

"Will you join us for lunch?" Mr. Weeks said.

"I'd love to, but I can't stay long. The telephone call—they want me back at work."

"It must be important," Miss Lane remarked. "Julian tells me that you usually only work half days."

"Well," Kitty said with a smile, "they want me to cover Mr. Wilson's visit."

"Is that so, Capability?" Her father stood, one hand on Miss Lane's shoulder. "That's wonderful news. We should celebrate."

"Well, not the entire visit. Just part of it," Kitty clarified. "He's meeting the Congressional Union, which is headed by Mrs. Belmont, whom I interviewed recently," she added for Miss Lane's benefit.

"Well, it's marvelous news in any case," Sylvia Lane said.

"And speaking of news," Mr. Weeks began.

Kitty held her breath.

"I've invited Miss Lane to accompany me to the Railwaymen's dinner, and she's accepted."

Kitty must have looked baffled, because he explained, "The association is hosting a dinner to honor the president during his trip. And I was lucky enough to receive two tickets."

"That's perfect then." Kitty would have to accustom herself to seeing Miss Lane at her father's side from here on. For Sylvia Lane to go out with him in public, without her brother, would be quite a statement. "I will see the president in the morning, and you will meet him for dinner."

"I hardly think we will meet him," Mr. Weeks said. "They're expecting a thousand guests or some such number."

"It should be quite the event then."

"Quite," Miss Lane said. "I'm really very excited about it." She looked up at Mr. Weeks and smiled. "Thank you for thinking of me, Julian."

Kitty rose. "Well, I should be getting back."

Mr. Weeks said, "So soon?"

"I don't want to keep them waiting. This is quite an opportunity for me."

"Yes it is, Miss Weeks—"

"You should call me Capability," Kitty said.

And what would she be expected to call Miss Lane one day? *Mother?*

⁂

Kitty met Mr. Mills in the *Sentinel*'s lobby. He wore a light jacket, woolen hat, and striped muffler.

"Don't you feel cold?" A gust of bitter January hit them as they stepped outside.

"I'm a warm-blooded fellow, Miss Weeks."

Kitty didn't want to know what that was supposed to mean so she cut straight to business. "Where are we going?"

"I have an address on Bowery."

She didn't go to that part of town very often. It was a notorious skid row. "He lives there?"

"Lives, works, I'm not sure. It would appear that he's part of some radical gang."

"He's an anarchist?" They'd been in the news lately for blowing up things.

"Worse. A pacifist."

"Is that so bad?"

"Those fellows never quit. They think God is on their side."

Kitty smiled, then started to shiver and wrapped her arms around herself. "Let's take a cab. I'll pay."

Mills burst out laughing. "If you want to be a real reporter, Miss Weeks, you travel by subway. Cabs are for emergencies. How else do you see the world?" He chuckled and slapped his hand against his thigh. "Taxicab indeed. That's too good."

Kitty followed him to the Times Square subway station and

bought herself a token. As much as Mr. Weeks allowed her to move freely about the city, he put his foot down when it came to mass transport—especially of the subterranean kind. He had an idée fixe that a young pretty woman would be harassed underground.

"We'll take a local to Spring and Lafayette and then walk," Mills said as they waited on the platform.

She scanned the map. New York's subways were the first in the world to feature both local and express stops in both directions. The ingenious system consisted of a single trunk line, which ran from South Ferry at the tip of the island to Ninety-Sixth and Broadway and then split into two, one branch going to 242nd Street and Broadway and the other to Bronx Park. An extension under the East River connected the southernmost stop to points in downtown Brooklyn—an engineering miracle, as far as Kitty was concerned. It would have been easy for her to board the train at Seventy-Second Street and Broadway, a few blocks from home, and hop off at Times Square, just a few blocks from work. But as it was, Rao drove her.

Their train arrived with a rattle, rumble, and screech, and the doors creaked open. A crowd of passengers poured out in every shape and color, like an advertisement for Ellis Island.

Kitty climbed in. All the seats were taken, so she grabbed a leather strap and stood in front of a Russian babushka with a colorful scarf on her head and a basket of potatoes on her lap. The train rumbled forward. Even in winter, she could smell the pungent odor of bodies packed close. In summer, she thought, it must be unbearable.

They arrived at their stop with amazing speed, and Kitty

followed Mills onto the street. She was glad to be back in daylight and the cold air of winter. The subway might be fast, but it felt claustrophobic down there. Mass transit, she realized, was one of the few forms of travel that didn't offer different classes of service. For the duration of the ride, it was a great equalizer.

They started to walk east, through streets cluttered with tiny storefronts and carts where men repaired umbrellas, sharpened knives, or sold roasted peanuts, kindling, shoelaces, and suspenders. A sooty-faced boy tagged along behind Mills, asking if he wanted a shine for a nickel. A newsboy yelled the news—in Russian—and then another cried out something in Yiddish. A voice spoke in German.

Urchins surrounded Kitty, begging for money. She tossed over a couple of coins, and they held out their hands until she gave each of them one.

"You shouldn't," Mills said. "It just encourages them."

Kitty closed her purse with a click. "I can't say no."

She heard the rumble of elevated trains on Third Avenue. It was the Third Avenue line that had transformed Bowery from a fashionable boulevard into a dump. The raised tracks cast the street below in perpetual shade; the deafening racket and debris from trains deterred decent types. Now vagrants huddled beneath blankets on its sidewalks or leaned against its dilapidated storefronts.

An old man sat on a canvas satchel, his legs outstretched. Kitty picked up her skirts and stepped over him when he wouldn't move. "This is where we'll find Mr. Emerson?"

Mills pulled the notepad from his pocket to check the address.

"Just a block farther," he said as they walked under the shadows of rails held up by giant metal pillars. Empty bottles and shards of glass littered the sidewalk.

"And He will come to save you," a drunk declaimed. "Raining down His righteous anger…"

Mills stopped in front of what looked to be an abandoned storefront and knocked on the door. There was no reply.

"You still haven't told me why you want to speak to Mr. Emerson," Mills said.

Kitty answered quickly. "I think he may have an idea who Elspeth Bright went to meet the night she died." Then she rapped on the door again. "Is anyone in?"

Mills said, "Wait a minute. Elspeth Bright went to meet someone of her own volition?"

They heard a bolt sliding and a chain fall, and a scruffy-looking fellow, still in his union suit, peered out. "What do you want?"

"We're here to see Mr. Phillip Emerson," Mills said.

"And who are you?"

Kitty stepped forward. "Friends."

He looked her up and down and must have decided she seemed trustworthy. "Give me a minute." The door closed.

"Never let the door close," Mills said. "That's rule number one of journalism."

"And what were you planning to do? Force your way in? He'll be back. He probably went to change."

"Sleeping here, I don't think he cares for such niceties."

"Let's see, shall we?"

The door opened again, and this time, the fellow was dressed in trousers and a shirt. He also wore gold-rimmed spectacles. "Come on in."

Kitty resisted looking at Mills to say "I told you so."

They entered a musty room that smelled of old cheese and cigarettes. A few rickety metal chairs and a table were the only pieces of furniture. The shutters were down, and the only light came from a single electric bulb that hung nakedly from the ceiling. It was about as cold in here as out on the street, so Kitty left her coat on. Newspaper clippings tacked to the wall caught her attention.

LUSITANIA SINKS, UNRESTRICTED SUBMARINE WARFARE, *ARABIC* TORPEDOED, E-2 DISASTER. Other than a story about Mr. Wilson's upcoming visit, the clippings catalogued a litany of horrors.

Mr. Emerson emerged from another room, wearing baggy trousers and a fisherman's sweater. His good looks shone brighter in contrast to the dingy surroundings. He stopped short when he saw Kitty. "I know you. From the navy yard."

She held out her hand. "I'm Capability Weeks, from the *New York Sentinel*. And this is my colleague, Phineas Mills."

"Goddamn it. She told me she was a friend. Sorry, Emerson," his comrade apologized.

Emerson lowered himself into a chair. "So, what can I do for you, Miss Weeks? Surely, this isn't about that E-2 mess."

"What's that?" For the second time during their visit, Mills flashed Kitty a look of bewilderment.

"You didn't tell your friend." Emerson chuckled. "Miss Weeks and I both happened to be present when the E-2 exploded."

"We're not here because of the submarine, Mr. Emerson."
Kitty sat down opposite him. "Though I will admit that I would
love to know what you were doing at the docks. Mr. Mills and
I have come today to talk to you about Elspeth Bright."

The cocky expression vanished from Emerson's eyes. He
blinked a couple of times. "Elspeth was a wonderful girl…the
very best."

"I heard you were at the Brights' dinner on Christmas Eve.
Strange that they should invite someone whom Dr. Bright fired
from his job."

Emerson shifted in his chair. "I wasn't fired. I quit. Now, cut
to the point, Miss Weeks."

Kitty didn't have a specific point, but she wanted to gauge
his reaction. "I have reason to believe that Elspeth didn't die in
her sleep." He didn't flinch. "I believe she went out to meet
someone that night and that the meeting had something to
do with the Edison batteries. There must be a lot of money
involved in naval contracts."

Emerson remained silent.

Kitty went further. "Surely you knew about her work,
Mr. Emerson."

He pushed his chair away with a scrape and began to pace up
and down. "I knew," he said finally, "that even with all those
experts looking at the proposals, it was Elspeth who understood
that the batteries might release too much hydrogen."

"Do you think someone wanted to silence her?" Kitty had
nothing to lose. Anything he said could yield a clue to work
from. "Well, Mr. Emerson?"

"What the hell." The handsome young man cracked his

knuckles. "I haven't told anyone this, and I'm probably giving you the rope with which to hang me—"

"Don't be so sure of my motives, Mr. Emerson," Kitty interrupted.

"Don't do it, Emerson," his friend warned.

"I owe it to Elspeth." Emerson's voice broke. He turned to Kitty. "It's me she went to meet in the park. I arrived late, but only by a few minutes. She was already dead. I hope you catch whoever did it, Miss Weeks. I'll wring his neck with my own hands."

CHAPTER TWENTY-NINE

T he room went quiet. No one moved. Then Mills said, "You expect us to believe this nonsense?"

"Believe it or not. It's your choice." Emerson shrugged.

"All right then. What did you do next?"

"I checked her pulse. Nothing. So I went away."

"You didn't call for help?" Kitty stared at him. "You just left her?"

He looked at her as though she were crazy. "She was dead. And how would I have explained what I was doing there in the first place?"

"What were you doing?"

He froze. "I've said enough."

"Look, Mr. Emerson…" Mills took a step toward him.

"No, you look, Mr. Mills. Elspeth wanted to speak in private. We agreed on a time, then she pushed it back. I arrived at midnight to find her lifeless in the snow. That's all you will get from me. You and your pretty friend should leave now."

"We could go to the police with this," Mills said.

"Be my guest." The reverent tone Emerson used when talking about Elspeth had faded away, and he spoke belligerently, like a thug, daring them to bring him in.

"Don't be a fool, Emerson," his friend hissed. "You'll ruin the plan." He marched to the door and held it open. "Now, the two of you"—he glared at Kitty and Mills—"bugger off."

Once they turned down a side street to leave the rumble of the trains behind them, Mills paused. "I'm sorry that fellow was so rude."

Kitty took a deep breath. "That's the least of my worries, Mr. Mills. It's Mr. Emerson's words that have hit me hard."

"You can say that again." He rubbed his hands together to keep them warm. "Do you think he's telling the truth? It's not at all what I expected."

Kitty didn't have a ready answer. "I don't know what to think. On the one hand, he seems to have truly cared about Elspeth. On the other, how are we supposed to believe that he arrived at the park at midnight, only to discover that she had died? It doesn't sit right."

"I wonder if there was anything between them."

Kitty didn't want to admit she had suspected something of the sort, and worse. It felt like a violation of Elspeth's privacy. "I'm tired, Mr. Mills. This may make me a bad reporter, but I'd like to take a cab home. May I give you a lift?"

He considered the offer. Then he tipped his hat. "That's all right, Miss Weeks. I'll walk."

That evening, Kitty and her father ate dinner at a restaurant. Mr. Weeks wanted a change, and every now and then, he enjoyed a taste of France.

A waiter poured wine into long-stemmed glasses and served a dish of snails sizzled in butter.

"You go ahead," Kitty said.

"You really should try them, Capability." Mr. Weeks pushed the plate toward her.

"No thanks." Kitty had an appetite for adventure but not when it came to her stomach.

"I hope you don't mind my inviting Miss Lane to the Waldorf."

She watched him spear the soft flesh and pop it in his mouth. "Not at all."

"I only had two tickets, and I didn't think you'd want to spend hours in a crowded hall listening to the president discuss preparedness for war."

"I can read about it the next day, and I'm sure I'll be tired from the morning. Miss Busby said that Mrs. Belmont and her friends plan to press Mr. Wilson to change the constitution."

"I don't envy the man." Mr. Weeks wiped away the speck of grease that had landed on his tie.

"Neither do I." Kitty began to feel queasy. She put it down to the sight of the buttery dish combined with the events of the day that had led to Mr. Emerson's unsettling revelation. She still didn't know what to make of it—she didn't trust him, but that didn't mean that everything he said was a lie.

Kitty fell onto her bed and closed her eyes. She saw Elspeth, Dr. and Mrs. Bright, and opposite them, Mr. Emerson, Prudence, and Georgina, as well as Mr. and Mrs. Marquand. They were all at dinner, talking over each other.

Why wouldn't Emerson say why he and Elspeth arranged to meet? Was it a secret lovers' rendezvous, or something to do with the batteries? Perhaps it was a mercenary plan to stop her from revealing their flaws. At any rate, Kitty couldn't hear the Brights and their guests clearly. If she could only piece together their stories, she felt sure they would lead her to the heart of the matter and allow her to discover why a seemingly healthy girl like Elspeth had passed away sometime during the dark, cold hours between the end of dinner and midnight.

The next day's paper printed the president's itinerary in exhaustive detail, leaving nothing to the imagination. Kitty read through it for incidentals, tidbits she could add to her story for color.

Mr. Wilson would leave Washington at midnight and travel by rail in his special car, New York, to Pennsylvania Station, where he would arrive at 6:05 a.m. He would eat breakfast on the train and then drive to the Waldorf Hotel, accompanied by Mrs. Wilson; his physician, Dr. Cary T. Grayson; his secretary, Joseph P. Tumulty; and Charles Swem, his stenographer. The party would be escorted by Collector Dudley Field Malone and two representatives of the Railway Business Association, H. H. Westinghouse and W. L. Saunders. In the morning, he would receive the delegation of women from the Congressional Union at his hotel. At noon, he would drive in an open car via Fifth Avenue to address the Clerical Conference of the New York Federation of Churches at Aeolian Hall. After luncheon back at his hotel, the president would take care of official business at the University Club at Fifth Avenue and Fifty-Fourth Street. Then, before he returned to the capital, again on the midnight train, he would deliver two speeches, one to the Railroad Business Association and another—which showed how important the fledging industry had become—to the first annual dinner of the Motion Picture Board of Trade. Somewhere in the time that remained, a German delegation would seek to approach him to have milk shipped to starving babies in Germany.

"Ooh, the motion picture dinner." Kitty turned to Mr. Weeks. "If you had tickets to that, you might have caught a glimpse of some of the popular actors."

"I wouldn't recognize a motion picture actor if he came up to me and shook my hand," Mr. Weeks replied.

"Don't let Grace hear you," Kitty said. The maid was pouring Mr. Weeks's morning coffee. "She might decide to stop working in this house."

Grace grinned.

Even Mr. Weeks smiled. "It's too early for jokes."

"I had to be up early," Kitty said. "Today is not a day for me to be running behind."

The account of Mr. Wilson's day concluded with a note that the Congressional Union meeting had been arranged in Washington, and a confirmation had been telegraphed to the

New York members last night. Among those expected to be present were Mrs. O. H. P. Belmont, chairman of the New York State Division. Kitty wondered whether Mrs. Bright would be there as well—she ought to tell Elspeth's mother about her conversation with Mr. Emerson.

Another division of the CU, led by Mrs. Harriet Stanton Blatch, would make for Albany to speak to the head of the Democratic Party state committee members.

Kitty reached the Waldorf Hotel on Thursday the twenty-seventh at twenty minutes past eight o'clock. She would have arrived sooner, but a crowd of tightly packed heads had formed outside the hotel, slowing her down.

The president's car pulled up at eight thirty, and the throng let out a roar. Kitty stood on her tiptoes and craned her neck for a partial view of the tall gentleman tipping his top hat.

"There's Mrs. Wilson," someone yelled.

"He looks so happy, talking to everyone in his party."

"Look at him laugh!"

Clutching her hat with one hand and her purse with the other, Kitty elbowed her way toward the hotel's main entrance, a massive, curving driveway cut into the building right off Fifth Avenue at Thirty-Fourth Street.

A uniformed doorman stopped her. "Excuse me, madam. Only hotel guests are allowed inside today."

"I'm a guest of Mrs. O. H. P. Belmont." Kitty adjusted her cloche, which had come dislodged in her push forward.

"Is that so? Just a minute." He whispered something to another man in uniform.

"Mrs. Belmont is sick, madam. She won't be coming today."

"I'm with the *New York Sentinel*." Kitty put on her most professional manner to hide her surprise. "I'm here to report on the president's meeting with the Women's Congressional Union. They're expecting me. I've been invited."

The second man said, "Let her in. The ladies are already here. They can decide."

"This way please, madam." The guard pointed her inside.

The president wasn't the first dignitary to stay at the hotel; everyone from generals to visiting princes slept at the two-decades-old Waldorf when they came to town. The hotel was built on land owned by the Astors, and it was joined a few years later by the Astoria, constructed on an adjacent plot. The two behemoths combined to boast a staggering thousand rooms, impeccable service, "tea" as a meal, and forward-looking restaurants that were among the first to serve ladies without escorts at any hour.

Kitty made her way upstairs to the East Room via the famed Peacock Alley, a three-hundred-foot hallway that, at certain hours, was filled with "swells" and was the best place to preen, to see and be seen in Manhattan. But before nine in the morning, on the day of the president's visit, it was just a corridor furnished with silk carpets and ornate chinoiserie placed on pedestals at suitable intervals.

At the entrance to the East Room, a woman took attendance from a list on her clipboard. "And you are?" she said to Kitty.

"Capability Weeks."

She scanned her sheet. "I'm afraid I don't have you here."

"Mrs. Belmont invited me." Kitty glanced into the room, where several dozen women milled about.

"You know Mrs. Belmont is ill?"

"I was informed."

A bell rang inside the room. "Ladies! I have bad news," a woman's voice called. "It seems that the president will not see us."

"How can that be?" someone cried.

"We had it all arranged!"

"It's a disgrace!"

With the attendance-taker distracted by the wave of indignation that had ensued, Kitty slipped inside. She worked her way to the back so she would be harder to spot.

"Ladies, ladies. Quiet please." The announcer waited until the chatter died down. "It appears that the president believes that an appointment hasn't been made, but it has. We have the confirmatory telegram."

"Well, we'll wait here all day," the women shouted.

Just as the situation seemed as though it would get out of hand, a man with slicked-back hair entered, checking the time on his gold pocket watch.

"Oscar," someone murmured, referring to the maître d'hôtel, Oscar Tschirky, who was such a fixture that he was known simply by his first name or as "Oscar of the Waldorf."

Oscar approached the woman who had made the initial announcement and whispered something.

"Who is he speaking to?" Kitty whispered to the lady beside her.

"Mrs. E. Tiffany Dyer, our Union's secretary. Haven't you met her?"

"I'm afraid not." She smiled, took a step back, and melted away before her ignorance aroused any further suspicions.

"Friends," Mrs. Dyer said, after she and the maître d' had finished their discussion. "In order to help us move beyond this impasse, Mr. Oscar has kindly agreed to convey a note from us to the president's secretary."

Kitty hoped they would be able to work out something if for no other reason than she would hate to miss her chance to see Mr. Wilson in person and forfeit her assignment. Besides, even the papers said the meeting had been confirmed.

The note was composed, and Mrs. Dyer read it out: "More than one hundred women in the East Room desire an audience in regard to the national suffrage amendment. They ask for ten minutes of your time."

"Written with all the care as if it had to deal with the sinking of a neutral ship," one of the few men present observed with a smirk to another. Their disheveled suits and cynical air marked them as reporters.

Kitty caught sight of Mrs. Bright speaking with a group of friends, and Mrs. Marquand, the Brights' neighbor, nearby.

She walked across. "How nice to see you here, Mrs. Marquand. I wasn't aware that you are also a supporter of constitutional reform."

"I'm not." She looked down her ski-slope nose. "I'm here to support Ephigenia. It's the first time she's really been out since Elspeth died."

Mrs. Bright noticed Kitty and peeled away from her group. "Miss Weeks. Are you here on business?"

"Yes, I am. Mrs. Belmont invited me."

Oscar returned. "I have here a reply from Mr. Tumulty, the president's secretary." He handed a note to Mrs. Dyer.

"'I very much regret that the president's engagements this morning make it impossible to arrange this matter as you have generously suggested,'" she read aloud.

"Shame! Shame!"

Mrs. Dyer waited for silence. "'When the representative of your committee called at the White House yesterday,'" she continued, "'the president informed her of the crowded condition of his calendar today.'"

"We will have a response," a shrill voice cried. "But first, all reporters must leave!"

"Ladies," the handful of men in the room protested.

"This is private business."

The men left, dragging their feet, and the door to the East Room closed behind them.

"Reporter here!" The attendance-taker had noticed Kitty and shouted, accusatory finger pointing.

Kitty wished she could disappear as a hundred pairs of eyes swiveled to stare at her.

"Miss Weeks works for the *Sentinel*," Mrs. Bright said. "I can vouch for her. She's all right."

"She can stay. Let's get back to work." Mrs. Dyer decided the matter.

The note-writing resumed.

"Thank you, Mrs. Bright. May I speak to you for a moment in private?"

"Excuse me, Jeanette." Mrs. Bright moved away from Mrs. Marquand. "What is it, my dear?" Her expression was open, honest, without a trace of guile.

"I thought you might like to know that I met Mr. Emerson," Kitty said in a low voice. "I'd like to tell you more about it. Perhaps, after this—if you have some time—"

The ruddy cheeks turned pale.

"Would you like to sit, Mrs. Bright?"

"No, no. I'm fine. What did he say?" Elspeth's mother grabbed Kitty's arm.

Kitty regretted her decision to bring up the topic. "I was hoping we could discuss it later."

Mrs. Bright anxiously eyed her up and down. "You're keeping something from me, Miss Weeks!"

Kitty stalled. She didn't want to cause a scene.

"Tell me, Miss Weeks."

"Mr. Emerson said that he had arranged to meet Miss Bright in the park the night she died."

Mrs. Bright went weak at the knees. "I think I'll take that chair now."

At that very moment, a baby-faced man with thinning hair walked in.

"Mr. Tumulty, the president's secretary!" someone said with a gasp.

"Please be patient, ladies. The president of the United States is on his way," Mr. Tumulty announced.

CHAPTER THIRTY

B efore Kitty knew what was happening, Woodrow Wilson strode in. Sixty years old and almost six feet tall, the slender president wore a dark suit, stiff-collared shirt, tie, and tie pin. His narrow, ascetic face with high cheekbones, the rimless glasses perched on his nose, and his watchful demeanor gave the former Princetonian the stern, cold look she had read about.

The president clasped his hands behind his back and addressed the assembly in a measured, careful manner. "I ought to say, in the first place, that the apologies I think should come from me, because I had not understood that an appointment had been made. On the contrary, I supposed none had been made and therefore had filled my morning with work from which it did not seem possible to escape."

Kitty thought she must be in a dream. She hoped Miss Busby would allow her to write about the brouhaha over the scheduling—the misunderstanding and Mr. Wilson's apology.

"It may be, ladies, that my mind works slowly," he continued. "I have always felt that those things that were most solidly built were built piece by piece, and I felt that the genius of our political development in this country lay in the processes of our states and in the very clear definition of the difference of sphere between the state and federal governments."

While he spoke, Kitty had heard a rustle behind her. Now, she looked back—Mrs. Bright's chair stood empty. Kitty scanned the crowd to see Elspeth's mother quietly wending her way to the door. For a moment, she considered following her, since Ephigenia Bright didn't look well. Kitty weighed her options. The president of the United States won.

"When I last had the pleasure of receiving some ladies urging the amendment to our constitution," he was saying, "I told them that my own mind was unchanged, but I hoped open, and that I would take pleasure in conferring with the leaders of my party and the leaders of Congress with regard to this matter. I have not fulfilled that promise, and I hope you will understand why I have not fulfilled it, because there seemed to be questions of legislation so pressing in their necessity that they ought to take precedence over everything else."

He was putting the women off, Kitty realized with mounting fury. He believed that other matters were more important.

"The business of government is a business from day to day, ladies," the president continued, "and there are things that cannot wait."

Like votes for half the population? If only Alva Belmont were here to challenge him. She would never let Mr. Wilson get away with such a feeble explanation.

"I have not forgotten the promise that I made, and I certainly shall not forget the fulfillment of it, but I want always to be absolutely frank. My own mind is still convinced that we ought to work this thing out state by state."

Kitty glanced around her. Many of the women were shaking their heads with disappointment. She spotted Mrs. Marquand listening intently; Mrs. Bright must have left without informing her friend.

"I did what I could to work it out in my own state in New Jersey," Mr. Wilson continued, "and I am willing to act there whenever it comes up; but that is so far my conviction as to the best and solidest way to build changes of this kind, and I for my own part see no reason for discouragement on the part of the women of the country in the progress that this movement has been making."

No reason for discouragement. No reason for discouragement? How long did they have to wait—until the war with Europe was over? Then some new "pressing" matter would rear its ugly head. The change to the constitution could be put off indefinitely.

"It may move like a glacier, but when it does move, its effects are permanent. I had not expected to have this pleasure this morning and therefore am simply speaking offhand and without consideration of my phrases, but I hope in entire frankness. I thank you sincerely for this opportunity." The president bowed.

A smattering of applause went through the room.

Mrs. Dyer thanked Mr. Wilson for his time. "We had hoped," she added, "that you would include the woman suffrage question in your address in the Middle West when you take up the campaign for preparedness. Yes, Mrs. Bruere?" She pointed to a woman who had raised her hand.

"You are urging a federal movement, sir," Mrs. Bruere said, "not a movement as separate states for preparedness. We believe and insist upon the necessity for an amendment to the federal constitution, because we feel that it is logical. We have the country behind us."

Mrs. Charles Beard spoke next. "No mobilization can be complete without the mobilization of women. Was the Clayton antitrust law gained state by state, sir?"

"I do not care to discuss that." Mr. Wilson responded with obvious annoyance.

Kitty stood there, taking it all in, and she finally understood what she had just witnessed. When it came to matters he cared about, the president didn't hesitate for a moment to campaign around the country to sway hearts and change minds. But when it came to woman suffrage, he took refuge behind states' rights. Somehow, war warranted the exercise of his powers of persuasion, while campaigning for half his citizens' rights did not.

No wonder so many women were enraged. No wonder so many felt they must browbeat and threaten, take matters into their own hands.

Mrs. Dyer stepped forward to thank the president once again, and he left as swiftly as he had arrived.

CHAPTER THIRTY-ONE

K itty pushed her way through the hubbub outside the hotel. Even though it was freezing, the president's admirers remained, stomping their feet and blowing into their hands to keep warm. This time, it was easier getting past the elbows and chests, the annoyed comments and stares, because she was one of the few who wanted to leave the vicinity of the Waldorf.

A woman in a mink coat argued with a policeman, telling him that she had dropped her ticket to tonight's dinner and demanding that he help her find it or allow her to enter without one. A gaily outfitted marching band had begun to tune up. Kitty passed a familiar face—Mr. Emerson's bespectacled comrade. Seeing him there made her uneasy—he couldn't possibly admire the cause that Mr. Wilson had come to New York to promote. She glanced his way, but either he didn't notice or preferred not to acknowledge her. Kitty didn't give him another thought. She felt guilty about springing her news on Elspeth's mother and then leaving her to fend for herself. All her energies were focused on reaching Mrs. Bright.

Finally, the crowd thinned. Kitty quickened her pace until she came to a block where the traffic seemed to be moving freely and jumped into a cab. Fifteen minutes later, the taxi pulled to a stop and she paid the fare. She walked up to the Brights' house and rang the bell.

The butler opened the door.

"Is Mrs. Bright in?" Kitty said. "I just need to speak to her for a minute."

"She is resting, Miss Weeks, and asked not to be disturbed."

A photograph of Elspeth stared out at Kitty from the étagère in the hall. A grandfather clock chimed once; it was half past eleven o'clock.

No one rested before noon. Mrs. Bright must be very upset. Understandably so. "Could you please knock and ask her if she will see me? She knows what this is about."

The butler sent a maid upstairs to check. There was no sign of Dr. Bright or the twin boys.

The maid came hurriedly back, looking worried. "She won't answer," she told the butler. "And the door is locked."

"Is that usual?" Kitty asked.

The maid turned to the butler, then back to Kitty. "No, miss."

"Is someone else at home who can check on her?" Kitty had a dreadful sense that something might be wrong.

"I think we should wait for Dr. Bright to come home," the butler said.

"By then, it might be too late. Excuse me." Before either servant could protest, Kitty rushed past and took the stairs two at a time. She would never forgive herself if something had happened to Elspeth's mother.

"I beg your pardon, madam!" The butler followed.

"She may be ill," Kitty said. "She left a meeting with the president before it was done." Kitty looked about on the landing. "Which door is it?"

The maid went over to one and knocked. "Mrs. Bright,

are you well?" Then she knocked again, louder. Still, no response.

Kitty fiddled with the doorknob. "How did she seem when she arrived home?"

"I've never seen her in such a state," the maid said. "Not since Miss Elsie passed."

Kitty turned to the butler. "You need to break this open."

"She may be sleeping," he said, horrified.

Kitty banged on the door. "Do you think she could sleep through this?"

He adjusted his jacket nervously, then swung his shoulder into the door a couple of times. It opened on the third try.

Mrs. Bright lay on top of the bedclothes, her face slack, one arm outstretched. A half-drunk glass of water stood on the bedside table beside a spoon and a couple of empty sachets.

The maid gasped. "Mrs. Bright!"

"Call the doctor," Kitty said at once.

"Dr. Bright?" the butler said, dazed.

"No, man, a real doctor! Then her husband."

Kitty approached the supine woman. She reached out and touched her wrist for a pulse. The skin wasn't entirely cold. There was still a faint pulse.

"Mrs. Bright," she whispered and laid a hand on the woman's forehead. She wished she knew what to do or how to help.

The maid took a look at the empty packets. "Her sleeping medication."

The butler returned. "The doctor will be here soon. He said to keep her warm."

What was she doing in a stranger's bedroom? Kitty watched

as the maid covered her mistress with a blanket. Death seemed to follow her. Elspeth's might have been unrelated, and Georgina's was an accident, but her words seemed to have precipitated this one.

The doctor arrived a quarter of an hour later.

"I'll take over from here," he said, opening his medicine bag. "Are you a friend?" he asked Kitty.

"An acquaintance. I'll give you some privacy." She left the room, ready to slink back home, when the front door opened and Dr. Bright stood in the entryway, silhouetted against the light.

Kitty made her way down the stairs, one hand sliding along the bannister.

"Wait for me in the parlor, Miss Weeks." He handed his bag to the butler.

She took the chair by the fireplace where she had first met Elspeth's mother.

The maid came in. "Can I get you something to drink, miss?"

"No, thank you. How is Mrs. Bright?"

"The doctor said she will pull through, but that it's lucky we found her in time…"

The maid put more logs onto the hearth, and the smoldering fire crackled back to life. Kitty gazed into the dancing flames, allowing her mind to go blank until Dr. Bright joined her.

"It seems I have you to thank again," he said. "But the fact that you're here, that you guessed something might be amiss, suggests to me that you might know why it happened."

Kitty didn't have a reply. How to explain to a man that she had almost killed his wife by telling her something of what had happened to his daughter.

Fortunately, she was saved by the bell—a buzzer rang, and the butler walked past to answer it.

"Is Mrs. Bright home?" She heard Mrs. Marquand's supercilious voice. "She left the Waldorf without me."

Dr. Bright rose and went out into the hallway. Kitty heard him tell her, "Ephigenia's fine. Just a bit under the weather. So kind of you to check."

He returned a minute later. "You were saying?"

She wasn't going to be let off the hook so easily. "I overstepped," Kitty said. "I involved myself in determining the cause underlying your daughter's death. If it is any excuse, I will say that it was because Miss Bright made such a strong impression on me."

"Elspeth was quite some girl, wasn't she?" He rubbed his hand across his forehead, stretching the skin beneath his fingers. "We should all have asked more questions about how and why she slipped away from us. But I felt responsible. I thought our quarrel had brought it on. Elspeth had stopped sleepwalking, you know—"

"She wasn't walking in her sleep, Dr. Bright," Kitty interrupted him gently. Now she would have to tell him what she had learned, and she had no idea how he would react. "Miss Bright had arranged to meet Mr. Emerson after dinner."

"No." He gripped the arms of his chair. His expression switched from disbelief to anger, and he jumped to his feet. "He killed her! That unconscionable, despicable— And to think I only have myself to blame for bringing him into this house."

"Please, Dr. Bright. He told me she had already passed away when he arrived in the park."

"He's a liar!" The scientist trembled with scorn. "That man is everything that is most rotten in this world."

"I did consider that." Kitty spoke softly, almost to herself.

Dr. Bright picked up a poker and violently jabbed the logs in the fireplace, causing sparks to fly. "I can't fault Ephigenia for straying... She's a woman of passion, and I was busy with my work, while she was at home, alone with the boys."

"I beg your pardon?" Mrs. Bright had strayed? With whom?

"I found out by accident." Dr. Bright was too caught up in his own thoughts to notice Kitty's confusion. "Ephigenia had written him some compromising letters. That ingrate was blackmailing my wife."

Mrs. Bright and Mr. Emerson? It didn't seem possible. A picture of them together flashed through Kitty's mind. She and her father had come to pay their condolences, and Emerson had been standing right there, right where Dr. Bright stood now.

"Did Miss Bright know about this?" Fool that she was, Kitty had assumed it was Elspeth that Emerson was keen on.

Dr. Bright hung his head. "I'm not proud of it, but I told her—only about the blackmail. I thought of confronting him myself, but Effie would have died of shame if she knew I had found her out."

"And then?" Kitty said.

"Elspeth invited Emerson to dinner on Christmas Eve. She told me she had a plan. But she didn't give me any details because, as it so happened, we fought. We argued over those godforsaken batteries that evening, and that was it. Dinner was uncomfortable, we finished early, everyone left, and Elspeth went to bed—"

"Except she didn't go to bed," Kitty interrupted again. "She went out to meet Mr. Emerson—most likely to get her mother's letters back." Now, that was more in keeping with what she knew about Elspeth.

"And that's why he killed her." Dr. Bright thumped his fist against the mantel. "I don't care what he told you, and I don't know how he did it, but he killed her. He's taking his revenge. He's hated me and my work ever since his brother died on the F-4. And poor Effie. She doesn't know that I'm aware of her transgressions, but she blames herself for Elspeth's death. In some profound way, she feels she failed her daughter."

"Excuse me, Dr. Bright." Kitty felt awful for the family, but something else he had said touched off alarms. "Did you say that Mr. Emerson's brother died on a submarine?"

"That's right. Chlorine gas from the old lead-acid batteries killed all the sailors on board that craft. You would think that, as a result, Phillip Emerson would be in favor of a better, safer cell, but then you don't know him."

"I'm afraid I don't follow." Kitty's pulse began to race.

"Emerson's mind is twisted. For him, better batteries mean better submarines, and better submarines mean a better navy, which, in turn, gives the government more of a reason to go to war. And that's where he draws the line."

"That's ridiculous. He thinks we'd go to war simply because our equipment has improved?"

Dr. Bright didn't seem to find the logic strange at all. "It's what the Europeans did. Once they developed their weaponry, built up their armies and navies, the pressure to unleash all that power became irresistible. All they needed was a pretext, and they found one.

"In fact, when you told me you had seen Emerson at the docks, I thought he'd blown up the E-2 himself. But later it became clear that the batteries weren't up to par."

Kitty scrunched her eyes, willing herself to concentrate. Emerson at the docks. Emerson prepared to take lives to further his cause. Emerson's friend outside the Waldorf where the president would be giving a speech that was, in effect, a call to arms. His warning to Emerson not to ruin "the plan."

"My Elspeth was right, and I wasn't." Dr. Bright gave a tremulous sigh. "And now I must go to the police. That fellow has to be put behind bars."

"I'm afraid not, sir." Kitty gathered her thoughts. "We can't go to the police without exposing Mrs. Bright and your daughter. But there is something else we can do." She hated to say it. She hated even to think it. "We must act to prevent another catastrophe that I fear may occur tonight."

CHAPTER THIRTY-TWO

T hat's preposterous." Dr. Bright shook his head once Kitty had finished.

"Why?" Kitty retorted. "You believed Mr. Emerson capable of violence when it came to your daughter. When it came to workmen at the navy yard."

"But this is the president of the United States."

"Exactly. And what better moment to put a spoke in the march toward war than to bring down Mr. Wilson right when he's presenting his preparedness plan to the country for the first time?"

"I don't know, Miss Weeks." Dr. Bright looked old and tired, and the furry muttonchop whiskers covering half his face made him seem out of step with the times.

"Do you mind if I use your telephone?" The more Kitty thought about it, the more she felt she might be on to something. If nothing else, the mere fact of such an act would demonstrate the strength of the antiwar factions' grievances. And if there was even the slightest chance that the president could be in danger, she had to warn someone. Of course, she couldn't be sure, and she had no hard proof, but one shot was all it took. One shot killed President Lincoln. One shot killed Archduke Franz Ferdinand and set off the war in Europe. And President

McKinley had been shot in public by an anarchist just fifteen years ago and died from the infection that resulted. How hard would it be to draw one's pistol at the Waldorf and aim? Kitty had been close enough to do it herself this morning.

The operator connected her to the hotel. "Could I speak to an Agent Soames?" she said to the switchboard attendant. "He's with the Secret Service. I think he may be staying at the hotel with the president."

"I'm afraid I'm not allowed to direct calls to the president," droned the voice at the other end of the line.

"I don't want to speak to the *president*. I want to speak to one of his Secret Service men."

"If the gentleman is a guest, then I can connect you. If not, I'm afraid it won't be possible."

"Can you check if he's a guest? The last name is Soames. *S-o-a-m-e-s.*"

A pause. Then, "I'm afraid he's not on the list."

"Can I speak to someone else then?" Kitty shook the earpiece in frustration. "Anyone connected to the president's party? This is very important."

"Would you like me to leave a message with the hotel's security?"

"I don't want to leave a message," Kitty said. "I need to speak to someone who can help me now."

"If you can't give me a name, madam—"

Kitty disconnected the line.

"No luck?" Dr. Bright said. He'd been listening to her conversation.

"I'm afraid not."

"I'll notify the police. I'll ask them to keep an eye out for him."

"That's a good idea, Dr. Bright," Kitty said. It was better than nothing. But more needed to be done.

The cab raced to the *Sentinel*. Kitty thought she ought to put in an appearance and tell Miss Busby about the events of the morning before she excused herself and tried to come up with her next steps.

Miss Busby tapped her table impatiently. "That took a lot longer than I expected."

"There was a lot going on, Miss Busby."

"And how was the president? Did he make any commitments to the ladies?"

"None whatsoever. He said that the pace of change would be glacial, but when change came, it would be here to stay."

"In other words, wait, be patient, don't fuss."

"Exactly."

"Why is it that women always have to wait?" Helena Busby's earrings, made of pink-and-blue cloisonné, swung back and forth. "Why don't men have to wait for what they want sometimes? By the way, did you happen to catch a glimpse of Mrs. Galt?"

"She wasn't with him, not at the meeting."

"What's the matter, Miss Weeks? You seem very down in the mouth for such an exciting day. Don't tell me you've become a secret suffragist and are disappointed by our president's lack of support."

"I'm just a bit frazzled."

"Go on home." Miss Busby waved her hand. "It's late for you in any case. I'll expect your story on my desk first thing tomorrow."

As Julian Weeks liked to say, he was suited and booted. He sported a carnation in his lapel. His hair was brushed to glossy brilliance.

"You look sharp." Worn out, Kitty collapsed in the study.

"I have a big evening ahead of me. How was the Congressional Union meeting?"

"Eventful... I think I'm going crazy. I believe someone might try to harm the president tonight."

Mr. Weeks adjusted the flower fastened to his chest. "How? Slipping poison into his drink? Or shouting partisan slogans?"

"I'm not joking."

"I was afraid of that." Julian Weeks grimaced, or perhaps he needed to stretch his lips. "I take it you know who this someone is and what his aims are?"

"He's Dr. Bright's former assistant." Kitty looked her father in the eye.

He returned her gaze calmly. "Well, if you have grounds for suspicion, you should alert your young man."

"He's not my young man. But yes, I tried to contact the Waldorf, and they wouldn't put me through."

"So who else knows about this possible plot?"

Kitty couldn't tell whether he was making fun of her. "Dr. Bright, who said he would notify the police, you, and I. That's all."

"May I ask why you believe this fellow wants to harm Mr. Wilson?"

"He's antiwar, like Erich Muenter." This past summer, the German-American fanatic had snuck into J. P. Morgan's mansion and, in the name of peace, shot the banker twice.

"Like Muenter, although perhaps not so cracked?"

"I think Mr. Emerson is very sane." She recalled Emerson's cool conduct in Brooklyn. His refusal to buckle under when Mills threatened to call the law. "You've seen him. He was the handsome fellow with Mrs. Bright the day we paid our condolences."

"I will keep an eye out for him over dinner then." Her father still didn't take Kitty seriously.

"I don't believe that will be enough."

"You've thought this through, Capability?"

"As best I can… I'll go to the Waldorf and look for Soames myself." Given the president's packed schedule, he was probably at one of his other appointments right now.

"Without a ticket? I doubt they'll let you in."

Kitty suspected he had a point.

"Why don't you come with me?" Mr. Weeks suggested.

"What about Miss Lane?"

"If there's even a chance that you're correct, then you must speak to an agent, and we're both going to have to be on the lookout."

"I'll find a different way." After all the effort she'd put into healing the breach between her and her father, Kitty didn't want to be the one causing a rift between him and Sylvia Lane.

"You have to put your money where your mouth is,

Capability." Mr. Weeks stood. "You told me that you had no choice but to delve further into the Brights' business. And now it's come to this. Don't worry about Sylvia. She will understand.

"This is about you, Capability. Do you have the courage of your convictions?"

The traffic was terrible going downtown, and there were gawkers on Riverside Drive.

"I heard that the president and Mrs. Wilson were motoring here this afternoon," Rao said as he drove the Weekses to the Waldorf.

"Alone?" Kitty asked. She pictured the Wilsons meandering along the Hudson, like Franz Ferdinand and Sophie near Sarajevo's Miljacka River. *Crack.* The Packard went over a twig, and Kitty jumped.

"You're nervy," Mr. Weeks said.

"Yes, I am." Anyone, anywhere, at any moment could get at the president. Nothing about his schedule was a secret. The entire city seemed to know where he was, and when, and for how long. And who was the fellow who started Europe's war? Just a young man, like Emerson, with ideals, like-minded friends…and luck.

A path had been cleared for vehicles carrying invited guests to approach the hotel. Still, the Packard inched along, as car after car stopped at the entrance, and one by one, prosperous couples stepped out and onto the red carpet.

A uniformed porter asked to see their invitations.

"This is quite a turnout," Mr. Weeks remarked.

"Five thousand applied for tickets, but we only have room for twelve hundred and fifty."

"Where will everyone sit?" Kitty held on to her father's arm.

"Tables have been arranged on the main floor, madam, as well as in the galleries and adjacent halls. Diners not located in the main ballroom will be invited to come in and stand while the speeches are in progress." He checked the card that Mr. Weeks proffered and marked it off on his ledger. "You have no cause for worry. You're seated in the balcony and will have a fine view of the proceedings."

"I'd like to speak to Mr. Oscar," Kitty said.

"You know our maître d' personally, madam?"

"Not personally, but I have an urgent message to convey. I'm sure he's busy, but it won't take more than a moment."

"Madam, could you leave him a note—"

"I'd really rather not," Kitty said. Five couples stood in line behind her, and more disembarked from their cars. She lowered her voice before adding, "I have concerns about the president's safety."

The porter looked flustered. "I will ask him to find you, madam. Table sixty-seven. He will come as soon as he can."

"Thank you." Mr. Weeks led Kitty away. "Keep calm, Capability. Remember, the president has constant protection, and, whether or not you are able to warn his agents, it's their duty to keep watch. If you start rushing around in this mayhem, it's you who will be arrested. Oscar has over a thousand guests to attend to. Let's go find our seats and wait for him to come to us."

They wove their way to their numbered table for eight, where the other six guests had already taken places. A huge American flag covered the ceiling of the ballroom. Thousands of smaller flags hung from the balconies and around every pillar. Chandeliers glittered, pearls glowed, and diamonds and conversation sparkled. Below, on a raised stage in the ballroom, sat the head of the Railwaymen's Association, behind a placard bearing his name, Mr. Post. There were dignitaries to the left and right of him, and an empty chair for the president between him and Mayor Mitchel. A row of Secret Service men stood guard at the back.

Kitty picked up her opera glasses for a closer look. Soames was there. If only she could write a note, fold it up into a paper airplane, and shoot it to him. She breathed in deeply and told herself not to worry; she must trust that he was able to do his job. He couldn't see her since his eyes were trained on the crowd on the main floor. No doubt Secret Service men and policemen had been assigned to survey every level of the ballroom.

Everyone stood when the president entered. He took his seat between Mr. Post and the mayor. Mrs. Wilson arrived shortly thereafter. She took a seat on the second balcony tier, above and to the right of her husband. The crowd rose and cheered. The president stood and bowed to his bride, his stern face breaking into a happy smile. Later, the papers would report that "scores of women who had brought opera glasses turned them on the Wilson box and frankly stared." Kitty was one of them. She took a long, hard look at the new Mrs. Wilson for her own and Miss Busby's sake. There she was, the former Mrs. Norman

Galt. Dark-haired, attractive, with strong gnashers that seemed to catch the light when she smiled.

"She's handsome," one of the ladies at Kitty's table remarked. "I have to hand it to Mr. Wilson—he chooses well."

The room went quiet as introductions began. Kitty fidgeted with the folds of her dress. Where was Oscar Tschirky? She hoped he would come to see her as promised.

The president rose. "Mr. Toastmaster and ladies and gentlemen," he began, "the exactions of my official duties have recently been so great that it has been very seldom indeed that I could give myself so great a pleasure as that which I am enjoying tonight. It is a great pleasure to come and be greeted in such generous fashion by men so thoughtful as yourselves and so deeply engaged in some of the most important undertakings of the nation."

Kitty closed her eyes for a moment. She saw a dead girl in the snow and another lying in the street, hit by a car. A submarine exploding, a body flying through the hatch—the president calling a nation to prepare for war...

"We live in a world which we did not make, which we cannot alter, which we cannot think into a different condition from that which actually exists," Mr. Wilson said. "It would be a hopeless piece of provincialism to suppose that because we think differently from the rest of the world, we are at liberty to assume that the rest of the world will permit us to enjoy that thought without disturbance."

Some in the audience stamped their feet to show their appreciation. The elegant lady beside Kitty who had been twirling her pearls now dropped them and brought her hands together in approval.

"America is young still," the president called, his words thundering through the hall like the preacher's son that he was. "She is not yet even in the heyday of her development and power."

Kitty observed the rapt faces around the room, the fluttering stars and stripes. The patriotic feeling was palpable, and the president was capable of drawing it out.

"America has been reluctant to match her wits with the rest of the world. When I face a body of men like this, it is almost incredible to remember that only yesterday, they were afraid to put their wits into free competition with the world." Mr. Wilson looked up at the balcony where his wife sat and smiled. She smiled back. They seemed very much in love.

"We have preferred to be provincial," he continued. "We have preferred to stand behind protecting devices. And now, whether we will or no, we are thrust out to do, on a scale never dreamed of in recent generations in America, the business of the world.

"We can no longer be a provincial nation!"

The applause that followed sounded as though it would never stop.

Kitty took a sip of water, dabbed her lips with her napkin, and resumed scanning the crowd with her opera glasses. So far, she saw no sign of Emerson or his friends, although whole sections of the room were hidden from her field of vision—so that didn't count for much.

"But, gentlemen, there is something that the American people love better than they love peace," the president declaimed as Kitty's gaze roved through the balconies. "They love the principles upon which their political life is founded.

They are ready at any time to fight for the vindication of their character and of their honor.

"We cannot surrender our convictions," Mr. Wilson continued as his wife turned to make a remark to one of her companions. "I would rather surrender territory than surrender those ideals which are the staff of life of the soul itself."

The door to Mrs. Wilson's box opened a crack. Kitty froze. Then she trained her glasses on the stage—the Secret Service men stared straight ahead. They had no idea what was happening above.

"And because we hold certain ideals," the president said, "we have thought it was right that we should hold them for others as well as for ourselves."

A figure had entered the First Lady's box.

"What's wrong, Capability?" Mr. Weeks whispered. Without realizing it, she had clutched his arm.

"In Mrs. Wilson's box," Kitty croaked, not daring to lower her glasses.

"Shh," said the gentleman beside her.

"Should I go?" Mr. Weeks asked.

"Here." She handed him the glasses. "I'll be back."

Kitty darted between the tables and ran out to the hallway. "Mr. Oscar," she called to the dignified, portly man heading up the stairs.

She could hear the president thundering on. "Nobody seriously supposes, gentlemen, that the United States needs to fear an invasion of its own territory. What America has to fear, if she has anything to fear, are indirect, roundabout, flank movements—"

"Mr. Oscar," Kitty said, at the end of her wits, "there's a stranger in Mrs. Wilson's box. I wanted to alert you. I wanted to alert the Secret Service. He may have a gun."

"You are sure he's not with Mrs. Wilson's party?" The maître d' straightened up, trying to hide his alarm.

"I know him," Kitty said. "Please hurry."

"Return to your seat, madam. I will take care of it at once." Oscar turned on his heel while Kitty made her way to her table, trembling.

"He's still there." Mr. Weeks handed Kitty her glasses.

Mr. Emerson sat in the row behind Mrs. Wilson. Why hadn't the president's wife noticed him? And what was he waiting for?

"America will never be the aggressor," President Wilson declared.

Above him, Phillip Emerson reached into his jacket.

Kitty stood, ready to scream.

The door to Mrs. Wilson's box opened again.

"America will always seek to the last point at which her honor is involved to avoid the things which disturb the peace of the world," the president said.

Dr. Bright's assistant leaned toward the First Lady.

"Excuse me," an annoyed guest at the table behind Kitty hissed. "Would you please sit down?"

Two Secret Service agents entered and clapped their hands on Emerson's shoulders, but not before he dropped a white envelope into Mrs. Wilson's lap.

Kitty fell back into her chair, her forehead damp with perspiration.

The agents led the interloper away. Mrs. Wilson sighed, patted her hair, and continued listening to her husband as though nothing had happened.

For the next several minutes, all Kitty could hear was the blood pounding in her ears. At one point, Julian Weeks squeezed her hand.

Every now and then, raucous applause broke out, and Mr. Wilson concluded on a rousing note. "Then there will come that day when the world will say, 'This America that we thought was full of a multitude of contrary counsels now speaks with the great volume of the heart's accord, and that great heart of America has behind it the supreme moral force of righteousness and hope and the liberty of mankind!'"

CHAPTER THIRTY-THREE

From the Railwaymen's dinner at the Waldorf, Mr. and Mrs. Wilson proceeded to the first annual dinner of the Motion Picture Board of Trade of America at the Biltmore Hotel. They arrived there at 10:50 p.m., and the president finished speaking to an audience of a thousand at 11:25 at night.

Five hundred members of the Ninth Coast Artillery escorted the couple to the Biltmore from the Waldorf, and Mrs. Wilson preceded her husband into the dining hall where a band played "The Star-Spangled Banner."

The Wilsons then drove in their automobile to Pennsylvania Station and took the post-midnight train back to Washington. Mr. Wilson would leave the following evening to begin his preparedness tour of the Middle West.

"Better him than me," Mr. Weeks said as he and Kitty read about it the following morning. "I don't know how he does it. I'd be reduced to a heap, while he appears fit enough to keep up this pace day in and day out."

"That's why he's the president and you aren't," Kitty replied and helped herself to marmalade. Her own brush with the Wilsons had been fleeting. As soon as the president had finished speaking at the Waldorf and everyone was on their feet, giving him a standing ovation, a waiter had come over to Kitty. She nodded at her father and followed the man out to the entrance of one of the balcony boxes, where a door opened, and Edith Wilson stepped through.

An aide whispered to the president's wife. Her white teeth flashed a smile, and she extended a small hand. "Thank you for informing the agents about that strange young man." Mrs. Wilson spoke crisply. "I'm new to public life and had no idea he had been sitting behind me for so long."

Before Kitty could even curtsy properly, the president's wife had already walked down the hall, ready to join her husband as they made their way to his next engagement.

The doorbell to the Weekses' apartment rang.

Mr. Weeks checked the time. "Who can it be at this hour?"

Grace came in a few minutes later, bearing an elaborate bouquet. "It's for you, Miss Kitty. It came with a note." She handed Kitty a thick card.

It was a brief thank-you letter, signed by Mrs. Wilson on Waldorf stationery, and tucked into the envelope was a chit from Soames: "I hear it was you who alerted us to the danger. I'll be traveling with the president and First Lady and now know to keep watch on all sides."

Kitty asked Grace to arrange the flowers in a vase and finished breakfast. Yesterday had been a dream. A world of flags, speeches, and larger-than-life personalities. A world in which, for a moment, she had played a brief part. Now, work beckoned. She had a story to write for Miss Busby.

With the sense of letdown that came after intense effort and excitement, Kitty climbed into the Packard and sat back as Rao drove her to the *Sentinel*.

Kitty wondered what had happened to Mr. Emerson. She had

clearly misjudged him. He may have crossed the line, entering Mrs. Wilson's box, but he hadn't harmed anyone.

She came in to work, composed her story, and typed it up. It met with Miss Busby's approval.

"Well done, Miss Weeks. Well done."

At half past noon, Kitty left the building.

"Back home, Miss Weeks?" Rao said.

"Let's go to the Bowery." Kitty gave her chauffeur the address. She would put this matter to rest, once and for all.

"Are you sure this is where you want to go, Miss Weeks?" Rao asked as he pulled up at the curb.

"Unfortunately, it's where I have to go." Kitty opened the door and climbed out.

A bum huddled under cardboard put out his hand as Kitty passed. "A penny, miss?" He had an alcoholic's bright-red nose. Kitty dropped a couple into his outstretched hand, its skin cracked, the long nails embedded with dirt.

She pounded on the shutter to the storefront where she had last met Dr. Bright's former assistant. Emerson's friend emerged, dressed and with spectacles on this time. He rubbed a finger into his eye behind his glasses. "You again?" He didn't seem pleased to see her.

"Is Mr. Emerson in?"

"He's sleeping. He had a late night. What do you want?"

"I was at the Waldorf. I saw him there, and I've come to finish what I've begun."

Emerson's friend raised a fist. "Did you unleash the Service on him?"

Kitty stood her ground. "May I speak to him?"

"'May I speak to him?'" the friend mimicked. "Fine. Come in. But this is the last time."

Kitty entered the storefront alone, hoping Rao would have the sense to come look for her if she stayed too long.

"Emerson," his comrade shouted. "Emerson. Visitor—Miss Weeks from the *Sentinel*."

A few minutes later, still in his evening clothes, Mr. Emerson limped out from the back. Kitty's hand flew to her mouth. The handsome young man had a black eye, fat lip, and dried blood caked around the edges of his nostrils.

"Go away," he snarled as soon as he saw Kitty.

"I came to apologize, Mr. Emerson."

"I don't give a damn." He turned and began to hobble away.

"Do you give a damn that Mrs. Bright almost killed herself yesterday? And that I know you were blackmailing her?"

Emerson stopped moving but didn't look back.

"What did you give Mrs. Wilson?" Kitty said.

"A petition to share with her husband," Emerson's friend replied with grim satisfaction. "They say the president only listens to his wife's advice, and since Emerson has such a way with the ladies, we thought he'd be perfect to plead our case."

Emerson slowly made his way to a cabinet and tossed a packet to Kitty. "Here, you can return these to Mrs. Bright or burn them, whatever you want."

She stared at the envelopes tied with string and addressed in a feminine hand. "Elspeth died for these letters."

"It didn't have to happen." He sounded resigned. "I don't know why she postponed our meeting when I told her it wouldn't take me long to fetch them and come back."

Kitty had slipped the letters into her pocket and had one hand on the door. Something still nagged at her. A tiny detail. "Was it Elspeth who told you that she wanted to meet later?"

His mouth opened slightly. "Now that you mention it, no. Her baby-faced friend from school passed along the message."

CHAPTER THIRTY-FOUR

Framed against a wintry, purple sky, Westfield Hall resembled a fortress. The gothic main building housing the dormitories and classrooms had a forbidding air; behind it stood the science laboratory and gymnasium and, in the distance, playing fields and wooded grounds.

Kitty entered the school shortly after three o'clock. A German lesson was in progress: "*Bitte*, translate for me, girls: 'His poor mother never drinks tea out of a little cup; she drinks it out of a big glass.'"

Girls studying French chorused with one voice: "*J'attends le train.* I am waiting for the train. *Cela dépend de vous.* That depends on you."

A geography lesson proceeded apace: "The southern slopes of the Himalayas are under divided control. Kashmir in the northwest, between Afghanistan and Tibet, stretching north to the Karakorams…"

The strains of "Blue Danube" on the piano and the patter of dancing feet followed.

Kitty hadn't yet decided how to begin. She had no doubt that the headmistress wouldn't be pleased to see her again. So, how to find the student she was looking for? How to speak with her one-on-one? The corridors were empty, the classrooms were full, and there was no one on the grounds to ask.

Portraits of Elspeth Bright and Georgina Howell hung in a display case. Handwritten tributes, mementos, ribbons, and memories had been tacked around them.

A small figure appeared at the end of the hallway, dragging a canvas sack behind her.

Virginia.

Kitty followed her into the mail room. "Hello, Virginia. Thank you for the book."

"It's nothing." Virginia didn't seem the slightest bit surprised to see her and began sorting letters as though she weren't there.

"That's a pretty extended punishment."

"I got in trouble again." She wiped her sleeve across her nose. "This time, for talking back."

"I read your note. You seem to know a lot about this school."

"Maybe I do."

"Was Elspeth Bright popular?"

"I wouldn't go so far. She's one of the few girls who seemed decent though. She didn't treat me like I was a pest."

"And Prudence Marquand?"

"She's a pill."

"Did she and Elspeth get on?"

No reply. Then, "What do you think?"

"I'd like to speak to Prudence. Do you know where I can find her?"

"Why should I tell you anything, Miss Weeks?"

"I don't know. Why did you give me that book and the note? I think you know things that I don't, and you want to help."

Virginia sighed the sigh of someone who was much older. She finished with the batch of envelopes in her hand and reached in the canvas sack for more. "You know what's funny about this punishment? So many letters, and sometimes, the envelopes aren't properly sealed. That's how I discovered that Georgina Howell was Miss Howe-Jones's niece. Her mother, Miss Howe-Jones's sister, ran away to the city and had a child."

That explained why the headmistress refused to let Georgina go—she was attached to the girl and didn't want to see her sister's mistake repeated. But Kitty hadn't come to Westfield to probe into Georgina's past.

"Please, Virginia, you must know where I can speak to Prudence in private."

"Privacy is for the birds." Virginia shrugged. "But since you seem so keen on it, you could try the yearbook office. She'll go there as soon as classes are done."

"Thank you, Virginia." Kitty checked to make sure the coast was clear.

"You won't tell me what this is about?"

"I'm afraid I can't."

Kitty took a right past the restrooms, the janitor's cabinet, and the photography darkroom. She opened the adjacent door and peeked in. It was empty. She slipped into the room, closed the door behind her, and turned on the light. The room was just as she recalled it when she had toured it with Georgina. Wooden desk, two chairs, massive typewriter. A corkboard overflowing with notices and reminders. A bookshelf lined with rows of former yearbooks. The current yearbook, the one in progress, lay on the top shelf.

To an outsider, life in boarding school could seem carefree. Schools provided everything: friendship, education, recreation, a chance to develop one's character. But inside, every small slight, every trivial incident, was magnified. A sharp word or look from a teacher or schoolmate carried the same weight as one from the president of the United States, or from an editor to her employee. When in school, school became one's entire world.

And this—Kitty picked up the yearbook—was its newspaper. A newspaper that had the added benefit of summarizing all the key players' feelings for one another.

She began to read:

Mary Albert: Mary meddles here and there,
Geometry is all her care;
She's taken most a peck of pills;
And comes to tell of all her ills.
Peggy Ashton: To basketball Peg loves to go,
Where she can shout and cry, oh!, oh! oh!

Elspeth Bright's entry was now surrounded with a black border, and her original epigram, *Judge thou me by what I am, so thou shalt find me fairest*, had been crossed out and replaced in pencil with the words *Bright like a spark, extinguished with a breath*. This was followed by her date of birth and the day she had been found dead, December 25, 1915. Georgina Howell received similar treatment, except that *"Let thine occupations be few," said the sage* hadn't yet been altered.

Beside Prudence Marquand's name were the words: *"Baby" we call her not unkindly, Merely because she seems in manner set, And hates the little epithet.* Baby. Baby-faced Prudence.

The end of the book listed all the contributors. Georgina

Howell, editor. Elspeth Bright and Lenore Hodgkins, deputy editors. Cancellations and arrows on the page showed that Miss Hodgkins had been promoted to editor. Another girl had taken Elspeth's spot. Prudence, formerly on the editorial committee, had been demoted to photography assistant.

The school bell rang, marking the change of periods. Footsteps resounded down the hall. The door to the office opened halfway.

"Do you need my help, Baby?" Two girls spoke in the doorway.

"No thanks, Sophie. And please don't call me that. You know I hate it." Prudence took a step inside and stopped in her tracks. "Miss Weeks?"

"Can I have a minute of your time, Miss Marquand?"

Prudence turned red. "I'll see you later," she said to the other girl and waited until the door closed. "What's this about?"

"I think you can guess." Kitty came straight to the point. "I'd like to know why you told Mr. Emerson that Elspeth wanted to meet him at midnight but allowed her to assume that they were keeping their original appointment. And then, when I came to speak to you, you sent me on a wild-goose chase to do with Elspeth's studies on batteries."

Prudence Marquand looked about uncertainly for a moment, then stuck out her jaw. "You must be mistaken. You're going to have to leave, or I will send for the headmistress. You should know that after Georgina's accident, she instructed us not to speak to strangers, especially reporters."

Kitty hadn't anticipated a flat-out denial. She had thought that Prudence, a mere schoolgirl, would fold like a pack of cards. She had forgotten how tough some schoolgirls were.

"On your way, Miss Weeks." Prudence moved toward the door.

Kitty cast her thoughts back to her days at the Danceys', tried to put herself in Prudence's shoes, tried to imagine what might have caused the girl to act as she had.

"Elspeth was so pretty, so clever." She had to remind herself that Prudence wasn't yet eighteen. She would soon be an adult, but at the moment, she was still a child. An angry, scared, sullen child. "It must have been hard to have Elspeth as both a schoolmate and a neighbor. I wouldn't have liked that... I went to boarding school myself. At times, it could be trying"— Kitty fished around for an experience that would resonate with Prudence—"to always be surrounded by other girls who were supposed to be one's friends."

Prudence didn't budge, but she didn't open the door either.

"One of the older girls, Mellicent, teased me mercilessly about having grown up in the East."

No response.

"She used to make silly jokes about it, and when she was bored, she would call me names."

"That's nothing," Prudence said. "The girls are much worse here. They do things to one."

"What kind of things?"

Before Prudence could reply, the door flew open and her friend Sophie pointed an unwavering finger at Kitty. "There she is, Miss Howe-Jones. She was right here when Prudence and I came in after class."

"Thank you, Sophia." The headmistress picked up her skirts and stepped into the room. A set of keys around her waist jangled. "Please leave us now."

Sophie darted a nervous look at the scene, then scurried away. Miss Howe-Jones turned to Kitty. "I am stunned, Miss Weeks. How dare you enter the school unannounced? Enough is enough. I will telephone your employer at once."

"Cruel things," Prudence went on. "When I first arrived, the girls played pranks on me. They said it was all in good fun."

Miss Howe-Jones burst out, "Haven't I told you never to speak to strangers, Prudence? Go back to your room and leave Miss Weeks to me."

But once she had started, Prudence couldn't stop. "There were pie beds—you know about those?—and salt in my tea," she said to Kitty. "Elspeth and her friends made me jump into the pond in my petticoat once. I nearly froze to death. I thought one day it would be my turn, but somehow, my turn never came."

"Oh, you stupid, stupid girl." Miss Howe-Jones vibrated with fury.

"What did you do, Miss Marquand?" Kitty prompted.

"I said go back to your room, Prudence."

"All I wanted was to disturb a lover's tête-à-tête," Prudence continued, her voice shaky. She continued speaking to Kitty. "Elspeth and her gentleman friend ignored me for the entire evening. They spent it chatting and whispering between themselves."

"How did you manage it?" Kitty asked.

"I put a sprinkle of Mrs. Bright's sleeping powder into Elspeth's wine. Just a sprinkle." She emphasized the word as though the quantity shielded her from blame. "I thought she would grow tired waiting for him and go home. Or perhaps she'd feel so sleepy that she would decide not to meet him at all… It's not my fault that she didn't. That she just stood there in the cold."

"Do you realize what you've said, Prudence?" The headmistress had gone pale with horror.

Prudence trembled and wiped the perspiration from her forehead. "Yes, I do. Elspeth died because of me—but I didn't mean it."

"And now the whole world will know about your misdeed." Miss Howe-Jones glared at Kitty. "Think, Prudence. Think before you speak."

With all the emotions swirling around, Kitty tried to do just that. Miss Howe-Jones was angry but not shocked or stunned as she ought to be. What seemed to bother the headmistress most was not what Prudence had done, but that her student had revealed the truth to a reporter. "Aren't you disturbed by Prudence's confession, madam? I know I am."

The headmistress didn't respond at once. Instead, she straightened herself and stood tall.

Kitty studied the proud, weathered face. The realization sank in slowly, and she staggered backward. "Have you known about this all along?"

Neither Prudence nor Miss Howe-Jones uttered a word. Both their faces became masks. Kitty couldn't grasp how the headmistress could conceal such a serious matter. "I know you don't want to see Miss Marquand behind bars—"

"You are right about that, Miss Weeks."

"Miss Howe-Jones told me not to tell anyone." Prudence finally found her voice. "She said I would shame my parents, ruin my future, and all for what—it wouldn't bring Elspeth back."

"You took my advice in the wrong spirit," Miss Howe-Jones said stiffly.

"Not at all. You were scared that my behavior would reflect poorly on Westfield."

The headmistress exhaled with a long sigh. "Are you happy now, Miss Weeks?"

"I'm sorry. What do you mean?" Kitty was caught off guard by the sudden accusation.

"I told you to stop meddling, but you couldn't leave well enough alone. What is your aim? To shut down this school and deny generations of girls a first-class education? To have me pilloried for believing that every young person is capable of change and deserves a second chance?"

"So, this is my fault now?" Kitty couldn't believe the head-mistress's audacity.

"In any case, you have no proof," Miss Howe-Jones continued. "What will you do? Write it up in your paper? Take it to the police? No one will thank you. You see, Miss Weeks, you won't be able to mention any of this without bringing shame on everyone involved. You will destroy Prudence's future and ruin Elspeth's reputation in the bargain. And Miss Marquand and I have no intention of helping you do that—isn't that right, Prudence?"

"Yes, ma'am." Prudence crumpled, her brief rebellion crushed.

"This isn't right—" Kitty began.

"I know it may be difficult for you to accept, Miss Weeks." Miss Howe-Jones resumed her unflappable, schoolmarmish manner. "After all, you must have been taught all about distinguishing right from wrong, good from bad, and crimes deserving punishment. But in this case, I believe it will be best if we all forget that Elspeth died because of Prudence's foolishness. Prudence will remain in school and continue to make amends while carrying the burden of her sins for the rest of her days. Westfield Hall will remain in business, and you, Miss Weeks, will go back to writing cheerful, uplifting stories for the Ladies' Page. Are we in agreement?"

She held out her hand, but Kitty allowed it to hover in the air.

"Come now, Miss Weeks, it's time you get off your high horse. What are you going to do, ruin the Marquands' lives, the Brights' lives, my life's work, all these girls' education, simply to satisfy your sense of justice?"

"What about your sense of justice, Miss Howe-Jones? What about Elspeth?"

"Elspeth is dead. Nothing we do or say will help her now."

"And what about you, Miss Marquand?" Kitty turned to Prudence in a last ditch attempt to find an ally.

"Please, Miss Weeks." Prudence's voice dropped low. "I can't undo what I did, but Miss Howe-Jones is correct. I will spend the rest of my life paying for it. You must believe that I never intended to harm Elspeth—not in any lasting way. Please, Miss Weeks. I don't want to hang because of one mistake."

The principal took a step toward Kitty. "What is your verdict now?"

"Why is this on my shoulders?"

"You chose to look into it." Miss Howe-Jones smiled.

The walls of Westfield Hall began to crack and crumble. Dust flew. The floor opened up at Kitty's feet. But somehow the headmistress in her rustling black silk dress and the student in her blue cardigan and gray skirt stood on solid ground, staring at her, waiting for her to speak.

There was no right choice, Kitty realized. There were no winners, only losers in this game. There was no point in learning right from wrong, truth from lies, justice from injustice if it couldn't be put into practice, except in the most extreme and clear-cut circumstances.

"Well, Miss Weeks?"

"So that's it, Miss Howe-Jones? You will keep Prudence here, keep her parents in the dark, keep the Brights in the dark?"

"How I handle the affairs of my school is my business. Allow me to escort you out now, Miss Weeks."

"I hope you know what you're doing, madam."

The headmistress didn't miss a beat. "I have forty years' experience."

"Good luck, Prudence," Kitty said. But Prudence averted her gaze as Kitty followed Miss Howe-Jones to the corridor.

They went past an empty French classroom and an empty German classroom. Past a student reading poetry on her own and a group of girls poring over a mathematics problem.

Betraying neither fear nor self-doubt, the headmistress watched from the main entrance as Kitty hurried down the path as quickly as she could without breaking into a run. She passed through the break in the low stone wall where the Packard waited. And only when Rao started the motor and pulled away did Kitty feel those eyes leave her and she was able to breathe again.

CHAPTER THIRTY-FIVE

At the high-ceilinged apartment in the New Century, with its parquet floors, warm electric lights, and windows sheathed in translucent muslin, Sylvia Lane was leaving. "I'm so glad you're home, Capability." She took her fur stole from Grace and wrapped it around her neck. "Your father was very worried that you'd been out for so long."

"I have a long story to tell." Kitty handed the maid her coat and gloves.

"I'm sure he will be glad to hear it."

"My sincere apologies for yesterday."

"You did what you had to do. I'm not upset." Miss Lane bent forward, a whiff of sweet Bulgarian roses permeating the air, and kissed Kitty on both cheeks. "Take care of yourself, my dear." In an instant, she was gone.

Mr. Weeks sat in his study.

Sylvia Lane was a lovely woman, Kitty thought, dropping down on the couch. She really hadn't given her enough credit.

"I'm sorry," Kitty said to her father, "that I disappeared without notifying you first."

"You've been gone for hours."

"If it's any consolation, I now know how Elspeth Bright died."

"No consolation for me. Didn't Sylvia tell you? She is leaving."

"Where to?" Kitty sank into the soft cushions. She could do with some food and a bath.

"To Kansas. She received an offer to teach at a school there some weeks ago, and now she's decided to take it."

Kitty sat up. "That's sudden."

"She told me that she's lived half of her life with her parents and the other half under her brother's care. Now, she wants a chance to live by herself."

"It doesn't have to do with you canceling plans yesterday?"

He shook his head. "She said not."

Kitty rubbed her face with her hands. She was so very tired. "Does Miss Lane know you want to marry her?"

"Not in so many words. But she's aware of my intentions."

"She will come back, won't she?"

"Her brother's here, so I suspect she'll visit."

"I am terribly sorry—"

"No need to worry about me." Her father's tone was gruff. "Let's hear the final verdict on Miss Bright."

"You predicted correctly." Kitty recalled their conversation from a few days before. "It seems to have been an accident. So many accidents." Something inside of her tightened into a knot.

"Slow down, Capability. Take it one step at a time."

"Miss Bright died because she planned to meet a friend outdoors at night—I'm not at liberty to tell you why. Her schoolmate, who didn't like the idea and wanted to trick her, told the friend that Miss Bright had postponed the meeting, then she slipped Elspeth some sleeping powder, thinking that Elspeth wouldn't go at all. The worst part is—"

"It gets worse than this?"

"The worst part is that the headmistress knew. She kept the student on at school, didn't alert the authorities. The Brights have no idea, and the student hasn't told her parents… I understand now why you didn't want me involved."

"The girl can turn herself in, you know. She has free will."

Kitty pictured Miss Howe-Jones against the imposing walls of Westfield Hall. "I'm not so sure."

At work on Monday, January 31, Miss Busby took a bite of a truffle from a box of bonbons. "Would you like to try one?"

"Thanks, I just had breakfast." Kitty pulled up a seat. She had come to a decision that something must change. If she wouldn't bend, then perhaps finally, her boss might.

"I enjoy our human interest stories, Miss Busby. But if we really are to do something new for the new year, then I'd like to propose this. That every now and then, we—I mean, I—take a stab at reporting crime."

Helena Busby's jaw dropped. "On the Ladies' Page?"

"Yes." Kitty could see no other way to keep working for the *Sentinel* and give rein to her investigative instincts.

The editor nervously unwrapped a fresh bonbon, the colored paper crackling. "That is most risqué. What did you have in mind: kidnapping, missing persons…arson?"

"Any or all of the above."

"Oh my." Miss Busby popped the chocolate into her mouth. "Oh my."

"I know you disapprove, but before you dismiss it, or me, will you think about it first?"

The editor exhaled loudly. "Do I have a choice? Only the other day, I told Herman, 'The world is moving too fast,' I said. Next year, you will see me in a skirt up to my knees, and the year after that, with my hair cut short."

Kitty grinned. The editor had a penchant for drama. But Herman was Mr. Musser, so Jeannie Williams had been right.

"You will think about it?" Kitty said as she left, carrying her assignments.

"I suppose I must. I don't promise anything though." Miss Busby raised her voice so that Kitty could hear her halfway down the hall.

"The Secret Service arrested a zealot in Cleveland," Jeannie announced from her seat in the hen coop. "He was close to the president's automobile and had a razor blade in his pocket. He told them that he had no idea that Mr. Wilson was even in town."

"I find that hard to believe," Kitty said. "The hubbub Mr. Wilson's trips cause is difficult to miss."

"I love Secret Service men." Jeannie idly drew and then erased a heart by the side of a typewritten article. "They're so dashing and handsome."

Kitty laughed. "That they are."

"I suppose Mr. Wilson has gone to the Middle West to convince the German-Americans there to support him if war becomes necessary. He's stopping in Milwaukee next." Jeannie turned to face her. "Aren't you scared of what the future holds, Miss Weeks?"

"I am a bit," Kitty replied. "But I intend to keep writing, keep asking questions. And beyond that, all we can do is wait and see what happens."

Author's Note

Murder Between the Lines chronicles Kitty Weeks's adventures during the period from December 1915 to the end of January 1916. The events that occur in the novel are closely based on historical fact. As Kitty lives these events, she doesn't have the benefit of hindsight. She experiences them as they unfold, and as they are reported by the main source of news in the 1910s—newspapers. As a result, newspaper accounts of the Edison batteries, the president's visit to New York, and more are woven through the text as Kitty would have encountered them. (I've provided a list at the end of the book in the References section.)

Where possible, I've also used period sources, whether it's yearbooks or math problems, to give readers a sense of what girls were learning, reading, and doing at the time. And when historical characters such as President Wilson, Mrs. Belmont, or Mrs. Sanger appear, I try to rely on their own words—from speeches, articles, or other sources—as much as I can. So, for instance, the account of President Wilson's meeting with the members of the Congressional Union that appears in the novel is almost identical to the account that was reported in the *New York Times*. I do this because, time and time again, I've discovered that what I learn about the 1910s from its own sources is far more fantastical, thought-provoking, and in some sense, "fictional" than anything I could make up.

Further Reading

For readers who would like to know more about the Edison batteries and Miller Reese Hutchison, I would recommend Patrick Coffey's book *American Arsenal: A Century of Waging War*, which traces America's transformation from an isolationist state to a world superpower.

As a parent navigating the school system, I was fascinated to learn about the ups and downs of girls' education in the early part of the twentieth century in *The Science Education of American Girls: A Historical Perspective* by Kim Tolley.

Before I began writing this book, I'm embarrassed to say I didn't know much about the woman suffrage movement. Aileen S. Kraditor's *The Ideas of the Woman Suffrage Movement, 1890–1920* provided an easy-to-read and thought-provoking introduction.

And I still haven't wrapped my head around the multifaceted Alva Belmont. Sylvia D. Hoffert's *Alva Vanderbilt Belmont: Unlikely Champion of Women's Rights* and Amanda Mackenzie Stuart's *Consuelo and Alva Vanderbilt: The Story of a Daughter and a Mother in the Gilded Age* gave me a start.

For more on New York in the early 1910s, see the further reading section of the first novel in the Kitty Weeks series, *A Front Page Affair*. Also take a look at www.radhavatsal.com.

Reading Group Guide

1. What are the first three words that come to mind when you think of Kitty Weeks? How do those words fit her?

2. What draws Kitty to Elspeth Bright and keeps her going when everyone else says that Elspeth's death wasn't a crime?

3. If you have read *A Front Page Affair*, how do you think Kitty has changed since the first book, and how does that influence how she handles situations in *Murder Between the Lines*?

4. What obstacles and choices does Kitty face in terms of her work? In what ways have things dramatically changed for women in the past hundred years, and in what ways have they not?

5. Describe Julian Weeks as a father and his relationship to Kitty. Does Sylvia Lane fit the bill as a potential spouse for him and good mother for her? Is Kitty right to be nervous about her father's relationship with Miss Lane and its effects on her?

6. What would you think of a president marrying in office today? What does Miss Busby's response to President Wilson's remarriage tell you about her?

7. Miss Busby is described as running the Ladies' Page with an "iron fist." Elspeth Bright says Miss Howe-Jones runs Westfield Hall like her "fiefdom." What parallels do you see between the two women? In what ways are they different?

8. What sense do you get of the life of a working woman in the newspaper business based on Kitty, Jeannie, and what we know of Miss Busby's experiences? Is Kitty wrong to advise Georgina Howell to be cautious? If not, how should she have advised her?

9. How would you characterize Dr. Clarke's theory about women's health and how it affects their education? Do you see any vestiges of that kind of thinking today? Are there similar theories today that you think might be debunked in the future?

10. What do you think motivates Mrs. Howe-Jones to shield Prudence Marquand from the law? What arguments does she use? Do you think she was correct? Should Kitty have taken matters into her own hands and gone to the authorities herself? Why do you think she didn't?

11. What are the reasons that President Wilson gives to put off promoting an amendment to the Constitution that would give women the right to vote? What arguments do the women at the meeting at the Waldorf use to counter his stance? Do you think their points are effective?

SELECTED REFERENCES AND RESOURCES

Newspaper articles

"Energy and Mr. Edison," *New York Times*, October 23, 1906.

"New Batteries Powerful," *New York Times*, August 10, 1907.

"Edison Lessens Submarine Peril," *New York Times* magazine section, April 18, 1915.

"Wilson Indorses Woman Suffrage," *New York Times*, October 7, 1915.

"President Weds Mrs. Galt in Her Home in Simple Ceremony; to Spend Honeymoon at Hot Springs," *New York Times*, December 19, 1915.

"Modified Conscription for Britain," *New York Times*, December 29, 1915.

"Our Relations with Austria Acute," *New York Times*, December 29, 1915.

"Girl Somnambulist Is Frozen to Death," *New York Times*, December 30, 1915.

"*Lusitania* Settlement Now Likely, Following Austria's Compliance on All Our Demands," *New York Times*, January 1, 1916.

"New Year Revelers Crowd the Hotels," *New York Times*, January 1, 1916.

"Liner *Persia* Torpedoed; Hundreds Perish. Three Americans, One a Consul on Board. Washington Sees a New Crisis Threatened," *New York Times*, January 2, 1916.

"Blow to Edison Battery," *New York Times*, January 16, 1916.

"Gas Explosion in Submarine Kills 4, Injures 10, at Brooklyn Navy Yard; Edison's New Safety Battery Blamed," *New York Times*, January 16, 1916.

"Many Submarine Deaths," *New York Times*, January 16, 1916.

"A Foreign Navy Uses Edison Battery Too," *New York Times*, January 17, 1916.

"Warned of Battery Danger," *New York Times*, January 17, 1916.

"E-2 Court of Inquiry Is Named by Daniels," *New York Times*, January 18, 1916.

"Admits Cooke's Warning; Navy Department Says No Hydrogen Detector Could Be Found," *New York Times*, January 21, 1916.

"Roosevelt Defense Plan," *New York Times*, January 22, 1916.

"Wilson Comes Here to Face a Busy Day," *New York Times*, January 26, 1916.

"All Cheer the President," *New York Times*, January 28, 1916.

"'Prepare,' President Wilson Pleads; 'No Man Can Be Sure of the Morrow,'" *New York Times*, January 28, 1916.

"President Tells of 'Humbugs at Large,'" *New York Times*, January 28, 1916.

Books and other sources

1915 Yearbook, Reading High School for Girls. Reading, Pennsylvania.

Belmont, Mrs. O. H. P. "Women of Today Are Making Their Mark as Modern World Builders," *New York Times* magazine section, November 22, 1914.

Belmont, Mrs. O. H. P, and Elsa Maxell. *Melinda and Her Sisters*. New York: Robert J. Shores, Publisher, 1916. https://archive.org/details/melindahersister00belmrich.

Bennett, E. A. *Journalism for Women: A Practical Guide*. New York: John Lane, 1898.

Clarke, Edward H. *Sex in Education; or A Fair Chance for the Girls*. Boston: Houghton, Mifflin, and Company, 1873.

Collaw, John M., and J. K. Ellwood. *School Arithmetic, Advanced Book*. Johnson series. 1900.

Crane, Laura Dent. *Automobile Girls Along the Hudson or, Fighting Fire in Sleepy Hollow*. Philadelphia: Henry Altemus Company, 1910.

Lunardini, Christine A., and Thomas J. Knock. "Woodrow Wilson and Woman Suffrage: A New Look." *Political Science Quarterly* 95, no. 4 (Winter 1980–81): 655–71.

Marcet, Mrs. *Conversations on Chemistry; in Which the Elements of That Science Are Familiarly Explained and Illustrated by Experiments*. London: Longman, Brown, Green and Longmans. 1853.

Morton, Eliza H. *Morton's Elementary Geography*. Chicago: American Book Company,1900.

Sanger, Margaret. Speech given at the Hotel Brevoort, January 17, 1916. Part of Margaret Sanger Papers collection, Library of Congress. http://wyatt.elasticbeanstalk.com/mep/MS/xml/b128167h.html#b128167h.

Stuart, Amanda Mackenzie. *Consuelo and Alva Vanderbilt: The*

Story of a Daughter and a Mother in the Gilded Age. New York: HarperCollins Publishers, 2005.

Thoday, D. *Botany, A Textbook for Senior Students.* Cambridge, UK: Cambridge University Press, 1915.

Young, Joe. "When the Grown Up Ladies Act Like Babies (I've Got to Love 'Em That's All)." Edgar Leslie and Maurice Abrahams, composers. Johns Hopkins University Levy Sheet Music Collection, 1914. http://jhir.library.jhu.edu /handle/1774.2/10133.

T *his* is whom they've sent to cover my party?" Mrs. Elizabeth Basshor was in her forties, plump, and well-preserved. As befitting a queen bee, she was dressed in crisp yellow silk, and the plunging neckline of her gown revealed an ample, bejeweled bosom.

"Hotchkiss?" She turned to her secretary, a boyishly hand-some fellow who coughed into his palm by way of reply. Behind them, workers put final touches on the dais for the band, and waiters scurried about, pushing chairs into place and arranging floral centerpieces on tables dotted across the lush lawns of the Sleepy Hollow Country Club.

Mrs. Basshor trained her gaze on Capability Weeks. "Are you sure you are up to this?"

Nineteen-year-old Kitty squared her shoulders. Today's Independence Day gala—held on Monday, July 5, since the Fourth fell on a Sunday—would be her first solo outing as a reporter. In a simple tea dress, her glossy chestnut hair pinned away from her heart-shaped face, her brown eyes sparkling, Kitty felt ready. "Miss Busby wanted to attend, but she sent me because she's indisposed. I've been working for her for the past sixth months."

"I know your Miss Busby." Mrs. Basshor sniffed at the mention of Kitty's editor at the Ladies' Page of the *New York Sentinel*. "She gives me a nice write-up." Her gaze drifted to the workmen on the lawns. "Too close, too close," she called, frowning and pointing to a string of lanterns, patterned in red, white, and blue. Her attention returned to Kitty. "Did Miss Busby tell you we're having a display of Japanese daylight fireworks this afternoon? You must observe them carefully and be sure to give them their due. They're quite spectacular, not at all flashy like the nighttime ones.

"Hotchkiss." She swung around to him. "See to it that Miss Meeks receives a copy of the guest list and the program. If you need further help, Miss Meeks, my secretary will be happy to assist you."

"It's 'Weeks,' actually," Kitty corrected, but Elizabeth Basshor had already stepped off the terrace and was busy making sure that the lanterns were being hung to her satisfaction.

"You mustn't take it personally." Hotchkiss tried to smooth things over as soon as his employer was out of earshot.

"Names aren't her strong point—I'll leave you to imagine what she called me when I first started working for her." He shuddered at the ghastly memory and handed Kitty a page from his clipboard.

She glanced at the notes: *Guests to arrive at three. Japanese fireworks from four to five. Illumination of the clubhouse terrace and Italian gardens at six. Dinner and dancing to follow.*

"Have you been with Mrs. Basshor for long, Mr. Hotchkiss?"

"About five years, Miss Weeks." He took a deep breath. "I must point out that we've had some cancellations because of Saturday's incident on Long Island."

Kitty nodded. He was referring to the shooting of Mr. J. P. Morgan, the nation's foremost financier, who had been attacked by an intruder who barged his way into the Morgan mansion. The story had made front-page headlines and pushed aside news of the war in Europe.

"Fortunately, Mr. Morgan seems to be recovering well." Hotchkiss pulled a handkerchief from his pocket. "Otherwise— who knows—we might have had to call off the party." He wiped the perspiration from his forehead. "Do you know how much work it took to get to today, Miss Weeks? Months of agonizing. Menus changed and changed again. The guest list vetted, entertainment fixed—and we have the impossible task of ensuring that each year everything is the same, and, at the same time, *utterly* different."

"It sounds extremely demanding, Mr. Hotchkiss." Kitty looked around her. "But this is a beautiful location." The patio gave way to green lawns, which sloped toward formal gardens and the Hudson River, and backed up against the majestic brick-and-stone clubhouse, which had once been home to a Vanderbilt granddaughter.

"It is much more pleasant than trying to do something in Manhattan."

"Hotchkiss!" Mrs. Basshor trilled just as a long-haired Oriental beckoned to her secretary from the far side of the terrace.

"If you will excuse me"—he sounded flustered—"I should go take care of business."

Kitty left him to negotiate the competing demands for his attention and wandered off to explore the grounds before the party began. She made her way past trimmed topiaries, through a vine-covered pergola, and down neatly graveled paths that led to a fountain burbling at the center of a peaceful Italian garden.

In the distance, ships steamed up and down the broad expanse of the Hudson. Kitty watched the water surge in their wake for a few quiet moments. Just a year and a half ago, in the spring of 1914, she had been nothing more than a recent boarding-school graduate arriving by sea to set foot on home soil for the first time. She had been born abroad and, as a child, had followed her businessman father on his travels through the Indies and the Orient; then, for almost a decade, she boarded at the Misses Dancey's school in Switzerland until he sent for her to join him in New York.

She had applied for the position at the Ladies' Page after she had settled in and grown accustomed to her new town. Without any practical experience, she had been certain she wouldn't be selected. But somehow, Miss Busby had hired Kitty as her apprentice—and then set her to opening mail, reading proofs, judging cookery contests, and, every now and then, writing a piece about domestic matters.

The Morgan shooting, which reawakened Kitty's urge to write a real news story, seemed like just the latest instance of how the world could turn on a dime. Last summer, an assassin's bullet in far-off Sarajevo had launched the entire continent into war. This May, a torpedo from a German U-boat had struck the majestic ocean liner *Lusitania*, which sank in a mere eighteen minutes, killing nearly twelve hundred passengers—128 of them Americans—and it felt as though the United States might be sucked into Europe's madness.

Kitty turned away from the river to a shady path that wound its way toward the club's golf course.

"The example of America must be a special example," the president had said in his rousing speech in the aftermath of the *Lusitania* tragedy. "The example of America must be the example not merely of peace because it will not fight, but of peace because peace is the healing and elevating influence of the world and strife is not."

The clack of hedge cutters jolted Kitty from her reverie. A gardener trimming bushes with a ferocious pair of blades scowled as she walked by.

She came across a groundskeeper shoveling manure into a wheelbarrow outside a two-and-a-half-story yellow-brick building. With its tiled roof and arched windows reaching all the way to the roofline, it looked formal, but the layout didn't seem right for a residence. "What is this place?"

"It's the stables, miss."

"Is that so?" Kitty smiled to herself. Some horses had all the luck.

A couple strolled along arm in arm. He was big and burly

in his formal attire; she was about half his size and wore a lavender gown with muttonchop sleeves that overwhelmed her petite form.

"I don't know what we're doing here," the woman said to her companion before her words were drowned out by the sound of touring cars crunching down the gravel drive.

Kitty hurried back to the party, where the band had begun to play, and chose an inconspicuous position beside a pillar on the terrace from which to observe the goings-on.

The lawns soon filled with gentlemen in dark suits and ladies in wispy organza gowns. Pearls glowed around necks; diamonds sparkled on languid wrists. Silver trays bobbed up and down as waiters made their way through the crowd, proffering bubbly drinks and savory appetizers. Children darted between the grown-ups' legs.

Bang! "You're dead, Willie!" A gunshot went off. Kitty searched for the source of the sound.

One of the boys had fired his toy pistol.

"I'm not Willie," his playmate cried indignantly.

"Are too."

"Why don't you play Cowboys and Indians?" Kitty suggested.

The boys stared at her in confusion. "Why would we want to play that?"

"Look at us," the first one demanded, "and tell me who looks like Kaiser Bill and who"—he stuck his hand in his pocket and assumed a debonair pose—"resembles King George."

Kitty laughed. No one seemed to care for the German kaiser these days. She wondered whether he was as bad as the press made out.

The boys ran off, continuing their battle, and she found

herself drawn to another conversation. Two men, one with a chest full of medals, discussed the details of the Morgan shooting. How Mr. Morgan's attacker panicked and fired when he saw the 250-pound banker charge toward him—and then found himself pinned below the massive financier, who toppled forward when the bullets hit his groin and thigh. How the Morgans' butler had conked the fellow in the head with a lump of coal after Mrs. Morgan pried away his guns. The would-be assailant was in police custody.

"Wouldn't you know, he's German," the man with the medals said. "Thank goodness he's safely behind bars," the other replied.

"Doing a little eavesdropping, were we?" Hotchkiss startled Kitty by materializing noiselessly beside her.

"I'm just doing my job." She felt her cheeks flush.

"Aren't we all?" Tiny moon-shaped gold cuff links flashed from under his cuffs as he clasped his hands together. "Would you like me to help you put names to faces?"

"That would be wonderful." Although Kitty and her father went to parties from time to time, they didn't hobnob with New York's high society, and it would be important for her to identify the most important guests in her article as well as to say who was wearing what.

"The woman with the turban"—he nodded toward a striking figure in iridescent Turkish-style pantaloons—"is Mrs. Poppy Clements. She's the wife of Mr. Clement Clements, the theater producer, and is a playwright herself. The handsome buck to her left is Justice Stevens, a cad of the first order."

"He's with his grandmama," Mrs. Basshor's secretary

continued with a smirk, as a good-looking fellow with an old lady on his arm made eyes at all the pretty girls going by. "She's richer than Croesus, and he has to keep on her good side." He turned to another cluster of guests. "Those over there are the Goelets in conversation with the Burrall-Hoffmans.

"Mrs. Wilson Alexander is behind them in red and blue. Mr. Wilson Alexander has the white beard. There's John Parson with the glasses. Miss Winnie Slade is wearing a wonderful bracelet—do you see those emeralds?"

Kitty nodded. She wished she could take notes, but Miss Busby had forbidden her from writing anything. "Notepads and pencils staunch the flow of conversation, so it all stays in here." She had tapped her temple.

"And... Oh no." Hotchkiss pretended to take cover. "Here comes Hunter Cole with his wife, Aimee."

Kitty spotted the couple she had seen wandering about the grounds stop to speak to the turbaned Mrs. Clements.

"What's wrong with them, Mr. Hotchkiss?" she said, surprised that he would be so indiscreet in front of a reporter.

"Have you seen her dress?" The secretary sneered. "He's a bully, and she's a nobody—but, of course, you didn't hear me say that."

Kitty watched the couple for a few moments; when she looked up once more, the secretary had vanished.

What a strange man, she thought to herself before she stepped out onto the lawns.

Kitty felt the urge to mingle. These were people whom a girl in her position might be expected to know, that is, if her father took more trouble to socialize. Realizing that she didn't have to wait to be introduced because she was there on business, Kitty approached the first lady she saw heading her way—Mrs. Goelet. The older woman seemed amused by the young reporter and was soon joined by the inquisitive Mrs. Burrall-Hoffman. Kitty had no illusions that the women were interested in her for her own sake. From their remarks she could tell that what they really wanted to know was how someone who dressed well and spoke well could be there to work, and that they wouldn't mind a mention in the Page's Social Scene column.

"Isn't she delightful?" Mrs. Basshor joined the group and took Kitty's arm as well as the credit for her being there. "I told dear Frieda Eichendorff that her husband's paper must send someone other than that beanpole, Helena Busby, who usually comes."

Kitty didn't care to hear Miss Busby described so disparagingly, but this was hardly the moment to leap to her boss's defense.

Mrs. Basshor beamed at her friends. "The fireworks will start in fifteen minutes or so." Her smile hardened as she turned to Kitty. "I look forward to your description, my dear. Don't let me down."

The women drifted away to find their husbands, and Kitty returned to the terrace, pleased with the results of her first foray into social reporting. She hadn't gone into journalism to become a society columnist, but she had to admit that the profession had its pluses: one could speak to whomever one wanted, for starters.

Given her lack of formal training, Kitty realized that she couldn't afford to be choosy. Moreover, the skills she required

today—to observe, ask questions, come forward when necessary, and disappear into the scenery when not—were all skills
required for any good reporter, even a newswoman.

A sudden flurry of movement caught her eye. A feminine
voice, shrill enough to be heard above the din of the party,
called, "I'm sorry!"

A figure in a lavender gown with muttonchop sleeves pushed
her way through the guests.

"She bumped into me on purpose," Mrs. Cole hissed to her
heavyset husband as they made their way toward the terrace.

A Conversation
with the Author

What inspired you to write *Murder Between the Lines*?

I knew I would like *Murder Between the Lines*, which is the second novel in the Kitty Weeks mystery series, to start a few months after the events of the first book, *A Front Page Affair*. I also thought I would anchor it to President Wilson's second marriage, which took place in December 1915. As I was browsing through the papers to see what else was going on at the time, I came across the headline "Girl Somnambulist Is Frozen to Death," and it caught my eye at once. I immediately thought that this was an occurrence that would fascinate Kitty.

That article described a situation similar to the one that takes place in the book—the girl, said to be a sleepwalker, goes out at night lightly clad and is found the next morning frozen to death. If I recall correctly, she was also a boarding school student and her sleepwalking was put down to too much stress on her nerves caused by studying, and that was it. There was no crime—it was just an incident that happened.

So, I asked myself, what if foul play had been involved? And I built the character of Elspeth Bright around that and gave her her own backstory. She's a completely fictional character inspired by a death, and an explanation for that death, that I thought Kitty would find very unsatisfying and would motivate her to dig deeper.

As an aside, when I was reading about suicide reports of young women during the 1910s, I noticed that whatever stress they were facing was often attributed to too much time spent reading and/or studying.

How has Kitty grown between *A Front Page Affair* and *Murder Between the Lines*? Will she change over the course of the series?

In *A Front Page Affair*, Kitty is new at the Ladies' Page. She's an apprentice, like an intern today. Over the course of the first book, Kitty learns a lot—she learns that she's able to investigate situations that trouble her and that she's willing to take risks for what she believes in. She continues to build on those traits in the second book. As we see from the way Georgina Howell reacts when they first meet, Kitty's work is now well-known, even though she isn't personally known by name. She becomes someone other girls look up to—but that's a problem, because while she appears to be independent (and in many respects, she is independent), she relies on her father financially and emotionally. When Georgina approaches Kitty for help, Kitty realizes there's not much she can do if some trouble should befall Georgina.

As the series continues, she will continue to evolve. (She's still just nineteen years old in this book.) We'll see how she balances her ambitions for her career with her relationships. As her understanding of the society and politics around her deepens, the problems she has to solve become more complicated. It's all part of her coming-of-age story, which mirrors the more general coming-of-age story of women at this time. Women were fighting to be taken seriously, to be considered full citizens, and to be given the right to vote.

You attended boarding school in Connecticut for two years. What was it like? Did it influence how you conceived Westfield Hall?

I grew up in Mumbai, India, and came to boarding school in Connecticut for the final two years of school. One thing led to another—I went on to college at Chapel Hill in North Carolina, then to graduate school at Duke, where I met my husband.

Coming to the United States so young, on my own, was definitely a life-changing experience in more ways than one. I was sixteen when I arrived. I'd had what I would say was a privileged upbringing in India, and then suddenly, I was in a new environment away from the support of my family. What I saw was a situation that in fundamental ways was the same as the one I'd left—there were "insiders" and "outsiders," but in India, I was on the inside, and here, I was on the outside. And, like Kitty, I think it made me a better observer, and it taught me not to take anything for granted.

I wasn't aware of any kind of hazing going on at school, but what I did draw on in terms of conceiving Westfield Hall was the sense of the small, enclosed world that a boarding school creates. Everybody knows everyone's business, it's hard to hide, problems can get magnified, and because you live there, there's no place to escape.

The sense of Westfield being its own world is also reinforced by its general layout, which is similar to the boarding school I attended. We had a low stone wall surrounding the campus, a pond, a main building, and some separate buildings, but basically, the school wasn't part of the town—it stood apart from it.

Can you say more about the strong female characters in this book?

Well, there's Kitty, Miss Busby, Miss Lane, and Mrs. Belmont, for starters. Growing up, my family was very female-dominated, and my great-aunt especially was a petite, fearless woman who was very much involved in culture and politics. Watching her be herself without any self-doubt made a huge impact on me. The women I read about from the 1910s—like Anne Morgan, who appears in *A Front Page Affair*, and Alva Belmont here—remind me of her in that they never seemed afraid to speak their minds, they set lofty goals, and they certainly don't seem to apologize for being who they are. I find those characters very refreshing, and we see them in different ways reflected in Miss Busby and Miss Lane and, of course, in Kitty. But Kitty is coming of age in a rapidly changing world, and she does have doubts about her place in it. What's fun is seeing how she responds to her doubts and everything else that's thrown at her.

Do you have the entire Kitty Weeks series plotted before the books are written, or does it unfold with each book separately?

I've had the general arc of the series planned from the beginning, with three parallel but related tracks: it's a coming-of-age story for Kitty; a coming-of-age story for women, who win the right to vote in 1920; and it's a coming-of-age story for the country, which goes from being essentially a second-tier nation at the start of World War I to a leading player at the end of it. The series feels Edwardian when it starts, and modernity starts creeping in as it progresses. I haven't plotted each book down to the last detail, but I have a rough idea of how the books will all play into the larger narrative.

Do you hear back from readers? How do you stay in touch?

I do—and I love hearing the feedback. It ranges from people who have really enjoyed the working girl and journalism angle, to suggestions of books set in the period that I might be interested in, to questions about what will happen to Kitty in the future. Readers mostly connect with me through my website, www.radhavatsal.com, and sometimes via Facebook. I always try to answer every message I receive, and I enjoy staying in touch. I also send out a newsletter with historical trivia and updates. Staying in touch with readers keeps me going!

ACKNOWLEDGMENTS

As they say, it takes a village. Many thanks to my family and friends, near and far, and also fellow readers and writers who I've met recently and who have made the first year of being in print so rewarding. We're in touch via email, Facebook, my newsletter, and in person—you know who you are.

Particular thanks to Anna Michels, my editor at Sourcebooks. It's a pleasure and privilege to work with someone who is so thoughtful, thorough, patient, and understanding. Kitty Weeks and I are grateful to be guided by such a steady hand. My sincere thanks also to Shana Drehs for her input. Liz Kelsch in publicity, Heather Hall, and the rest of the team at Sourcebooks have all been a pleasure to collaborate with. Liz has made working on book promotion something I look forward to!

I feel very fortunate to be represented by Mitch Hoffman at Aaron Priest, who brings more to the table than I could have asked for and who has tirelessly helped me make sense of the challenges facing a working writer—which is no small feat. And thank you to Kathy Daneman for her efforts and hard work on *A Front Page Affair*.

Neither this book nor the series would be possible without Daniel Welt's invaluable advice. I can't thank him and our daughters enough for their good humor, love, and unfailing support even when I appear to be missing in action.

About the Author

PHOTO CREDIT: JULIETTE CONROY

Radha Vatsal is the author of *A Front Page Affair,* the first novel in the Kitty Weeks mystery series. Her fascination with the 1910s began when she studied female filmmakers and action-film heroines of silent cinema at Duke University, where she received her PhD from the English department. She was born in India and lives with her husband and two daughters in New York City.